"Jack
All the best
Warm regards
[signature]

CACIQUE ©

(pronounced: Ka-seé-keh)

A historical novel of monocracy,
reverence, corruption
and disillusionment

by

Bernard Bennett

CACIQUE©

Copyright© 2002
by Bernard Bennett

Bernard Bennett, Author
Palm Beach, Florida

ALL RIGHTS RESERVED. NO PART OF THIS BOOK MAY BE
REPRODUCED OR UTILIZED IN ANY FORM OR BY ANY
MEANS, ELECTRONIC OR MECHANICAL, INCLUDING
PHOTOCOPYING, RECORDING OR BY AN INFORMATION
STORAGE AND RETRIEVAL SYSTEM, WITHOUT PERMISSION
IN WRITING FROM THE AUTHOR.

Published 2003 by
Panam Associates
Houston, Texas

Written for film/television adaptation

Library of Congress Cataloging-in-Publication Data
Bennett, Bernard
    CACIQUE© / Bernard Bennett

ISBN 0-9673681-1-1

Also by the author

MEXICO
from within

ISBN 0-9673681-0-3

About the cover

The cover depicts the *Aztec Calendar Stone*, commonly known as the *Aztec Calendar*.

The stone, measuring twelve feet in diameter and weighing twenty-four tons, remains a unique Mexican achievement. It is calculated that it required fifty-two years to complete (1427-1479) and was produced by the exclusive use of stone tools. The calendar is 103 years older than the Gregorian calendar that is used worldwide today—evidence of the Aztec's profound understanding of astronomy and mathematics.

The stone portrays the Aztec's days, months and suns comprising their cosmic cycle. It was painted in vibrant red, blue, yellow and white. In the expanded center circle of the calendar, as pictured on the cover, is the face of Tonatiuh, the Aztec sun god and god of all warriors. Around the face are four squares known as the Four Movements. According to Aztec legend, these squares represent the ways that the previous suns (or worlds) had come to an end—the first by wild animals, followed by wind, then by fire and finally by floods. The Aztecs believed that they were living in the fifth and final world.

The calendar, mounted vertically and facing south, was placed prominently atop the main temple in Tenochtitlan, the capital of the Aztec empire. When the Spaniards conquered Tenochtitlan, they buried the stone. It remained lost for over 250 years until December 1790 when it was discovered during reparation of Mexico City's cathedral, which now stands on the site. Today the stone rests in a place of prominence in the Museum of Anthropology in Mexico City.

Dedicated

With heartfelt reverence and in loving memory of my parents

So long as society is founded on injustice, the function of the laws will be to defend injustice. And the more unjust they are the more respectable they will seem.

Anatole France

TABLE OF CONTENTS

Preface
Introduction | 1
1. A Very Special Valedictorian | 7
2. A Presidential Assignment | 13
3. Pursuing a Mission | 25
4. The All-Important Letter | 37
5. The Start of a New Life | 45
6. Don Alejandro and Santa Anna | 55
7. An Introduction to Business | 65
8. A Troubled People | 73
9. The Indoctrination Continues | 79
10. Plotting for a President | 85
11. Unrest in Soledad | 93
12. The Colonel Passes On | 99
13. A Time for Correction | 109
14. The Oil is Ours! | 119
15. Transformation of an Idealist | 125
16. The Family Visits Maria | 131
17. About the Family | 139
18. A Problem Resolved | 145
19. Maria's Thesis | 151
20. Nick's Thesis | 159
21. Maria's Graduation | 167
22. Start of a Confrontation | 177
23. A Request is Granted | 185
24. A Family Tragedy | 199
25. The Cacique Becomes a Publisher | 209
26. The Porfiriato Era | 215
27. Inauguration of Casa Rosita | 229
28. A Startling Revelation | 239
29. The Hernandez Family Unites | 249
30. Don Eduardo Passes On | 257
31. Probate of Eduardo's Estate | 267

Preface

Since prehistoric days when small bands of spear-throwing hunters roamed the earth, man has exercised his inhumanity on his fellow man. Within each roaming flock, there emerged one rapacious, overpowering individual who would dominate all and assume the role of tyrannical leader.

Throughout the ages and regardless of the realm, the practice of despotism remained unchanged whether under the reign of Ivan the Terrible, Tamerlane, Charlemagne, Genghis Khan or some other autocrat. Century after century, the tradition remained with only a change of monocrat coming about through death, succession or by being overthrown.

Rule by the despot was absolute. An individual could be rewarded by assignment to service in the local administration and just as easily, by the nod of the head, be returned to servitude.

The oppressed could expect little in the way of a just form of life. With good fortune, he could be assigned to the quarry to spend long hours working to produce stone projectile points and other spear-related items. Others were ordered to hunt animals for food and then prepare clothing from the skins.

There was no consideration for just and fair treatment. They were overworked and undernourished, which resulted in epidemics and reduced life span. The more fortunate were ordered into combat where the subsistence was somewhat improved. The disgraceful history of despotism is one of complete enslavement and the inglorious chronicle of man's implacability to his fellow man.

In the recapitulation of totalitarianism through the ages, it would serve the reader well to explore the genesis of the respected, though fiercely feared, Mexican autocrat—the *cacique*. To do so, it is necessary to turn the clock back to the era of the Prophet Mohammed, who ruled under the banner of religion and democracy.

It was Mohammed, born in the desert of Arabia in A.D. 571, who was revered for miraculously instilling in that desolate wasteland new life, culture, civilization and the creation of a new kingdom that extended from Morocco to the Indies. With the embodiment of Islam, it was proudly proclaimed, "When the minaret is sounded and the worshipers are gathered together, the democracy of Islam is embodied five times a day when the peasant and king kneel side-by-side to proclaim 'God alone is great!'" This declaration would prove to be the mere utterance of meaningless words.

It was in A.D. 632 that the revered Mohammed left this world. Tradition of succession was respected by the designation of Abu Bakr. Lacking the religious status of Prophet Mohammed, the title of caliph, the religion's temporal and spiritual leader, was created with Abu Bakr being the first to hold the exalted position. In addition to his theological responsibilities, the caliph was empowered to direct the Islamic armed forces, which, in turn, were ordered to pursue the jihad or holy war, which was, in effect, a camouflaged justification to acquire new lands by force. It was, in the truest sense of the meaning, the perversion of a religion.

It was during this period in history that there was absolutely no semblance of rule by the people for the people. Democracy was unheard of. As the all-powerful dictator of the populace, the religious leader of all Muslims, and the general of the armies, Abu Bakr embarked on crusades where he ferociously attacked, murdered and acquired new lands. These campaigns were carried out under the pretext of religious aggrandizement or holy war but were, in reality, a means of territorial expansion.

Pursuing an agenda of zealous aggression, the caliph dared to cross the Strait of Gibraltar to mercilessly attack, pillage and subdue the defending Spanish forces on the peninsula of Spain. Having completely conquered and subjugated the populace, the caliph brought into existence a new jurisdiction under control of an appointed emir. The newly acquired territory was named Al-Andalus, which was later to become known as Andalusia. Following this acquisition and during the ensuring two hundred years, two additional emirates were created—Cordoba and Granada—each to be governed by an appointed caliph. While there existed discord between the three caliphs wherein their territories were involved, there was never discord involving military strategy. Their similar heritage allowed for relatively peaceful rule.

During this period of Muslim occupation, the devout Christian Spanish army was being restructured and reinforced to the point where in A.D. 1250 the Christian military machine proved to be too much for the Muslim forces. It was at this point that the title of caliph was changed, in name only, to the Spanish equivalent, caudillo. While there remained Muslim resistance, it was finally, in the fourteenth century, vanquished with Christians in complete control.

Crusades were the order of the day. It was during such a search for new territorial gain that in 1519 Hernán Cortés with a force comprised of 11 ships, 508 Spanish foot soldiers, 32 archers, 13 musketeers, 16 horses for his officers and 200 Cuban Indian burden-bearers vanquished his Indian adversaries in a land that would become New Spain. In rapid succession over a two year period, during which time there were temporary set backs, Cortés was victorious in claiming the new country for the Crown.

With but limited troops to maintain order over an occupied nation in which there existed a potentially rebellious populace, Cortés negotiated alliances with local tribes naming a tribal leader as *cacique*, a regional version of caliph or caudillo, all possessing despotic control over the populace. The appointed *cacique* was one who portrayed some degree of military skill and personal magnetism capable of commanding allegiance from the masses.

However, with time and lacking confidence in the unequivocal loyalty of the Indian *caciques*, Cortés and his successors methodically replaced the Indian *caciques* with native-born Spanish military officers and men of wealth and prominence affording them autocratic power.

As such, the Spanish empire, with its *cacique* structure, endured for three hundred years. Thereafter, with the program solidly imbedded, it continues in Mexico in a somewhat modified form to this day. Its continuity is best evidenced by a never-to-be-forgotten encounter between Mexico's chief of state President Ruiz Cortines and Gonzalo N. Santos, a *cacique* from the state of San Luis Potosi.

It was following the presidential campaign of 1952 during which many *cacique*s, including Señor Santos, labored obediently on behalf of the successful incumbent candidate. Santos was to be rewarded with the post of ambassador to Guatemala. Shocked by the offering and with an uncontrolled outburst at the president, Santos remarked, "You're going to send me to Guatemala!? I'm going to send you to go f#@! your mother! I'm not Don Dumbo Nobody that you can just send me out of the country!" The disturbance brought the commander of the Presidential Guard to the scene of the confrontation where the infuriated *cacique* demanded, "Get this m!#!@! f!@#!#! cop out of here or I'll do it with the barrel of my pistol." The president remained calm and collected, politely responding to the *cacique* by saying, "Go back and rule over your caliphate."

Just as we cannot establish the precise date of the inception of monocracy, we likewise cannot predict the finality of the subjugation of man by the despots of tomorrow.

INTRODUCTION

INDEPENDENCE AND CHAOS

The year 1873 continued to be plagued with political chaos since the day of independence from mother Spain. It is fascinating to reflect on the conditions under which the Spaniards, led by Hernán Cortés, were subdued and driven from their adopted land.

With the launching of an invasion from Cuba in 1519, history teaches that the Spanish venture was one of alternate successes and failures, covering a period of three hundred years. Their subjugation of an entire country gave birth to the terms *mestizos* (those of mixed European and Indian decent) and *criollos* (Creoles – people of pure European decent born in what was to become New Spain).

There was, however, a third privileged group sent by the Crown to oversee and supervise the Crown's interest. They were *peninsulares*, native-born Spaniards, who were disliked by both the *criollos* and the *mestizos*. Coupled with their dislike was fear and envy.

It was approximately one year after their overwhelming victory and control of Tenochtitlán, the Aztec capital (present day Mexico City), that they suffered the tragedy known as *la noche triste* (the night of sadness) on June 30 and July 1, 1520. They were besieged by the Aztecs, which resulted in the countless loss of life to their forces, both Spaniards and their Indian allies. The following summer, the European invaders, enforced by thousands of Indian mercenaries, attacked and besieged the same Tenochtitlán they had previously surrendered. With the capital virtually destroyed, ransacked, and their emperor executed, the Aztecs were completely defeated and consequently surrendered. Again in complete control, Cortés named the seized land New Spain.

The conquerors, in typical fashion, ransacked their newly acquired land of its wealth to the benefit of their mother country so much so that by late in the seventeenth century the economy of New Spain had collapsed. Disease introduced by the invaders and the overwork of the Indians resulted in the loss of much of the Indian population. By 1700, only slightly more than one million natives had survived out of an estimated population of fifteen million of the 1520 era. During the time leading to this period of collapse, the Spaniards had diverted their efforts from farms to vast cattle and sheep herds, products sorely needed in Spain. With the existing mining activity of minimal interest and with self-gain a principle interest, the controlling parties retreated into rural estates called haciendas, thereby establishing self-sufficient centers of political and economic power. As a consequence of their creating the haciendas, water became a basic and essential commodity with the result that the monopolization of the water supply forced the Indians to abandon their own small farms and to seek employment on the haciendas.

It was more the rule rather than the exception that Spaniards who came to this conquered land would amass unbelievable riches and then, with their gains in hand, return to the mother country, Spain.

Through greed, corruption and mismanagement, New Spain languished until the mid-eighteenth century. Although the new territory was sorely in need of financial assistance, Spain itself was in economic difficulty and could provide no help. It was not until late in the eighteenth century, during the regime of the Bourbons in Spain, and through reorganization, planning and control that the situation in New Spain was reversed, with particular emphasis placed on an expanded mining industry. The population at this time numbered approximately 6.5 million – about 42% Indian, 18% white and 18% *mestizo*. However, this newly found success would become the root of its own destruction. It was through the native-born *criollos* that the discontent presented itself, in that these *criollos* of Spanish origin deeply resented Spanish domination of a political and economic power of a system that pointedly favored the Spanish-born. These *criollos* formed a union with the rural masses who were without land and purchasing power and who were forced, by necessity, to live in slum areas. It was merely through the sheer number of *criollos* and discontents that Spain, without ample troops and the will to attack their adversary, was forced to retire from New Spain in 1820. History records that the uncontrolled destruction of Mexico during the Hispanic period (1519 to 1821) ranks as one of time's greatest tragedies.

Hence, since its inception, this new and thoroughly unprepared nation readily understood that formulating and establishing an acceptable functioning administration would entail continued tragedy and hardship. The longed for independence was finally achieved by a combination of Spanish officials who renounced their loyalty to the Crown, conservative *criollos* and select members of the high clergy in the country. Change was the order of the day. All production was at a standstill inasmuch as the Spaniards had monopolized government.

There had been agricultural and animal production that along with gold and silver mining served as substantial income producers. All such production had now become non-existent.

No native-born Mexican, whether *criollo* or *mestizo*, had any experience in government. With the transition, a new and powerful class, the military, had come into being. Generals, either in the presidency or behind the scenes, were to control the country's destiny, almost without interruption, for the next one hundred years.

Incredibly, between 1822, when Agustin de Iturbide proclaimed himself head of state, and 1876, when General Porfirio Diaz established a dictatorship that would endure for thirty-five years, Mexico would have two emperor heads of state, forty presidents and a number of provisional or interim governments. Of the many who held control during the nineteenth century, one in particular, Antonia López de Santa Anna, was in and out of the presidency eleven times.

While pandemonium prevailed in most of the nation, calm and serenity was the order of the day in the beautiful city of Guadalajara, state of Jalisco. Being the second largest city in Mexico, Guadalajara did not try to compete with Mexico City, the capital and the country's largest metropolis.

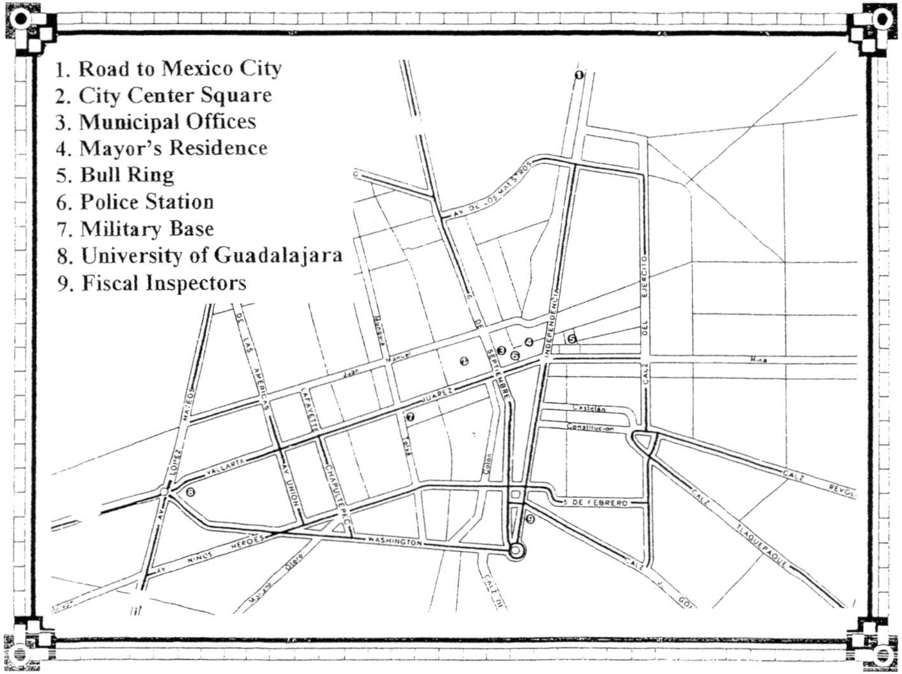

1. Road to Mexico City
2. City Center Square
3. Municipal Offices
4. Mayor's Residence
5. Bull Ring
6. Police Station
7. Military Base
8. University of Guadalajara
9. Fiscal Inspectors

Guadalajara, Jalisco
Circa 1870

CHAPTER I

A VERY SPECIAL VALEDICTORIAN

In spite of the ongoing regional turmoil, the uncertainty of the day did not interrupt the peaceful existence in Guadalajara, which was under the watchful eye of the caudillo in Mexico City.

This picturesque metropolis prided itself in its culture, music, painters and, most importantly, its production of tequila. Politically, it reacted against the left and even the center particularly when it had perceived threats to its strictly Catholic and conservative way of life. It exhibited enormous pride in its Spanish ancestry.

It was under such a notable background that graduation ceremonies were underway at the University of Guadalajara. The school was founded in 1791. With an excellent faculty, the institution produced many of the nation's literary figures, scientists, lawyers, doctors, theologians and, equally important, engineers.

The university was the Spaniard's crown jewel of education and was situated in a town that bears the present day name given by its founder, Nuño de Guzmán. As a lieutenant of Hernán Cortés, he ordered the slaughter of its entire Indian community to free the prefecture of Indian influence. It was he who gave the name to the cleansed community in honor of his hometown in Spain.

It was Guzman's belief that his selection of the site for the university was ideal for it was situated on a mile high plateau insuring it from unwelcome intrusion.

The university was a series of majestic structures

with approximately twelve hundred students in attendance. The buildings resembled dramatic fieldstone chateaus, each with an impressive twenty-foot high entry foyer. There were heavy stone walls and European style small-paned windows. The interior of the buildings was as drab as its faculty.

And so it was, on a humid Saturday, June 7, 1873, under a broiling sun in an open stadium, graduation exercises at the University of Guadalajara were in progress.

Under a blue sky, the rector of the university was delivering his address to the assembled throng of graduates, undergraduates and guests. The sun was oven-like in the cloudless sky creating extreme discomfort to those assembled. There was a punishing temperature of ninety-five degrees in a completely breezeless day. Consequently, it was the wish of all that the ceremony would not be lengthy.

Valedictorians are commonplace on such occasions; however, this valedictorian was most uncommon. He had excelled in completing the extremely difficult five-year prescribed course in engineering with a perfect record in every course. This was a feat heretofore never accomplished in a Mexican institution of higher learning.

Seated in the audience were the valedictorian's parents, Luis Hernandez and Maria Gonzalez de Hernandez, both native born Spaniards. He, prematurely gray at fifty-two years of age and at six feet tall, sat ramrod erect. With glasses over a Sephardic nose and pencil fine mustache, he exuded an air of Spanish aristocracy. She, ten years his junior, was petite with coal black hair and a slender nose with delicate nostrils. She emanated sincerity and kindness. There existed an extremely close resemblance between father and son with the exception of the father's moustache.

Both had been professors at the University of Salamanca, Spain, in the city of their birth, and were, perhaps unwisely though strongly, dedicated to openly condemn the Crown's treatment of the underprivileged. After repeated warnings, and threats and short-term jailing, their government ordered them to leave their homeland. As a result, they were exiled to what was then New Spain. It was at the University of Guadalajara that they found employment and where their pronouncements relating to the disadvantaged were directed to the Indian population. Such manifestos were not considered objectionable. They were of one mind in their quest for equality for all mankind in a classless society. The son, of whom they were so proud throughout his life and particularly on this day, had been lectured to by both parents in their driven belief of equality, compassion and benevolence for all people.

As the rector, Professor Antonio Juan Cardenas, delivered his address, it was obvious to all that he was severely curtailing his oration in consideration of the extreme discomfort being experienced by his audience. The intense heat was now accompanied by wind—the kind of wind that blows dirt in your eyes and hair and even between your teeth.

After concluding his warm words of greeting, the rector introduced the valedictorian, Eduardo Hernandez Gonzalez, who was being hailed as the notably distinguished son of the university.

Once presented, the young engineer did not hesitate to direct his remarks to both the graduates and undergraduates alike. His message was a reiteration of the pronouncement he had repeatedly heard since his early years. He pointedly lectured his fellow students on their responsibility of honor and duty to their country. He reminded them that they were beholden, throughout their lives, to strive for the welfare of their fellow man. This valedictorian was a true transcendentalist whose message was direct and unwaveringly idealistic.

In his closing remarks, he reminded his classmates

that the diploma, for which they toiled long and hard, was their pass to continue up the ladder of life. "The ladder shall not be easy to climb and there are no short cuts. You must start at the bottom. You will find that from all you have learned, that there is yet much to be learned. And so, my friends, it is up to you. Yes, you and you alone, are the architects of your future. Fear not if you encounter a closed door for God will open another for you." In closing, he offered a few lines of verse.

> "When you find your hope is waning and
> your tries in life are gone,
> Seek the love of God the Father for he will
> lead you on."

Upon completion of the valedictory, the rector once again came to the lectern to inform the now sun-boiled and exhausted assemblage that in view of the prevailing discomfort being endured by everyone, the individual presentation of diplomas to each of the 236 graduates would be foregone. What a welcome proclamation! What a sigh of relief! It was but moments later that the ceremony was concluded with everyone being invited and retiring to the auditorium for a traditional lunch with entertainment.

The auditorium was a cavernous room that resembled a graceless mausoleum – drab and damp. Nevertheless, it was a welcome change from the uncomfortable site of the graduation observance. While the air in the hall was damp and disagreeable, there was a gentle breeze created by the large overhead fans.

With the customary pre-meal offering of beer, tequila, pulque (fermented maguey juice), and wine, everyone appeared to be quite relaxed. Together, they presented themselves in an atmosphere of camaraderie, willing to forget the ordeal of sun, heat and wind.

The meal, as well as the music, was typical of the

mid-Mexico region, which is quite distinct from either the northern or the southern areas of the country. A group of seven mariachis set the tone of the merriment. It would be more in order to define the meal as a banquet.

There was lamb, pork, chicken, rice, beans, a variety of peppers and sauces in addition to the customary tortillas. With it all, the hit of the feast was the taco table. There were *tacos al pastor* (marinated beef, annatto seed, spices); *tacos de barbacoa* (shredded beef, cilantro, spices); *tacos de bistec* (steak, cilantro, onions, beans); *tacos dorados* (crispy corn tortillas, lettuce, tomato, sauces, cheese) plus a selection of fajitas and burritos. It was a satisfying way to reward the many who suffered their earlier discomfort.

For those who had already enjoyed a sufficient intake of alcoholic beverages, there was a refreshing soft drink punch made from apples. For all, it had been a long, somewhat trying, though enjoyable day. With the ceremony and festivities now concluded, the Hernandez family retired to their home where Eduardo, not yet twenty-two years old, could commence pondering what the next step would be for a highly proclaimed valedictorian engineer.

CHAPTER II

A PRESIDENTIAL ASSIGNMENT

Eduardo passed the first few days as a new member of the potential work force, relaxing and weighing his options related to his professional future. He was aware that the government was the prime employer in the country though he considered entering the private sector. With each passing day, he assessed his alternatives.

His cogitating came to an abrupt halt one morning two weeks later when he received a letter from the president of Mexico, Sebastián Lerdo de Tejada, a former chief justice of the Supreme Court. On October 19, 1872, Lerdo de Tejada succeeded President Benito Juárez who took office in 1871 and died of a heart attack while in office.

The president's letter was warm and cordial. He extended his congratulations to the highly successful graduate citing that Eduardo had now established a new benchmark for achievement. He expressed his desire that Eduardo enter government service proffering employment where the engineer would be answerable solely to the president himself. He further suggested that if the offer was accepted, the young engineer should report for work in Mexico City in two weeks prepared to start his career in public service.

Eduardo was honored and overjoyed to have received such an overwhelming proposal from such a prestigious office. Without delay, he immediately began preparing for his trip to the capital.

The journey to Mexico City was long and

exhausting. The antiquated steam locomotive traveled over narrow gauge track, malfunctioning occasionally, which resulted in delays of several hours on each such occurrence. Temperatures alternated between hot and cold as the train traveled through the low lands and around mountains. In over half of the passenger cars, windows were either broken or missing. The sole sources of obtaining food throughout the trip were the village trackside vendors who were always present for each stop whether scheduled or unscheduled. As if there were not enough distressful moments, to add to the discomfort, there were passengers traveling with their meager belongings including their chickens, goats and other small farm animals. A clean, functioning restroom was a rarity

  The distance from Guadalajara to Mexico City was 315 miles, an uncomfortable junket of four days' duration. As the train approached Mexico City, Eduardo could not avoid reliving the horrendous trip. He recalled, amongst other incidents, the four-hour delay in Ococtlan where the deep well pump malfunctioned. Consequently, it could not provide essential water to the steam locomotive. Then there was the almost two-hour delay, reason unknown, in Zitacuaro.

  Inasmuch as the Mexican rail system operated on a single track, when trains approached from opposite directions, one was compelled to divert to a rail siding so that the other could pass. As misfortune would have it, an oncoming train stalled on the principle line preventing it from reaching the siding. The consequence being a four-hour prolongation of an already horrendous experience.

  Needless to say, Eduardo was overjoyed to reach his destination.

  Arriving hungry, exhausted and disheveled, it was imperative that he retire at once to a small, inexpensive hotel for a full day of rest prior to reporting for duty. While the hotel he selected would possibly be rated below standard, it was by comparison a most pleasant change from the trip by train.

Early the morning following his day of rejuvenation, refreshed and presentable, he believed it to be prudent, prior to presenting himself, if he were to possess some degree of knowledge regarding the history of the president.

Seeking out a nearby bookstore, he discovered that Lerdo de Tejada, while chief justice, demonstrated fairness and understanding. He enjoyed an undisputed reputation for keen intelligence, great administrative ability and unquestionable sympathy for the long abused and impoverished Indian population. This compassion was profoundly appreciated by the young graduate.

He further discovered that the president firmly believed that Mexico's future progress rested heavily on the establishment of peace, which would not be possible without law and order, which, in turn, depended on firm executive control.

It was now 4:00 P.M., the pre-set hour for Eduardo to appear at the presidential office, which was located in the Palacio Nacional (National Palace), which was in the capital's *zocalo* (center square). The *palacio* was an enormous structure built by the Spaniards during their both shameful and glorious occupation of the country. The spacious building was the epitome of luxury and graciousness, resplendent with its winding marble stairways and evidence of past glory.

From his research, Eduardo learned that this magnificent structure occupied the site of Aztec emperor Moctezuma's palace. It had been built by slave labor under Hernán Cortés. In past years, he discovered, it was the official residence of viceroys. Today, it housed the office of the president and other government officials and administrative offices.

By custom, the bureaucracy enjoyed their mid-day

meal from 2:00 P.M. until 4:00 P.M. The upper echelon, however, would not normally return to their desks until somewhat after 4:00 P.M. Arriving earlier than the appointed hour, Eduardo awaited the president's secretary who arrived at 5:00 P.M. The bureaucrat welcomed him warmly, offering him a cup of coffee and asking his visitor to wait for the chief of state.

President Lerdo de Tejada finally arrived at 6:45 P.M., greeting the protégé with a *"Bienvenido, aqui esta su casa."* (Welcome, this is your home.)—a greeting of a most cordial nature. The president was a tall, erect, dignified man of some sixty years of age. His mop of gray hair matched his untrimmed mustache and scraggly beard. His long, narrow, brown face deeply seamed and with piercing eyes appeared to have been chiseled from granite.

Eduardo was ushered through rococo arches into the president's office of opulent elegance with its high frescoed ceiling and wedding cake chandeliers. There was an impressive grandiose desk complete with ornate gilt trim. In every direction, there were sofas and overstuffed chairs strewn with needlepoint pillows.

This private meeting with the president was of short duration, approximately forty minutes. During that time, Eduardo was informed that he would be cared for by a middle-aged army captain, Armando Vegas, who was summoned and then introduced to the engineer. It was apparent from both the verbal and visual exchanges between the military man and his boss that there existed a long relationship between the two.

The officer was well beyond the age of a person who would normally hold such a rank, which indicated that, perhaps, this captain had progressed through the ranks from enlisted status. He was a stocky individual with a face bronzed by sun and wind. His olive skin stretched over his high cheekbones. Eduardo, after requesting and receiving permission of the president to leave, departed with his newly appointed host.

Vegas escorted his guest to the Hotel Majestic where the visitor would be domiciled. The hotel was a five-story structure. It was located on the opposite side of the expansive city center square and somewhat similar in style to the National Palace. Just as its name implies, it was a majestic building. The hotel functioned as a housing facility for the many official guests from Spain during the occupation period. It was particularly popular for its close proximity to the now functioning federal government offices.

The hotel's quarters were most impressive with a private bath for each bedroom. When assigned to his room, Eduardo was overwhelmed by the lavishness and asked himself, "Is this what it's going to be like working for the president?"

The captain, who was serving as both a guide and a guardian, was very precise in explaining the schedule of activity for the guest. Eduardo was quick to conclude that the captain, who asked to be called Armando, was an *hombre de confianza* (man of trust) of the president. Once installed in his lodgings, Eduardo was left on his own until the following morning.

The two met for breakfast at which time Eduardo was told that he would be in Mexico City for ten days. During that time, as directed by the chief of state, he would become familiarized with the points of interest in and about the city. It was planned that he be a tourist for five days. After that, he would report for four days of indoctrination at the Department of Hydraulic Resources, the government agency that controlled the nation's water supply. Upon concluding the four days of enlightenment with the department's engineers, he would learn of his first assignment directly from the chief executive. Armando further clarified that he, personally, with government carriage and driver, would serve as his guest's tour guide

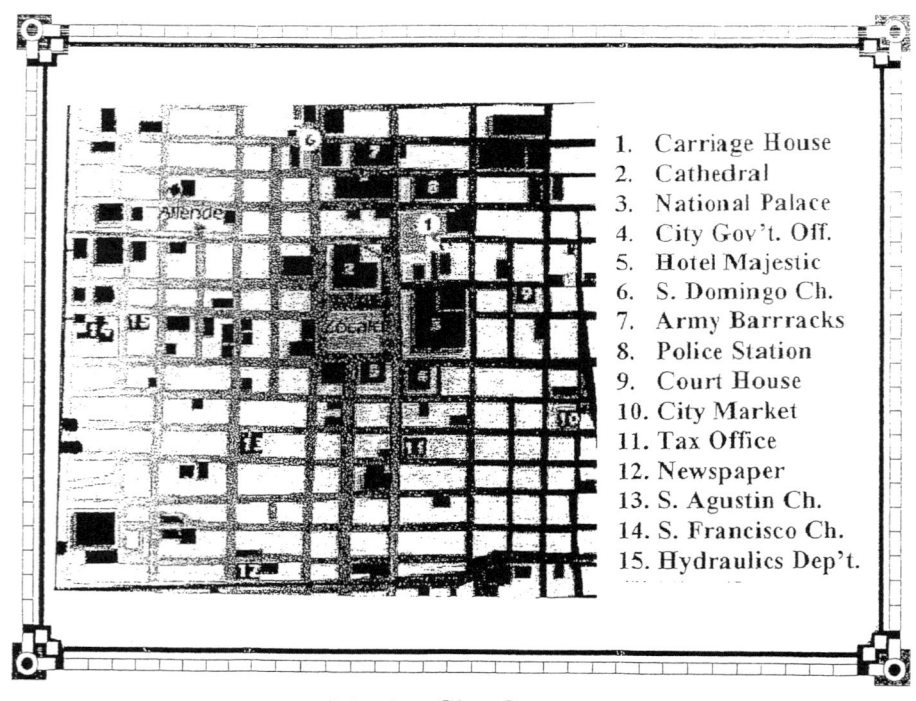

1. Carriage House
2. Cathedral
3. National Palace
4. City Gov't. Off.
5. Hotel Majestic
6. S. Domingo Ch.
7. Army Barrracks
8. Police Station
9. Court House
10. City Market
11. Tax Office
12. Newspaper
13. S. Agustin Ch.
14. S. Francisco Ch.
15. Hydraulics Dep't.

Mexico City Center
Circa 1870

during the period allocated to visitation.

There existed exceptionally good chemistry between the two, their differences being few and far between. Their likes ran a parallel course.

Among the sites to be visited, and as a first choice of the visitor, would be a room-by-room tour of the National Palace. Built by slave labor under Hernán Cortés, the original structure was almost completely destroyed by anti-Spanish mobs in 1862 and had to be rebuilt. Accompanied by a clergyman, he next toured the Metropolitan Cathedral located at close proximity to the center square. It was originally built as a small church in 1525 by the Spaniards and later demolished in 1573 in order to make way for the present cathedral, which was one of the prestigious houses of worship in the hemisphere.

Continuing the tour in the city, the host guide was most enthusiastic in relating the historic military background of Chapultepec Castle. The castle stands atop a two hundred foot hill overlooking the city and the valley of Mexico. Construction of the fortress was begun in 1783 and was completed in 1840. After fortification, it was made the home of the military college. In a voice choking with emotion, the captain explained to his guest, "See those columns over there? They honor the six cadets who were among those defending Chapultepec Castle against American troops at the height of the Mexican American War in 1847. They reputedly leaped to their deaths wrapped in the Mexican flag rather than be captured." Eduardo approached the columns, bowed his head and stood silent for several minutes.

The excursion continued fifteen miles to the southwest to the pueblo of Xochimilco whose name was given to it by the Chichimec Indians and means "the place where the flowers grow." Traveling by canoe through the multitude of canals emanating from the village center was a true delight. Eduardo was further elated when offered a picnic lunch arranged for by his most hospitable host. He was amazed to find that at such close proximity to Mexico City the natives continued to converse in Náhuatl, the Aztec tongue.

With the inspection of each site, the young engineer's fascination grew, for he had not previously ventured from his home of Guadalajara. Rounding out a memorable five days, there were visits to the provincial towns of Ixtapalapa, Coyoacán and the convent of Churubusco. It was now time for the new employee to get to work.

As per schedule, he reported bright and early to the hydraulics department, which was nearby. The director of the department was awaiting his arrival and extended a most cordial *"Bienvenido."* The department was housed in a deteriorated three-story building of concrete and glass that could best be described as rigid, unimaginative and ugly. Once inside, he was invited to join two other engineers at a table about the size of a diaper. The next four days were spent with staff members who enjoyed endless coffee breaks and three-hour lunches. In summation, there was little accomplished. With Eduardo now having completed his program of indoctrination, he was unimpressed with his mentors.

The following morning the captain joined Eduardo for a mutually enjoyable breakfast meeting for the two men had now established an extremely close rapport. From the moment of their initial coming together, they were on the same wavelength having similar preferences. In just a short period, a strong link had developed between two newly acquainted compatriots. This concord was accentuated by the fact that they were both warmly regarded by the president who addressed them both by their given names.

Immediately after breakfast, Armando delivered a large envelope from the president to his friend. Included in their good-byes was a warm exchange, the customary *abrazo* (embrace) and a parting *"Hasta luego."* (See you later.)

Once in the privacy of his hotel room and gushing with his body's adrenalin flowing, Eduardo opened the envelope. There were two standard size envelopes in the large envelope he had received. One of the envelopes contained a government approved expense authorization allowing the bearer the facility to make purchases for the account of the Treasury. In addition, there was a substantial amount of cash. The other envelope contained a letter of instructions from the chief executive addressed as "strictly personal" that clearly detailed the particulars of Eduardo's mission.

Upon reading and digesting the subject matter of the missive, he experienced a tinkling jolt to learn that he had been ordered to immediately proceed to the town of Soledad in the nation's southernmost state of Chiapas. Once there, he was directed to meet with the town fathers in order to discuss the installation of a potable water system that would replace the multitude of hand operated well pumps, many of which were inoperative. Without hesitation, he gathered his belongings. With a strange cold excitement filling his whole being, he was on his way to his first professional assignment.

The mode of public transportation to Soledad from the capital was by train to Veracruz and then by carriage to Soledad or, for the brave-hearted, direct by carriage. While his train trip from Guadalajara to Mexico City was an unforgettable experience, this new journey would prove to be a nightmare. The traveler would soon learn that the carriage drawn by four horses and carrying eight passengers, would stop, for one reason or another, at every town, village or pueblo en route. Among the many discomforts encountered were bare-wood slab seats and the odorous passengers boarding with poultry and other small farm animals.

Early in the trip, he wondered whether this might have been the carriage driver's first attempt at managing such a large conveyance. As for controlling the horses, it was either walk or run with nothing in between other than coming to bone-jolting stops. All attempts to withdraw into a vague half sleep were interrupted by the intolerable weaving of the carriage as it traversed the essentially mountainous route.

The days passed slowly with procession like monotony. His weariness grew with each passing hour. Finally, after three tortuous days and nights and with eyes burning and bones aching, he arrived in Soledad. As he joyfully departed his "home" of almost sixty-five hours, he released a long exhalation of relief.

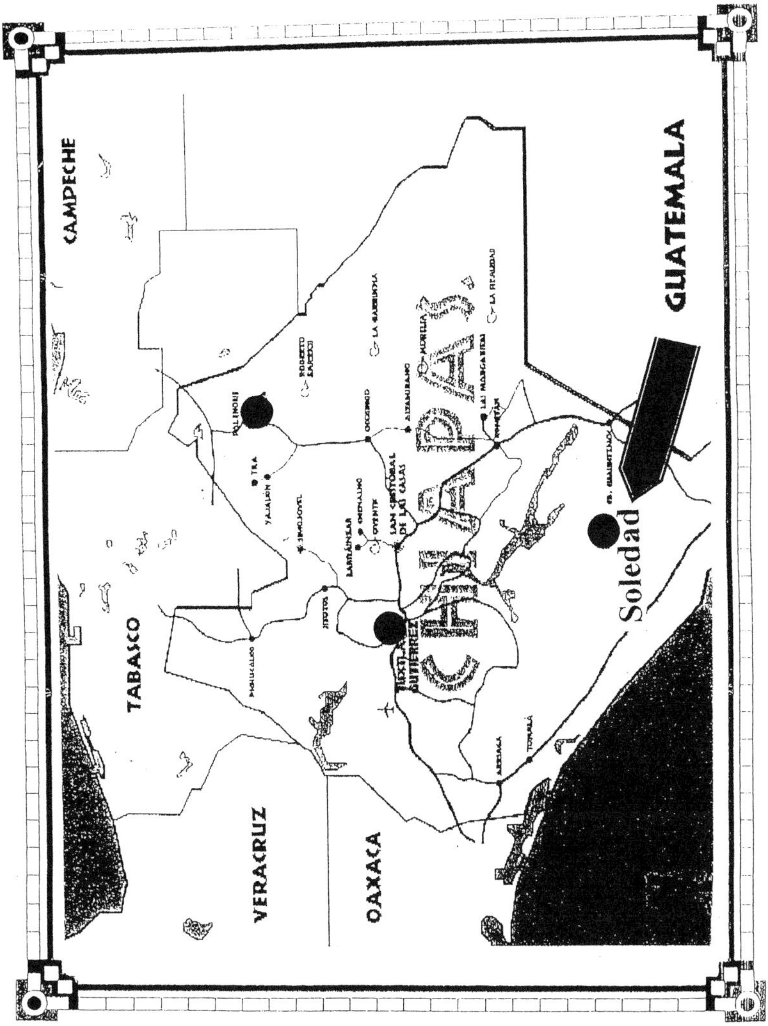
CAMPECHE
TABASCO
VERACRUZ
OAXACA
GUATEMALA
CHIAPAS
Soledad

CHAPTER III

PURSUING A MISSION

Without delay, he sought out a small though acceptable hotel, the Hotel Emporio, where he slept throughout the night and half of the next day. Once refreshed and well fed, he set out to become acquainted with this provincial municipality. He quickly discovered that this was a livestock, farming and general commerce community of approximately thirty-five thousand inhabitants, principally peasants, with an intermingling of successful ranchers, farmers and small business owners. It was not difficult to observe that there were more than a desirable number of howling dogs.

As he wandered about the town, he could only marvel at the timeless images that were present—donkeys ambling down dusty paths while the deteriorating government buildings, covered with a patina of dirt, stood silhouetted against the sky. There was a tree-lined public square, typical of so many Mexican towns, with its many tables dedicated to the customary domino games that were in progress.

Pursuing his inbred interest in the common man, he sought out the area of workers' housing. He noted the makeshift adobe homes of one or two rooms devoid of running water or even a hand-operated pump, electricity and bathroom facilities. In most cases, windows were either broken or non-existent. These homes of Indians and less fortunate *mestizos*, with their leaking thatched roofs, caused the visitor to be most disheartened.

Being the perennial student, Eduardo found the

local library. It was his wish to become knowledgeable, to some degree, with the historical background of Soledad as well as the state of Chiapas. He was disappointed to find the library terribly lacking in reference material. Making the best of the inadequacy of the available textbooks, he gathered whatever information was available and departed.

From his inspection, he learned that the township was a former Indian commercial center where the abundant agricultural production of the region was both sold and traded. It was its plenteous crops throughout the year that attracted Cortés to this vital source of food for his troops. Consequently, the Indian community was easily overwhelmed by the Spanish forces, which dominated the area for three hundred years. He further learned that the area possessed many interesting historic sites such as churches, convents and the like that were constructed by the invaders during the period of occupation.

The following morning, at precisely 8:00 A.M., he presented himself at the town hall only to learn that no one would report for work until 10:00 A.M. After a prolonged wait, he was finally ushered into the office of a town underling at 11:30 A.M.

He was coolly greeted by the bureaucrat, Fernando Silva, a short, stocky and unshaven individual who, for whatever reason, appeared to be perspiring profusely. So much so, that the exudation on his forehead resembled water beads on good quality butter. Upon meeting the public servant, Eduardo greeted him, *"Muy buenos dias, señor."* (A very good morning to you, sir.) The response was a most uncordial, simple *"Hola."* (Hello.)

At that point, the young engineer, with a creeping uneasiness at the bottom of his heart, initiated the conversation. "My name is Eduardo Hernandez Gonzalez, and I am here by order of the president. I should like to speak with your town administrator."

With that, Silva excused himself to pass to an

adjoining office where he repeated his visitor's remarks to his superior, Pedro Vargas. With a smirk and an eyebrow raised in amused contempt, Vargas responded, "Not another one. He's an agent of the president just as I am a distant cousin of Moctezuma. Don't waste my time or your time, get rid of him."

Having been given an irrefutable order, Silva returned to inform his visitor that the administrator was extremely busy and that Eduardo should return the following day at noon.

Punctually at noon the following day, he reported as instructed. He waited patiently until 2:00 P.M. when he was advised by the receptionist that the entire office force would be retiring for the normal two hour lunch period and perhaps it would be prudent that he return the following day at 4:00 P.M. Now realizing that he would have at his disposal an abundance of uncommitted time, he returned to the library to borrow reading material to help him pass idle hours.

Once again, punctually at 4:00 P.M., he sat and waited for an audience with his initial contact, Fernando Silva. Again, he was informed that Silva had been called away from his office, for reasons of urgency, and would not return. He was extremely disappointed. As before, he was given another appointment for the following day. And so it went the following day and the days thereafter and ultimately week after week. Through it all, Eduardo remained a man of composure and patience though he was experiencing an uneasiness spiced with irritation—an uneasiness that was masked by his controlled steadiness.

After three frustrating weeks of meaningless deceptive scheduling of appointments, he correctly felt as though he was moving at a snail's pace around a giant turnstile. Always the ultimate optimist, he fought the thought that his optimism might possibly be based on faulty logic. At long last, he convinced himself that he must adopt another approach in pursuing his commission.

Inasmuch as his proposition involved the installation of a potable water system, he decided to approach the town's civil engineer. It was his belief that a one-on-one approach of engineer-to-engineer would level the field and bring positive results. To his delight, he was given an immediate appointment. This could have been due to the fact that engineers preface their names with their title *Ingeniero* (Engineer); hence, *Ingeniero* Eduardo Hernandez would meet with *Ingeniero* Francisco Pedraza without delay.

Eduardo, punctual as usual, announced himself to the secretary of his peer at the appointed hour. Unlike past unsuccessful attempts for an interview, he was immediately received by his fellow professional. Upon meeting, Eduardo extended a cheery, *"Muy buenos tardes, Señor Ingeniero."* (A very good afternoon, Sir Engineer.) Unlike past responses, there was a warm reply, *"Buenos tardes. Bienvenido a Soledad."* (Good afternoon. Welcome to Soledad.) Francisco Pedraza was a tall, handsome *mestizo* of about forty years of age. In some ways, he resembled a younger version of Eduardo's father even though he had pronounced cheekbones, a sharp clear chin with hawk like features arresting an elegant, serious and dedicated face.

The meeting was most cordial up to the point where, as before, he identified his sponsor and his intention to see the town administrator. Pedraza instantaneously informed his colleague that it would be essential to see Fernando Silva even offering to call on his behalf which he did from an adjoining office.

Within minutes, an assistant to Pedraza appeared to advise that her boss had been urgently called away and that he regretted that he could not be of assistance in any way. A glazed look of despair covered Eduardo's face.

With great persistence, the young engineer returned to Silva's office several times a week for almost a month

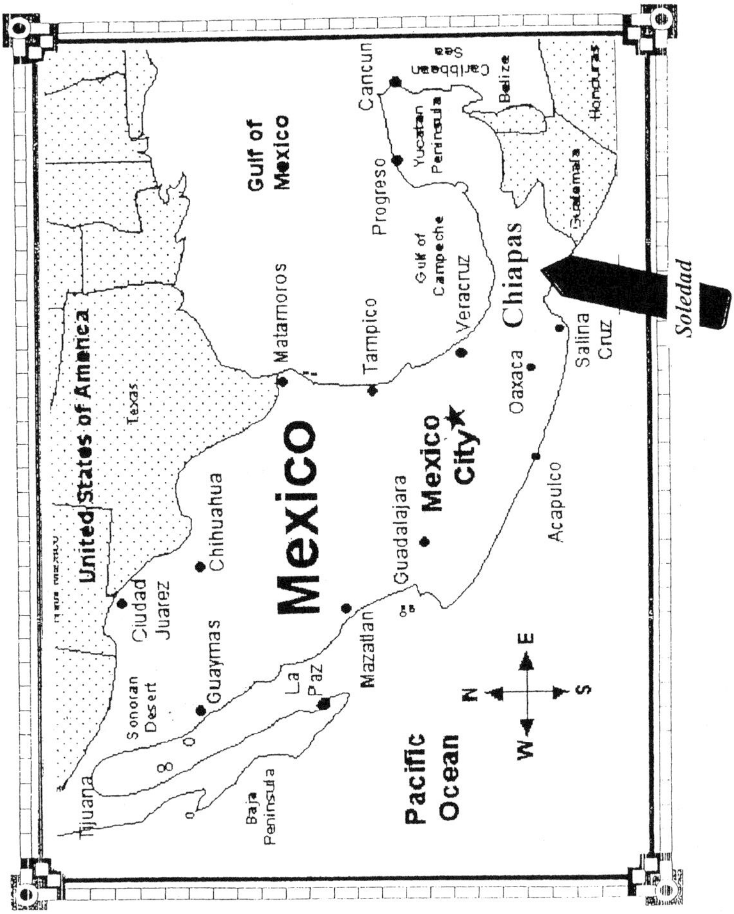
United States of America
Texas
Mexico
Gulf of Mexico
Tijuana
Ciudad Juarez
Chihuahua
Sonoran Desert
Guaymas
Baja Peninsula
La Paz
Mazatlan
Guadalajara
Mexico City
Matamoros
Tampico
Veracruz
Gulf of Campeche
Progreso
Yucatan Peninsula
Cancun
Caribbean Sea
Belize
Guatemala
Honduras
Chiapas
Oaxaca
Salina Cruz
Acapulco
Soledad
Pacific Ocean
N
E
S
W

only to be rebuffed as before. During this extended period of exhausting disillusionment, the now fatigued and frustrated valedictorian found himself suffering depression from introspection and self-doubt. He was aware that remorse could, perhaps, motivate him to continue though it would certainly not achieve his goal.

Profoundly dejected, he likened himself to an energetic individual who vigorously rows his boat with but one oar only to discover that he had affected one gigantic circle having returned to his starting point. He realized that he, too, since his arrival and after untiring travail had come full circle. Consequently, Eduardo was experiencing great difficulty in attempting to rid his conscious of the dull throb of grief which he was suffering in his heart and mind.

During the endless days of trial, tribulation and exhausting disillusionment, the engineer sensed that, at this point, time was his enemy. The days of idleness weighed heavily upon him and grew increasingly longer. The eternal student filled his days with reading and visiting the surrounding area. Yet, there was hour after hour of sheer boredom.

It was now six weeks since he arrived in Soledad, an enthusiastic idealist certain that the door of opportunity was unbelievably wide and open. In the last month, he had become bewildered as a child who had come upon something he did not clearly comprehend. After extensive periods of deliberation and prayer, he remembered that his religious upbringing would direct him to the church for guidance. Without a minute of hesitation, he was on his way to seek counsel from the parish priest, Father Agustin Diaz.

The father was a somewhat short, bald, rotund, middle-aged man with a square wall of forehead and heavy unkempt graying eyebrows. His rimless eyeglasses afforded him an intellectual appearance that accompanied a face exuding warmth and compassion.

Eduardo greeted the priest in his usual courteous salutatory warm manner, "Señor *Padre.*" (Lord Father.) The priest reciprocated with a sincere meaningful blessing of welcome.

Prior to entering into discussion, the priest invited his visitor to join him in a snack—a tray of assorted cookies and coffee. Their initial exchange was of their personal backgrounds. Father Diaz explained that he was of *mestizo* parents, born in the city of Veracruz where he was ordained, after which he was ordered to a diocese in Mexico City. There, not being permitted to express his sympathies by open censure of the government's treatment of the Indian population, he was unceremoniously banished to the backward and isolated town of Soledad.

At this point in the conversation, Eduardo grasped the opportunity to express his shared accord relating to the abusive manipulation of the native Indian populace as well as all underprivileged. From the outset, it was obvious that there existed a sincere rapport between the two transcendentalists. The young visitor was extremely concise in giving an account of his antecedents for he was most anxious to bring to the priest's attention his utterly disappointing experience thus far.

He commenced by explicating all that had transpired in his continued effort with the town bureaucrats. He meticulously and comprehensively commented on each and every occurrence. He concluded by portraying his disappointment in being rejected.

The cleric listened most attentively throughout the recitation. Hesitatingly, he told he young visitor that there existed a procedure in Soledad that governed all offerings such as that which his guest had proffered. He went on to explain that, as a compassionate friend, he would attempt to enlighten Eduardo as to why his effort to date had been futile.

While pouring another cup of coffee for each, the

reverend determined it was the appropriate time to reveal precisely what made the wheels turn in that isolated community of Indians and *mestizos*. He wished, however, to first point out that the inhabitants were living under a colonial system dominated by someone who held the all-powerful office of *cacique* (autocratic ruler). "My son," he was most emphatic in mentioning, "*cacique* is one word you should never forget nor fail to respect." At this point in the conversation, Eduardo's eyebrows rose in obvious question while his bottom lip pushed forward to accentuate his anticipation as to what might follow.

The priest continued, "He is the local boss whose power touches every individual and determines the economic and political relationship with the central government in Mexico City as well as the rest of the country."

He was quick to point out that this dominant form of life was not new, that it dated back to the days of the conquering Spaniards. He further explained that since 1519 there existed native chieftains who would, by order of the invaders, be designated *caciques*. It was intended that the *cacique* system, controlled by Spain, would be responsible for maintaining order of the native population. The father went on to point out that the *cacique*, normally *mestizo*, was the principal land owner in the region, owned all or a major part of the town's commerce and reigned with absolute power, particularly over the Indians. He was usually the sole purchaser of the crops they harvested. His power was boundless, for he would be called the owner of the prayer books as well as the people's souls.

While it was fact that in some remotely isolated areas *caciques* were Indians, with time and progress they were being displaced by *mestizos*.

He went on to explicate that irrespective of location, the Indian was exploited and forever became indebted to the *cacique*. Regretfully, the reality of the matter was that the Indian toiled daily to provide for his own survival and to pay off his debts to the *cacique.*

To thwart off any challenge to his power, this despot maintained his own personal corps of *pistoleros* (hired gunmen) and a strong favorable relationship with the state government, which, in turn, depended on the local dictatorial boss to insure that peace was maintained and unrest was non-occurrent.

It was common practice to rent large tracts for planting. Once scrubbed for planting, the land was repossessed for cattle grazing. In some isolated cases, the autocrat, in a rare demonstration of benevolence, permitted the Indian to occupy a portion of the cleared property to plant coffee, cotton, corn and the like. It was underscored that such a course of action could, as it had in the past, result in rebellion. It was this type of incident that occurred in the nearby town of Tzatziland Tzeltal in 1712. Unfortunately, the revolt caused many Indians to be jailed or killed. This reprisal brought humiliation to the state government.

He hastened to add that these regional rulers, generally *mestizos*, sought to conform to the image of Spanish gentlemen by constructing elaborate homes for themselves. In an effort to further emulate their image, they wore European clothing, carried swords and muskets, and rode horseback with saddle and spurs. They even acquired Spanish names hoping to be looked upon as Spanish *hidalgos* (noblemen).

Now having elevated themselves to an aggrandized social position, they supervised all that was related to land within their region, maintained order by force, ruled in all matters relating to labor, established administrative departments and enforced church attendance all the while acquiring land, commerce and huge personal fortunes.

As the discussion continued, the hour grew late. Somewhat exhausted, Father Diaz suggested, "In view of the late hour and my energy level waning, let us thank God for each finding a new friend and continue tomorrow morning, let's say about 10:00 A.M." They concluded a most cordial meeting with an affectionate *abrazo* after which they bid each other a pleasant evening.

Meeting once again, and after a short blessing by the clergyman and over a cup of coffee, they resumed their discourse. Eduardo was asked to address his new friend as *Padre Agustin* (Father Agustin). The curate then said, "Let's talk about Soledad." Hearing these words caused the young man's brow to crease. He nervously moistened his lips while his normally expressive face became almost somber. He sat attentively, slowly sliding to the edge of his chair.

The father continued, "In Soledad we have, and are governed by, a *cacique*—this is a fact we all respectfully accept. His name is Don Alejandro Fernandez Bravo. I would recommend that you not use the familiar prefix to his name, that is Don Alejandro, until he indicates you may do so. Our leader was in the army under command of General Antonio Lopez de Santa Anna when, in 1836, his forces laid siege to and overran the Alamo. Don Alejandro attained the rank of colonel and prefers to be addressed as colonel; and I would strongly suggest you address him that way. He also enjoys being greeted as *"Mi jefe."* (My leader.)

The cleric then went on to say that he would spell out just how his compatriot should pursue his mission. He stressed repeatedly that no business could be conducted without the previous accord of the *cacique*. Eduardo, approaching a point of exasperation, apologized for interrupting, "How can I get to see the *cacique*?"

"Patience, my learned son, patience," Father Agustin replied. He went on to reveal that before anyone could present an offering of any type to Don Alejandro, it must first be presented to the *cacique*'s private secretary,

Raul Molina, a huge man who doubles as a body guard and is commonly referred to, though not to his face, as *el Toro* (the Bull).

Again breaking in, Eduardo asked, "And how do I approach *el Toro?*"

The clergyman replied with a significant lifting of his eyebrows and a smile that tipped the corners of his mouth, "That is something we shall have to consider together at some future time. Perhaps through prayer God will assist us."

With those closing remarks, they kneeled side-by-side reciting a synoptic prayer. As per custom, they exchanged *abrazos* and parted.

CHAPTER IV

THE ALL-IMPORTANT LETTER

Befuddled by the multitude of revelations and attempting to put all of the pieces of the puzzle together, Eduardo returned to his hotel to ponder how he would eventually arrange an interview with the Bull.

After fighting through the cobwebs of a tense, sleepless night, he was without an answer as to how he would resolve the problem at hand. He searched anxiously for any feasible solution.

Even though he was as yet without a resolution to his quandary, he pondered how he would be received by the Bull if he were fortunate to obtain the hoped for audience. Would it be another disastrous reception similar to past attempts? He constantly wondered why the office of the president had not assisted him with an influential introduction. Was this meant to be a test of his ability to accomplish the mission on his own? He was, indeed, a troubled young man praying for direction.

It was just prior to noon ten days after he spoke with the priest as he remained in his room searching for any practical approach on how he might obtain the sought after interview, when there was a knock on the door. The caller was the desk clerk of the Hotel Emporio. With hands trembling and a facial expression resembling a mask of stone, he delivered a letter that, for obvious reasons, had the presentment of being very important. Delivered to the hotel by government courier, the upper left corner of the envelope was embossed with "President of the Republic, Palacio Nacional, Mexico, D.F."—unmistakably a letter from the president.

Once alone, Eduardo sat motionless and flattered though not surprised to receive a letter of such import. He had very clearly been told that he would be a direct employee of the chief executive, free from intervention by the bureaucracy. While he was not overwhelmed by receiving the letter, it was not so with the clerk who delivered it and found it to be mind shattering.

Never before had anyone in the town received a direct communication from such an authority. The clerk, excited beyond description, was experiencing an increased heartbeat, elevated blood pressure and difficulty in breathing. It was but a matter of minutes that word of this first-ever event spread throughout the ever-present groups in the town square. The topic of conversation centered on the young man in Room 207 in the Hotel Emporio and his prized possession.

It was not unusual that the story passed to the barbershop, grocery store, post office and every corner of the town center. Understandably, it was within hours that the news had reached the office of the *cacique,* where Raul Molina notified his boss. No longer would Eduardo be required to rack his brain as to how he would communicate with *el Toro.*

It was late afternoon when the aspiring engineer was utterly shocked to receive a hand delivered letter from no other than Raul Molina that read, "Colonel Alejandro Fernandez Bravo invites you to be present at the *Palicio Municipal* (Town Hall) tomorrow at 1:00 P.M." It was signed by Molina as *secretario particular* (private secretary). It was a well-established fact that such an invitation was non-negotiable. For Eduardo, he finally was enjoying, in a small way, the sweet smell of success.

The invitation, or more accurately the directive, caused Eduardo to pass a sleepless night even though he peacefully exhaled long sighs of contentment. He appeared to have gathered a strong inner sense of strength while his lingering despair was vanishing. He continued to be astonished that a single letter could alter his life so quickly and drastically. He would forever be grateful for it.

Not being able to sleep, he arose to rehearse his prepared presentation for a water system. He repeated it over and over to the point where he virtually committed the proposal to memory.

Arriving at the massive pyramid-style building at 12:45 P.M., he announced himself and was ushered into an outer reception area where he anxiously awaited the longed-for meeting. He had waited almost two months for this moment and not knowing what to expect, recalled the words of Livy, the great Roman historian who, in the sixteenth century, said, "We fear things in proportion to our ignorance of them."

At long last, and promptly at 1:00 P.M., he was directed into the office of the *cacique* by Molina. Eduardo was startled to see the size of *el Toro* who by best estimate was seven feet tall and whose dark, hawkish face seemed never to have known a smile. Coupled with his arrogant sallow features and full lips set in a perpetual sneer, he was someone with whom one would not choose to argue.

To be received punctually by the colonel was most unusual. His chamber in the government building was a massive room trimmed in dark wood. The oak furniture was bulky, unattractive and ornate. The *cacique* was seated behind a monstrous desk on an equally monstrous high-back chair. There were two rose-colored couches that faced each other on a carpet that was a shade of gray designed to hide dirt.

Once comfortably seated in a mammoth lounge chair, Eduardo initially observed a most imposing and obese soldier-like individual who was slightly shorter than Molina. He was a most impressive sight with a full head of hair and a long, gray, drooping handlebar mustached face of pronounced battlefield wrinkles. The overly wide suspenders supporting his trousers were stretched over a very robust abdomen.

In his typical dictatorial fashion, the colonel ordered his visitor to move to an overstuffed chair closer to his desk meanwhile commanding Molina to leave the room. His first words were *"Bienvenido, mi hijo."* (Welcome, my son.)

Eduardo wisely responded, *"Gracias* (Thank you), Señor Colonel." By prefacing the title with "sir," the normal form of greeting assumes the highest degree of respectability. As expected, the conversation was both initiated and completely dominated by the *cacique*. Throughout the one-sided discourse, Eduardo was never given the opportunity to plead his case or tender his prepared plan for potable water.

Throughout the meeting, the *cacique* fired probing questions at his visitor, at times asking a new query before Eduardo had completed answering that which was last asked. At one point, and in a most direct manner he asked, "Do you personally know the president? Have you met with him in Mexico City?" The answer was a simple "yes." There were even somewhat personal questions regarding the young man's parents and family history. The questioning continued, almost without end, during which time it was evident that the *cacique* was most impressed with his guest.

He found the engineer to be handsome, immaculately groomed, well mannered and equally well spoken. His Spanish ancestral background, incredible academic success and keen comprehension all combined to leave an extremely favorable impression on *el jefe* (the chief).

As the colonel scrupulously appraised his caller, his thoughts were on his only child, a daughter, Rosita, now eighteen years of age. Even while the questioning continued, the colonel reminisced on the tragic day when his beloved wife, Rosa, his companion for less than a year, passed away during childbirth. He was fully cognizant that in the isolated provincial town of Soledad, there was no young male who could even approach possessing the multitude of attributes he had encountered in the young man seated nearby. It was at that moment he ascertained that he had selected a husband for his treasured Rosita.

The one-sided discussion was, in reality, a four-hour, in-depth, exhaustive interrogation of Eduardo. As the confabulation came to an end, the two rose. The *cacique* approached his newly-adopted friend, placed his hand on Eduardo's shoulder and said, "This is an order, son. You shall remain in Soledad and assume the dual duties of Director of Education and the municipality's chief engineer." Eduardo stood motionless, stunned by the decree, particularly in that his future boss asked neither for his comment nor for his acceptance. He quickly realized that he had no option other than comply with that which was given as an undisputable order.

The autocrat then told his visitor to come to dinner at his residence at 8:00 P.M., the normal dinner hour, adding that a carriage would call for him at his hotel.

Precisely at the appointed hour, the invited guest was ushered into the living room of the gargantuan custom-designed Spanish-style hacienda. It was obvious that the conquerors' architects, though they employed Indian labor, left their imprint on the building, notably the decorative design, the façade and the majestic elegance of the structure giving it its name, the "mansion."

The arched entrance was encircled with statuary, sculpted columns and engraved decoration of celestial cherubs peering from wall indents.

It was a monstrous fifteen thousand square foot home of five bedrooms, seven baths, living room, dining room, den and kitchen. There was also an adjoining dining area for the hired help. At close proximity, there were servants' quarters, stables and a carriage house.

Eduardo perceived that the house exuded a feeling of comfortable decay, as there was an unavoidable dampish odor. He felt dwarfed by the soaring pilasters, frescoed ceilings and shoddy massive furniture. In typical fashion, a spiral staircase led to the second floor.

It was only a matter of minutes before the colonel, resplendent in his military uniform, appeared accompanied by his lovely daughter, Rosita. She was a truly beautiful, tall, slim *mestizo* young lady—a striking blend of a black-tressed Spanish beauty with some traditional Indian features. Her glowing eyes maintained a gleam that make-up could not improve. Her smile was eager and alive with affection and warmth.

Once introduced, there was immediate eye contact between the two with the *cacique* immediately recognizing that negotiating a union would not require the potency of his office. After a brief exchange, niceties and mutual toasts with fruit punch they passed to the massive dining room with its sixteen-foot ceilings and floral design carpet. The furniture was old, heavy and well crafted of Spanish colonial motif giving the appearance of antiques accented with timeworn distinction.

Seated at a dining table capable of accommodating thirty people, the colonel ordered wine for all. Not being one to perform in true diplomatic fashion, he offered a toast, *"A tu, Rosita, y tu, Eduardo. Un brindis por buen salud y una vida larga."* (To you, Rosita, and you, Eduardo. A toast for good health and long life.) Using the familiar *"tu"* for a young man he had just met, he implied that the two would be together through life. He was not one to beat around the bush.

Accustomed as he was to monopolizing a conversation, in this case he refrained allowing the two young people to converse freely. It was only when the dialogue slowed that he interjected an occasional word to stimulate the exchange. There was an obvious mutual attraction to the extent that Don Alejandro felt assured that he had at last found the son he had always wanted. As he sat and observed the two conversing, a flicker of a smile rose at the edges of his mouth.

As the evening drew to a close, Eduardo, in his true gentlemanly fashion, grasped Rosita's hand and planted a kiss causing a blush of pleasure to color her cheeks. With the hour growing late, her father accompanied their guest to the door. Again placing his hand on the visitor's shoulder, he bid him goodnight saying, *"Buenos noches, mi hijo. Mañana a la 10:00 de la mañana—tenemos much que hacer."* (Good night, my son. Tomorrow 10:00 A.M. – we have much to do.) Eduardo was then taken by carriage to his hotel. For all practical purposes, he was now a member of the inner circle. He was totally amazed and clearly confused by the speed at which events were occurring.

Early the following morning the newly appointed town engineer was awaiting the arrival of his boss. His first day was spent in the company of Molina who introduced him to the many municipal employees, after which he selected an adequate office and secretary appropriate for the newly appointed Director of Education and chief engineer. Prior to departing in late afternoon, he was again invited to dine with Don Alejandro and Rosita.

As before, he was carriaged to the mansion and, as before, virtually passed the entire evening conversing with his female dinner companion. Within minutes after enjoying desert, the *cacique* excused himself allowing the two to continue their discussion alone in the living room.

Each day was a repetition of the day before. Eduardo had demonstrated his capabilities by rapidly grasping the every day challenges of his office and efficiently resolving them. Each evening was a carbon copy of the evening past. Sundays were different as they attended church together with the traditional Sunday dinner served at 2:00 P.M. Life for the three became routine with but one exception. Rosita had been given permission to accompany her admirer to local receptions, activities and restaurants in the evening subject to one inflexible condition. The two, without exception, would be escorted at all times by a *dueña* (chaperone) who happened to be an elderly distant cousin of the colonel.

Throughout the period of courtship, the colonel was extremely mindful not to mention, either in general or in detail, any of the businesses that he owned and operated. He was more than aware of the young man's ultra visionary quixotic connections.

Since the inception of the relationship, the *cacique* could not recall when he had been more elated. He was ecstatic with the turn of events. It was unavoidably visible that the normal scowling expression was a thing of the past. Now, his dark, sparkling eyes looked out from his sun-toughened face while an easy smile played across his face.

And so it went for one month when, as per plan and wish of the absolute ruler, Eduardo asked for Rosita's hand in marriage and, needless to say, permission was granted. For all, there was intense pleasure, particularly for the future bride, which was evidenced by her happy, bubbling expression. She was blissfully elated and fully alive. Without consultation, and as one might expect, Don Alejandro set the wedding date.

CHAPTER V

THE START OF A NEW LIFE

The colonel, in the warm exuberance of his inner feelings, took complete charge of the wedding preparations. He loved every minute of it. Everyone became involved and participated in the arrangements for the wedding—the entire staff of town's employees, merchants, ranchers, farmers, grocers, musicians, and trades people.

It was on a beautiful Sunday, November 9, 1873, afternoon at 5:00 P.M., that Rosita Fernandez Vasquez and Eduardo Hernandez Gonzalez would be joined in holy matrimony by Father Agustin Diaz. Everything was in place and the town sparkled with red, white and green bunting from every treetop. During the course of the ceremony, the colonel could not refrain from quietly reminiscing about the past. He remembered the day his baby girl was born and the tragic death of his beloved wife, Rosa.

He looked back on how a beautiful Indian maid, Marta Moreno, much his junior, cared for and raised his daughter while he attended to his obligations as town administrator meanwhile acquiring and managing numerous business enterprises. He remembered how, during the course of Marta's twelve years of mother-like attention, he would have the caretaker join him in his bedroom once the child was asleep. His guilt was constant during the illicit relationship and once Rosita had grown into adolescence, he banished his mistress to the distant *Isla de Mujeres* (Island of Women) in order to safeguard his shameful behavior.

Isla de Mujeres was a tiny, desolate land mass situated some five miles off the coast of the Mexican territory of Yucatan. This diminutive island, consisting of but forty square miles, was discovered in 1520 and was initially utilized as a haven of isolation by Indian chiefs and Spanish noblemen who banished their mistresses to the island when they were no longer desired. The residents had developed small farms to facilitate their survival. For decades, they also received periodic deliveries of supplemental food and clothing arranged for by the men of power responsible for their placement on the island. Stringent security measures prevented escape. It was not until 1705 that an order of nuns, funded by a grant from Spain, established a convent on the islet.

As the ceremony progressed, his strong sun-creased face rearranged itself into an admiring smile of approval. With his eyes brightened with pleasure, this stalwart military man could not keep the tears from flowing down his cheeks.

Rosita's tenth birthday remained vivid in his memory. A memorable birthday celebration had been arranged by Marta. It was on this occasion that the father presented his adored daughter with a St. Christopher medallion. It was a gift to treasure—gold with the image of the saint in the center and encircled with diamonds.

The party was an overwhelming success and would not have been complete without a lengthy dissertation by the colonel who was never at a loss for words. He proceeded to explain that Christopher meant Christ-bearer and why Christopher, who died in the third century, became a martyr. Continuing he said, "Legend tells us that when Christopher was crossing a river, a child asked to be carried across. However, when Christopher put the child on his shoulders he found the child to be unbelievably heavy. The child, as the fable portrays it, was Christ carrying the weight of the world. This, my child, is why

Christopher is the patron saint of all travelers. Wear this medallion as you travel the road of life and you will have a protector eternally watching over you." The child was too young to fully appreciate the beautiful, costly gift she had just received. It was not so with Marta who could not remove her eyes from the pendant.

The prolonged religious service afforded the colonel an opportunity to return to thoughts of the past. However, when his name was called in the ceremonial procedure, his return to thoughts of the past came to an abrupt end. Once the couple had been united in holy matrimony, the festivities commenced.

A twelve-piece mariachi band set the convivial tone of the reception. The six hundred guests had brought a myriad of wedding gifts that covered the gamut from fine gold and silver offerings to horses, cows and other livestock. Such an event had never before occurred in Soledad. To add to the festivities, there were male and female vocalists, acrobats and magicians. There appeared to be no end to the serving of food consisting of barbecue, chicken, lamb, rice, beans, sauces, peppers and, of course, the essential tortillas. The tortillas of the region were distinct in that the farmers raised a blue corn resulting in blue tortillas. Normally, they were made much larger, about nine inches in diameter. With an open bar of soft drinks, tequila, pulque, mescal and beer, the celebrants lingered until 5:00 A.M. Gratefully, the colonel knew that while men had built his residence, Rosita would once again make it a home.

Too exhausted to proceed on their planned honeymoon at the archeological ruins of Santo Domingo de Palenque, some ninety miles distant, the newlyweds remained at the mansion departing late afternoon the following day. Upon arriving at the Mayan ruins of Santo Domingo de Palenque in late evening, the newlyweds checked into the Hotel Superior, which was owned, in part, by the bride's father. The hotel, a massive, weather-beaten structure of Spanish colonial design, was snuggled in the hillside and surrounded by eucalyptus trees.

Still exhausted, the couple decided on a restful night before touring the hotel site. As expected, the honeymooners did not leave their presidential suite until after noon. Patiently waiting for them in the lobby was their tour guide, Mario, who, as planned, was ready to go at 9:00 A.M. After a profound apology to Mario, the trio was off on their sightseeing trip. Mario was thoroughly familiar with the estate, as his father had served as caretaker for the past thirty years with Mario passing his entire life at the hotel. In precise detail, he commented on the history and surroundings of the impressive property.

He explicated that the principal structure was built in 1720 with rock from a nearby quarry and with tile imported from Spain. It was strikingly beautiful with its loftiness, majestic appearance and grandeur. Secreted in dense jungle, the crumbling, intricately decorated structures imparted the feeling that ghosts of the past continued to inhabit the edifice. He went on to say that it was believed that the architecture at Palenque was similar, in some degree, to that of southwest Asia. It was thought that this similarity provided a link between Mexico and the Orient.

He continued by pointing out that the Palenque complex occupied the lower foothills of the Sierra Madre in one of Mexico's wettest, most lush, forested territory. Further explanation indicated that development of the site began as a farming settlement about 100 B.C. and flourished between A.D. 600 and A.D. 700 at which time the community controlled vast land areas.

He added that for unknown reasons the area was abandoned some two hundred years later. He concluded by saying that the interpretations of inscriptions carved into Palenque's structures have given insight to the names of the inhabitants, rules of behavior, dates of birthdays, marriages and even the point in time of the start and finish of armed military campaigns.

With the tour completed, it was the hour for a specially prepared candlelight dinner as ordered by the colonel. From the flickering of the flame, a bright light twinkled in the depths of Eduardo's dark eyes while Rosita's green eyes were full of life, warmth and unquenchable love. A strong sensuous radiation passed between them.

The following day it was off again with Mario who wished to supplement the previous day's tour with a visit to La Cascada de Agua Azul (The Blue Water Waterfalls), which was nearby. The trio walked through long rows of palm trees and exotic flowers for forty-five minutes before reaching the falls. The waterfalls emitted a sound similar to the roaring warning clamor of an awesome storm.

It was now day three of their visit to the historic site of Palenque. Mario had suggested that they start at 9:00 A.M. the following day, however, the "lovebirds", now exhibiting signs of weariness, prevailed upon their guide to delay the hour until noon allowing them time to enjoy a late breakfast. Upon hearing his guide's suggestion, Eduardo thought, "No wonder he is ready to go at an early hour. He had a full night's sleep while I had to attend to my husbandly duties."

As planned, promptly at noon they were off to visit one of the principal attractions of Palenque—the Templo de las Inscripciones (Temple of the Inscriptions), which takes its name from the three gigantic limestone tablets located at the entrance and inscribed with hieroglyphics.

At close pursuit to their escort, they labored for almost thirty minutes to climb the stairs to the top of the pyramidal structure from where they could marvel at the panoramic view of the surrounding structures. Mario pointed out that from their vantage point, the Palace of Palenque was in clear eyeshot.

He went on to explain, "This Temple of Inscriptions is the resting place of Pacal, the king who ruled Palenque for almost seventy years beginning at the ripe old age of twelve. It is believed to be the only temple in Mexico constructed expressly to be a tomb."

After a short rest period, they followed Mario through the crypt after having been told that as a result of the ever-present humidity, the floor and steps were quite slippery and consequently they should proceed with extreme caution.

Mario was most precise in narrating the meaning of the inscriptions and carvings on the walls as well as the sarcophagus itself. As the hour was approaching 4:30 P.M., in addition to their being exhausted, Eduardo suggested that they commence the long trip down the Temple's steps and then return to their lodging.

Once back at the hotel, Mario proposed, "Tomorrow we shall visit the Palace—it is a complex of stepped buildings and court yards connected by corridors and an extensive system of underground passageways. You will find it most interesting.

Merely hearing the word "stepped" was enough to send electrifying shock through the visitors for they were now experiencing an extreme case of "honeymooners' fatigue."

At the risk of appearing unappreciative, Eduardo, in his most delicate and diplomatic manner, explicated that they had seen enough and would most appreciate time to rest prior to returning to Soledad.

After presenting Mario with a meaningful gift, they exchanged *abrazos* with their attentive guide bidding him a warm and sincere "*Hasta luego*." With this, they had come to the end of their three-day familiarization tour. They would spend the remainder of the week doing only what they wished to do.

With the *luna de miel* (honeymoon) now over, the

couple returned to Soledad having decided, at the request of the *cacique*, to establish their residence at the mansion. It was now on to a normal day-to-day life. Eduardo went to his office each morning while Rosita passed her day at home or socialized with friends.

Prior to departing on their honeymoon, the colonel petitioned, as a special favor, that Rosita become pregnant, as he sorely wished to have a grandchild. Always the manipulator, he believed that the addition of a newborn would solidify the marriage.

With but several months since they exchanged wedding vows, Eduardo proudly informed his father-in-law that in approximately eight months he would become a grandfather.

Life was good! The colonel had mellowed somewhat, Eduardo was performing beyond expectation and Rosita was a lady in waiting, constantly being cautioned by both men not to bend, stretch, lift or walk excessively. Don Alejandro, as he was now addressed by his son-in-law, decided to delay introducing his adopted son to his many business enterprises. He would defer until after the long awaited birth of a grandchild. He was more than satisfied that his *cacique*-in-training was almost ready for active participation in his diverse commercial ventures.

The day was Wednesday, September 16, 1874, Mexico's anniversary of its independence from Spain and a very special day in the family's household. The Gonzalez family was blessed with a little girl who, at the colonel's solicitation, was named Maria in memory of his mother. The parents were exuberant, only being out done in their joy by the proud grandfather.

Always in control, the *cacique* took complete charge in placing all the wheels in motion regarding the baptism. As expected, Father Agustin Diaz was called into service and entrusted with all things religious including rehearsing the choir. As always, Father Diaz performed magnificently. From the church, the assemblage moved to the mansion where everyone enjoyed a seated dinner that resembled a royal banquet complete with a string quartet and strolling violinists. No such event would be complete without the endless toasts to health, happiness and long life. Eventually, the wining, dining and salutations culminated a day that no one, particularly the parents and the grandfather, would ever forget.

The daily family routine continued as before with the exception that there was a new addition in the home and her *niñera* (caretaker), Josefina. The caretaker was thoroughly experienced in her job having performed the same service for two other prominent families in the community.

As the days passed into weeks and the weeks into months, the family bonded enjoying a sense of glorious happiness. Rosita directed the management of the mansion while Eduardo capably assumed many of the administrative responsibilities of the town, allowing the proud grandfather freedom to derive unbounded pleasure from his grandchild.

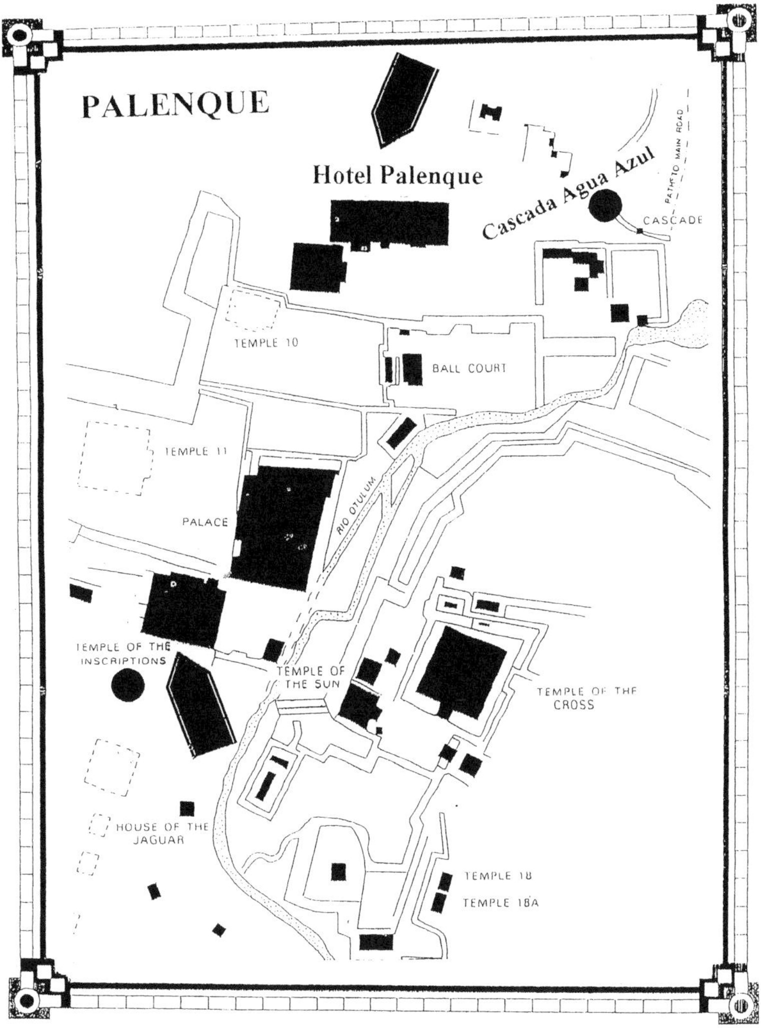
PALENQUE
Hotel Palenque
Cascada Agua Azul
PATH TO MAIN ROAD
CASCADE
TEMPLE 10
BALL COURT
TEMPLE 11
PALACE
RIO OTULUM
TEMPLE OF THE INSCRIPTIONS
TEMPLE OF THE SUN
TEMPLE OF THE CROSS
HOUSE OF THE JAGUAR
TEMPLE 18
TEMPLE 18A

CHAPTER VI

DON ALEJANDRO AND SANTA ANNA

It was at this point that the colonel decided to initiate the indoctrination of his adopted son. Diplomacy was not an attribute of the *cacique*; and being an advocate of telling it like is, he believed the moment had arrived to discuss his past and clarify the "whys" of the present.

Selecting a day when his daughter would be away, he suggested that the men remain at home for a man-to-man discussion. From past experience, Eduardo knew the so-called discussion would be one directional.

Once comfortably seated, the younger, with his normal calm and dazzling smile, anxiously awaited the opening remarks. The colonel opened the conversation by declaring, "In days past, the *cacique*, as we know him today, was head of a region and titled *gobernador* (governor). He was installed by Spanish fiat and entrusted to run the Indian pueblos, supervise their communal lands, maintain order, organize labor groups, enforce their religious conversion, including church attendance, control the clergy and see that the required royal tribute was promptly paid."

Shaking his head he emphasized, "Those were terribly difficult days, terribly difficult days. There was little contrariness in being an Indian or a poor *mestizo*.

"As poor *mestizos*, we were ordered to work for the Spaniards in their lumber cutting, mining or other profitable businesses. We considered ourselves fortunate when they would allow the male heads of families time to plant and harvest their own crops.

"With so many epidemics of small pox and measles, diseases brought by the invaders, there was widespread death. The death toll was so great that the decline in the Indian/*mestizo* population created a labor shortage. It was plain and simple slavery in its worst form.

"Unlike yourself, I was born of third generation *mestizos*—extremely poor. I envy so much the fine formal education and success you have achieved. I did not have the privilege of attending school nor enjoy even the most basic essentials of life. Now, I'll get on with the story of my past. At the age of ten, my father abandoned my family—my mother, two brothers, sister and me. It was then necessary for me to work to assist my mother with every day expenses in maintaining our home. First, it was working in the fields and then later on a ranch cleaning the horse stalls—an undesirable and unforgettable job.

"Some years later, I had the good fortune of being noticed by a town merchant who allowed me to work in his general store. There I had the opportunity to learn how business was conducted and how the storeowner exploited the Indians. His practice was to offer them credit to the extent that the borrowers were never liberated from their financial commitment. The theory behind it was that by keeping the Indians in a constant state of indebtedness, their only escape was to surrender to the *mestizo* way of life.

"At age twenty-two, I left Soledad to journey to Veracruz. You must know that Mexico, at that time, had achieved its independence; however, there remained pockets of Spanish military scattered throughout that refused to recognize the new nation. Hence, there were skirmishes in all areas, and it was my wish to help enforce Mexico's right to self determination."

Immersed and glued to every word spoken, Eduardo attempted to better understand his father-in-law's lack of compassion and tyrannical behavior. He pondered whether the savage-like oppression forced on Don Alejandro as a young man might have caused him to now become the oppressor.

Continuing, Don Alejandro said, "It was in Veracruz, as a young patriot, I enlisted in the army. I wished to have the honor of serving with General Santa Anna—I wished for this more than anything else, for the general was hailed by all for his successes in routing remaining Spaniards from the area.

"I had repeatedly read about the general and admired him. I was spellbound, as I would analyze his glorious victory against superior forces at San Luis Potosi—a battle to end all battles. With eighteen thousand men, mostly raw conscripts, he led his troops across miles of arid land during mid-winter without sufficient food and water for his lightly clad and poorly armed soldiers. He substituted his lack of supplies with fiery motivation. He repeatedly reminded his men that the best soldiers were not warlike, however, a military man dishonored was worse than death.

"This was to be a test of superior command. Bitter cold winds lashed his troops by night, forcing them to huddle around campfires. In contrast, during the day, with the desert sun ablaze, the heat parched the mouths of his weary troops. Dead horses and oxen; broken wagons and leftover supplies; rotting carcasses of soldiers marked the route of Santa Anna's army.

"Just prior to engaging the enemy, the general reminded his troops, 'To kill one person you are a villain—to kill a thousand you are a hero. I want only heroes in my army.'

"Finally, the day of combat arrived. The war raged unmercifully for three days with heavy losses on each side. With the final shot, Santa Anna emerged victorious, subduing the Spaniards in a major critical engagement.

The final accounting of the general's army laid bare four thousand losses made up of the dead, the sick and the deserters with no stomach for combat. Never to be forgotten was the sight of Santa Anna, riding along the long line of troops shouting words of encouragement, dismounting to help load gunpowder on a wagon or scolding cowards.

"From that point in Mexico's history, Santa Anna was proclaimed the man of the hour. He played a vital role in executing the Veracruz-formulated Plan de Casa Mata in 1823. This was a blueprint by which the troops under Santa Anna would march to Mexico City, subduing all opposition, with the intent of wresting undisputed centralized control from Agustin de Iturbide, the self-proclaimed Creole president. Santa Anna was a courageous, cruel, disconsolate and charming man who was never happier than when he was waging war.

"My son, this was a most momentous occasion, for on this day I was a part of the general's army fighting for my nation's freedom. Even with Iturbide proclaimed 'father of the nation,' there continued to be lawlessness in many parts of the country. Consequently, he was overpowered and exiled. General Guadalupe Victoria assumed the presidency. It was unimportant to me who served as president, as long as Santa Anna controlled the army. Much to my delight, in 1829, General Santa Anna deposed the indecisive Victoria and assumed the highest office in the land.

"By that time, I had spent six years by my general's side. I was promoted to the rank of lieutenant; and for the first time in my life, I achieved respectability.

"In the year 1833, while we were on a mission to quell an uprising, Vice President Gomez Farias installed himself as president. However, and as I expected, upon our return, the general promptly ousted the rebellious vice president and reinstalled himself as the chief of state. It was during this ouster that I proved myself under fire. In recognition of my performance, I was presented to my general. I had never met General Santa Anna, and I always wondered what he would be like. He was all that I had imagined and more—tall, stately, and strong with a square wall of forehead, heavy brows and scraggly beard. His troubled, long and bony granite-like face, leathery skin and sallow complexion combined with a warm, arresting smile made me feel privileged to have met him.

"He rewarded me with a field promotion to major and appointed me his aide. My son, that was the most memorable moment in my life.

"These were, indeed, turbulent times. In an effort to subjugate continued internal chaos, the president abolished all regional autonomy. This action brought on regional revolts, which were crushed by our overpowering strength. However, Texas was the exception.

"It was shortly after Santa Anna's abolition of autonomy that the Texas community of American colonizers, along with the Texas Mexicans, staged a movement to separate Texas from the republic.

"In November 1835, seeing themselves once again subject to Mexican rule in their local affairs, the Texans openly rebelled and drove out Santa Anna's troops. In just four months, they declared themselves an independent republic. Fifty thousand Americans poured into the new republic.

"I can tell you, son, the general was no office general—he didn't send anyone to undertake his perilous missions. As president, he led an army of six thousand men into the biggest battle of the time. I was by his side throughout the engagement at the Alamo. It was there he massacred all of the defenders. I was seriously wounded in combat to the extent that I knew my days as a soldier had come to an end. Prior to my retiring my commission, the general awarded me the medal that you see in that case on the wall and honored me with the rank of colonel. No longer a soldier, I returned home to Soledad.

"Once home, I decided to engage a qualified local professor to quickly instruct me in proper Spanish and mathematics. I so wanted to be better educated. At home, as a decorated colonel, I was at long last a highly respected citizen. I was surprised to learn that since leaving seventeen years ago, that the central government's appointed regional bureaucrat had had been replaced by a *cacique*, General Alfonso Corona del Rosal, a retired pre-colonial army hero who gained fame fighting the Spaniards in the late 1700's. The general noticed, as good fortune would have it, a relatively young retired colonel who had distinguished himself in combat.

"In view of the general's advanced age, he was conducting a search for a successor. During the past decade, inasmuch as presidents were previously military men, it had become a practice to choose all regional chiefs and local *caciques* from among those with military distinction. This program of conversion was, in effect, a way of rewarding militarists for service to their country.

"Now, let me tell you about General Corona. He was a man of few words and quick decisions. I was summoned to his quarters where he confronted me by asking if I wished to serve as his deputy. I immediately accepted his offer. After a pleasant lunch and familiarization tour of the town's administration building, we proceeded to his office where he assigned me a desk.

"Throughout my years of service to the general, I was repeatedly lectured on the fact that riches translated into power, although getting rich was no assurance of staying rich nor retaining power. He also repeatedly told me that it takes a certain discipline to amass wealth and another form of discipline to retain it. This hypotheses was repeated over and over, each time with the same closing remark, 'If you long for power and wish to stay powerful, you must acquire both forms of discipline.'

"And so, my son, for the next sixteen years I served the general as a loyal servant and understudy until his death in 1854.

"The intervening years since returning to Soledad were certainly rewarding to me. As a rising understudy and as a result of the beneficence of the general, I was given numerous insider business opportunities and rewarded with land tracts, operating farms and even a cattle ranch.

"Later, as *cacique*, I diligently pursued an untiring effort to perfect my mastery of Spanish and proficiency as a speaker. My determination to improve was such that I contracted with a professor of English at the University of Mexico in the capital to come to Soledad. Once here, I placed him in a leisurely, though well-paying, position in our town's administrative organization. I devoted one hour each day to instruction by him.

"As I look back on my life, how vividly I can still see that young boy who worked as a farm hand, cleaned stables and accepted any and all odd jobs. My, he has come a long way.

"Life was good to me in those days. It became even better when I met and began courting a young nurse, Rosa Vasquez Aguilar—a true *mestizo* who adored her man. She was slender, dark and fiery with piercing eyes that glowed. With all of her spontaneity, she was also gentle, serenely wise and charming.

"The chemistry was certainly there for it was after only a brief courtship and just two weeks after I assumed command of this region that we were joined in holy matrimony. Out of respect for my benefactor who had recently passed away, the wedding was small and private with only a few of my intimate friends in attendance.

"As *cacique*, I, Alejandro Fernandez Bravo, made it unmistakably clear to one and all that I would, hereafter, be addressed as colonel or, by very personal friends, as Don

Alejandro. I ordered that my wife be respectfully addressed as Doña (Madame) Rosa.

"Together we enjoyed a life of luxury. One of my first acts was to expropriate my home—a massive residence constructed by the Spaniards, owned by the government and maintained as a historic site. That privilege was but another perk of being *cacique*.

"Each day I fulfilled my responsibility as town administrator while Rosa performed her wifely duties at home by day and especially at night. To the extent that in just nine months after exchanging marriage vows, Rosa gave birth to a little girl we named Rosita.

"Unfortunately, life is strange for while we remember the good, we cannot forget the bad. With the joy of an addition to our family, there was an accompanying tragedy. As a result of complications during childbirth combined with inferior medical facilities, Rosa passed from the earth. I was crushed beyond description. It was a heart-wrenching end to a loving, though much too short, life together."

Wiping tears from his eyes, the *cacique* continued, "After a month of mourning, I knew that, somehow, life would go on, as my mind, body and soul were concentrated on a one month old baby girl.

"It was vital that I locate a suitable caretaker for little Rosita. After numerous interviews, I selected Marta Moreno, a strikingly beautiful Indian maid. With the period of lamentation now concluded and Rosita being properly cared for, I returned to my daily administrative commitments with unharnessed energy and bitterness. The limited compassion for the oppressed and underprivileged I once possessed had vanished. I harbored an unrelenting drive to acquire, by whatever means, additional businesses and wealth. Except for my days at the office, I became a social recluse devoting each evening to the company of Rosita, my sole pride and joy. Marta was my only relief from frustration once my little girl had fallen asleep.

"And so it went, year after year, with my daughter and myself growing older and closer with time. Our lives were quite routine until a young engineer came into our lives. Eduardo, my son, I have, through this day, detailed the life of joy and adversities of a *cacique* once again contented. You have brought great happiness to this house.

"Now, my son, you've heard enough for one day, so let's join our family for an enjoyable dinner."

Throughout the entire narration, except for a lunch break, Eduardo did not speak, for he was both fascinated by the account and completely aware of the colonel's displeasure when interrupted.

CHAPTER VII

AN INTRODUCTION TO BUSINESS

Now having passed his life in review for his son, Don Alejandro believed it was the appropriate time to introduce him to his varied business interests in preparation for future time engendered situations.

The indoctrination began one morning at the mansion when he surprised his understudy by advising him that he was about to become acquainted with the family businesses. The first stop was at the wholly owned soft drink bottling plant where many distinct flavors of soft drinks in two distinct sizes were produced.

The larger of the two sizes, called Jumbo, was a sixteen ounce nutriment and sold for one peso, while the smaller, called Superior, was twelve ounces and sold for two pesos. The common belief was that the reduced size drink was of higher quality, hence its name, and was preferred by those who could afford it, while the less affluent masses consumed the less expensive Jumbo. It was a highly profitable business that operated day and night. The plant production was distributed over an area of one hundred square miles and not restricted to Soledad.

Eduardo toured the facility, step-by-step, beginning with the basic raw materials, through the mixing process, testing and so on to the final stage of filling the bottles. It was during the filling process of the Jumbo bottles that this keen observer noticed that once the line of larger bottles had been completed, the same liquid was discharged into the smaller, more expensive bottles. Without hesitation, he rushed to the side of his father-in-law to call this to his attention. He was thoroughly befuddled when told, "Yes, I know." Bewildered as he was, he did not ask for an explanation.

With his tour of the production facility concluded, he was introduced to the office staff and was given a briefing on the components of the liquids employed and a cost analysis. He was amazed to learn of the enormous amount of sugar employed in the manufacturing process and the apparent above market price paid for the ingredient. It was pointed out that while the price was, indeed, considerable, it was, in reality, a transfer from one pocket to another, as the sugar purchased was grown in the colonel's sugar cane fields and processed in his refinery.

It was further noted that inasmuch as the daily diet of the Mexicans was deficient in energy, utilizing abnormal amounts of sugar served as an energy supplement to the daily food intake. Both the large amount of energy-producing sugar utilized and its substantial cost afforded the *cacique* the opportunity to demonstrate to the authorities in Mexico City that he had the consumer's welfare at heart.

The perusal continued. It was explained that the pumps in the patio were a somewhat detached business. It was from these deposits of kerosene and lubricating oil that distribution was effected to the *cacique*'s retail petroleum product outlets.

Thus, the day of enlightenment had come to an end. It was during the return trip to the mansion that Eduardo could no longer refrain from asking, "Don Alejandro, would you please clarify, for my benefit, why you were not dismayed when I mentioned the fact that both the Jumbo and the Superior bottles were filled with the same liquid?"

Calmly, the colonel responded, "My dear son, let me tell you in just a few words. What the public doesn't know won't hurt them. Let this be a lesson in psychology, where presentation is the most important element in merchandising a product. It is assumed by the consuming public that the smaller, costlier product must certainly be superior just as its name implies."

Somewhat stunned, Eduardo sat speechless, his face a combination of defiance and disappointment. What he had just learned was in direct conflict to that which he had been taught and believed throughout his young life. Still not speaking, he remained dumbfounded with disbelief, suppressed rage and disillusionment.

Throughout dinner that evening, he concealed any sense of disenchantment while maintaining his normal pleasant and distinguished demeanor. He knew from deep within that it would be necessary to cogitate and evaluate a most distressing situation.

Throughout the following day, without displaying his internal anguish, he questioned himself as to right, wrong and all in between. Don Alejandro's words continued to haunt him. However he might resolve his predicament, he was cognizant that he would be incapable of doing anything that might jeopardize his cherished relationship with his adored Rosita. Inasmuch as he was so deeply immersed with the colonel in both business and family, he realized whatever his determination might be, he could, in no way, imperil his relationship with him.

It was a beautiful fall day, perfectly suited to celebrate Maria's first birthday. It was, as well, September 16, 1875, the revered day on which Mexico celebrates its 1810 Dia de la Independencia (Independence Day). The nation's freedom was heralded when a poor priest, Miguel Hidalgo y Costilla, uttered his cry for an uprising from the balcony of a small church in the town of Dolores Hidalgo in the state of Guanajato. The unforgettable *"Grito de Dolores"* (Cry of Sorrows), "Death to the Spaniards! Long live the Virgin of Guadalupe!", called for revolution, a new government and the redistribution of land. The rebellion led by Father Hidalgo, and supported by the Indians under the banner of the Mexican Virgin of Guadalupe, marched on Mexico City. Thus began the revolution for reform, which, after years of conflict, eventually resulted in the Constitution of 1824.

Out of respect for the national holiday and, more particularly, in homage to the *cacique*, all of the town's citizenry participated in one form or another. The town was adorned with the tri-colors of Mexico.

There were flags in every direction. Bunting and lights were strung from pillar to post. Picture posters of the president were hung from buildings and posted on all available wall space.

In early forenoon, the local school children, police and fire departments paraded interspersed with makeshift marching bands. At approximately 3:00 P.M., an enormous barbecue was offered, provided by local vendors at the suggestion of the *cacique*. Don Alejandro's bottling plant contributed the soft drinks.

On this special day, all schools and businesses were closed with the townspeople donning their Sunday best. The music and entertainment continued until 11:00 P.M. Precisely at that hour, the colonel, resplendent in his army uniform, waved a large Mexican flag attached to a long pole from the second floor balcony of the town hall. As he waved the colors from side-to-side, he recited the words uttered by Father Miguel Hidalgo sixty-five years earlier. With the waving of the flag and as the colonel spoke, the assembled throng loudly shouted, "*Viva* (Long Live) Mexico". It was truly an impressive and colorful celebration. Along with the festive recognition of the national day, Maria was given quite a notable birthday party, which would be repeated each year.

The following day, Soledad returned to normal. Eduardo remained in a quandary questioning the business ethics of his boss. It was mid-morning when his inculcation in the Fernandez enterprises resumed. On this day, he would visit a venture that bottled drinking water in heavy, durable five-gallon glass jugs.

Potable water in Soledad was a treasured commodity. It was normally, and without cost, pumped from an individual's well or from one of the town's communal hand-operated pumping stations. However, two distinct problems existed. There were few private wells and most of the town's water-dispensing stations were inoperative or, if functioning, were at great distances from the peasants' modest abodes, causing great hardship in transporting the weighty filled containers.

The colonel, being extremely astute and profoundly pragmatic, understood that to insure a successful business venture it was essential to find a need and then fulfill it. This was precisely what he did by offering to deliver bottled potable water to the home site. With delivery of the bottled water, the purchaser was required to make a substantial refundable deposit for the container. The product was named *"Agua Pura"* (Pure Water) and was marketed as spring water from the well-known Agua Azul springs near the resort of Palenque.

The Agua Pura plant was extensive and located approximately twenty miles from the town center. It was completely enclosed by a six-foot high wall of adobe with an armed guard stationed at the main entrance. Eduardo questioned why it was necessary to have such protection at a basic industry.

Once in the enclosure, the visitor was staggered to see the great number of five-gallon containers scattered in every direction. In the center of the property was a large kerosene-driven deep well water pump that gushed a stream of water at the push of a button.

There existed a somewhat disorganized process whereby the returned containers were washed, inside and outside, with the spurting water and then refilled with the identical liquid that was used in the cleansing process. He could not believe what he was seeing. His forehead grew together in an agonized expression while his dark eyebrows slanted in a frown. With clenched jaws and narrowing eyes, he did not wish to believe what he thought to be fact.

He did not ask for an explanation of the obvious. He found it to be incredible that water, which was believed to be from renowned springs, was actually nothing more than locally pumped well water. It was inconceivable that such a fraud was being perpetrated on unsuspecting citizens who were paying for something they could obtain at no cost.

During the ride home, the idealistic engineer suppressed any visual chagrin relative to that which he had witnessed. He did not initiate any conversation and responding courteously, though briefly, to any comment by the colonel.

Now having visited two businesses of the *cacique*, Eduardo remained in a state of turmoil and bewilderment. Completely frustrated, he decided he must discuss the matter with someone; and, as expected, he once again turned to his respected friend, Father Agustin Diaz.

Within a matter of days, Eduardo met with the man who had become his trusted confidant, ally and friend. The two met for breakfast to allow ample time for discussion. The young man, shaken and mortified, related in minute detail his experience of the past two days and how, unavoidably, he was confounded, disappointed and extremely antagonized.

As he had done on previous occasions, the priest begged his guest to be tranquil, to sit back and to relax while the two good friends had a meaningful discussion.

The cleric commenced, "My poor boy, you have suffered much. However, what you have told me is not news—it is common knowledge by the town's inner circle, though no one would dare to condemn the activities that you describe. Prepare yourself, for you will be further distressed in time as you become further aware of other ventures."

He explained that his young friend was the heir apparent to the *cacique;* and if he would not follow closely in his father-in-law's footsteps, perhaps aside from the corrupt business practices, he would not be an effective leader.

He went on to mention that being an autocratic chieftain was not for the faint of heart. While the position designated a regional dictator who, hopefully, might be inclined to be benevolent, history had proven that to be unlikely in order to be effective.

The cleric continued to articulate, "One day you shall be our leader; and while it would be gratifying to have your people like you, whether they like you or not, it is essential that they respect you.

"You shall be required to maintain absolute control over the local army garrison as well as the police force, for it shall be your responsibility to maintain order and prevent civil unrest. Like any overlord, you shall be obliged to reward, with land or money, those who assist you in carrying out your mandate.

"I am fully aware of your sympathy for the Indians and the disadvantaged. You are cognizant that these depressed individuals purchase, through credit, from the colonel's store, which, one day, will become your store. There, they spend their meager pay and savings on mescal and remain forever indebted to the store. The sight of drunk or even unconscious Indians is tragically familiar. The final crushing blow is that when they regain awareness they are without funds and in debt. You shall have to come upon some resolution of this long-standing problem.

"Eduardo, you are like my son. I united you and Rosita and baptized little Maria. You are my family. You must prepare yourself for the task ahead, which is not designed for a romanticist. You must start now to prepare yourself for the future."

With those closing remarks, it was a moving sight as the two held hands, prayed and then embraced. Eduardo, his face expressing pain and bewilderment, departed, still somewhat perplexed, to continue his deliberation.

It appeared as though, with the passage of time, the young engineer remained disillusioned with the persistent shameful corruption encountered. Adding to his repulsion, he learned that the local police force, composed of men who could neither read nor write and were given their uniforms and sidearms, received no salary. Their sole source of income was that which they could exhort from real or created violations of the law.

It was during his many moments of privacy that he attempted to reason why any man could, with such despotism, so abuse his fellow man. He repeatedly asked himself, "Why? Why?"

CHAPTER VIII

A TROUBLED PEOPLE

In his never ending attempt to find an answer to his "why?", Eduardo reflected back to his people and their past. As a student of history, he was mindful of the composition of the population of his region. There were *criollos*, *mestizos* and Indians many of whom were Guatemaltecos—refugees who fled the militaristic persecution in their homeland and the neighboring country of Guatemala.

The mix of *criollos* and *mestizos* had not always been one of harmony and acceptance. As years passed, this mixture of highly emotional and short-tempered peoples developed a plan of existence, one with the other, that was, in effect, a means of tolerance.

While there existed mutual forbearance between the two, they were unified in their utter contempt for the downtrodden Indians. It appeared as though the impoverished Indian populace was regarded as sordid by *criollo* and *mestizo* alike.

So very often, Eduardo would dejectedly ask himself, "What is it with my people? What makes them do what they do?" He was quite cognizant of the fact that, like his people, his country was a land of extremes—from its towering mountain ranges to its many sea coasts, from its overheated plateaus to the rain-soaked forests, and from its quaint villages to its over populated centers.

With so many diversified backgrounds and differences, he sought to chance upon the "why?" after which he so desperately toiled.

He pondered the reason for the great divide in his people. Was it the earth-shattering tremors that occurred on a regular basis? Or, perhaps, it was the fear of volcanic eruptions or even the bloody past of a nation born of revolution. Perhaps it was their lack of identity because most citizens were of mixed origin.

This pursuer of ideals had experienced in his sheltered life that the Mexican lacked self-confidence and was, consequently, vulnerable to attack from without. He further had observed that, in general, there was security within the family clan. There was meaningful support between members of the typical Mexican family. In response to Eduardo's oft-pondered question of why the Mexican male was so prolific, he had come to the conclusion that, first and foremost, it was a means of evidencing that he had the ability to perform and, secondly, by having many offspring, he was insuring his own support in later life.

The Mexican, though sad and troubled from within, exhibited a false impression of carefree happiness. His life was difficult, and the prospects for a better life were few. It was for that reason that he sought every possible avenue of escape, even for a few fleeting moments.

Eduardo was keenly aware that it was this harbored insecurity and the accompanying lack of potential for an improved lifestyle that resulted in the search for escape from the hardships of daily life. He perceived that the common man had discovered alcohol and gaiety to be an escape. Constantly in search of a reason to exist in his daily toil, he was forever ready to join a friend in a drink or two or partake in the convivial celebration of one of the nation's numerous saints' days. As an additional means of release, the depressed toiler would vent his ire on the underprivileged, defenseless Indians.

When reflecting on those disadvantaged souls, he was thoroughly knowledgeable regarding their complete and absolute abuse. As a young man not yet in college, he spent two summer vacations in an Indian village, some thirty miles from his home, instructing the natives in reading and writing Spanish. By the process of osmosis, he became somewhat fluent in the local dialect and extremely familiar with their pre-Hispanic culture. The temperament and the modus vivendi of the natives in the state of Chiapas closely resembled that with which he was familiar.

While he sympathized with the multitude of hardships endured by the Mexican workers and most profoundly understood their hope for an improved existence, he could not accept, even to the slightest degree, the shameful disrespect directed toward the Indian population. He often wondered how the Indian race had managed to withstand the constant maltreatment over the many years since the conquest. They had been insulted, ridiculed, belittled and subjugated. For over three hundred years, they had plodded laboriously to serve their masters. Any attempt to flee to the safe haven of nearby mountains was quickly foiled by their oppressors.

Without solution, Eduardo agonized as to the troubling question of "why?" Why did the *criollos* and *mestizos* do battle with each other and still join together to torment and exploit the impoverished Indians? There was no let-up by this *cacique*-in-training to justify this controversial treatment.

The date was February 5, 1876. Outwardly, there was no indication of the ongoing indecision deep within Eduardo. He was his normal warm self and harmony prevailed in the mansion. This day was particularly significant. It was not only the anniversary celebrating the signing of the Constitution, *Dia de la Constitucion* (Constitution Day); it was also the colonel's birthday.

All Mexico rejoiced on this day. In Soledad, the town was bedecked just as it was on September 16 in observance of another historic date. In addition to the décor of the nation's tri-colors, there were marching bands and parades by diverse groups. All businesses were closed for the day.

The colonel recalled that in 1823 a constituent assembly had gathered to formulate a new national constitution. He looked back on the trials and tribulations of the assemblage that was created by the ineffective President Agustin de Iturbide and how his hero, Brigadier General Antonio Lopez de Santa Anna defeated the forces of Iturbide and wrested control of the nation. Santa Anna's victory was solidified with the support of the puppet constitutional assembly, which, in general, accepted the conditions of the proposed body of laws.

Finally, on February 5, 1824, the reform-minded body adopted a governing document that divided Mexico into nineteen states and five territories, with each state electing its own governor and legislative assembly similar to that of the United States. As such, it provided for a president, vice president and a supreme court. Interestingly, the constitution retained Catholicism as the state religion, prohibiting the practice of any other religion, while it hypocritically decreed freedom of the press and free speech.

The composition of the new congress was varied—lawyers, journalists, landowners, military officers and clergymen. While there were many who were learned and qualified for such a commitment, there were others who were not. Nevertheless, the body, once organized, functioned harmoniously but only for a brief period. It was shortly thereafter that almost every matter under consideration was debated endlessly with very little resolution. There was, as might be expected, the ongoing battle between *criollos* and *mestizos*, each group pursuing their personal interests. Nevertheless, the fact remained that there was a national congress in place along with the widespread hope that it would succeed in its efforts.

Don Alejandro Fernandez Bravo was being hailed as well on this day—his seventy-sixth birthday. He was celebrating his birthday just as he had done every year since becoming *cacique*. In reality, he knew he had been born in February 1800, though there was no record of the day. Since assuming his elevated office, he decided to establish February 5, 1800, as his birth date to coincide with this national day, which had become reality as a result of the efforts and success of his almost God-like hero, Antonio Lopez de Santa Anna.

By custom since 1854, Don Alejandro assumed the position of honor during the local festivities marking the anniversary of the constitution. Nevertheless, the evening also belonged to him, as his guests were seated at a formal birthday dinner at the mansion. The evening was identical in substance to the evening the year before and the years before that. There was the traditional cocktail hour followed by a most bountiful dinner.

By tradition, the guests feared what was to follow. It was normal procedure for the colonel to give his canned, endless speech, which did not vary from year to year. As a result of past tutoring, he was an enthusiastic, though boring, speaker. His captive guests were subjected to a repeat of his annual address with Eduardo experiencing the after dinner oration for the second time.

Each time, as he courteously focused on the speaker who reiterated the life and accomplishments of his idol, General Santa Anna, Eduardo reflected on life's coincidences. He thought that it was, indeed, fortuitous that the colonel's life was completely altered as a result of his encountering Santa Anna; while he, as a young graduate, was completely transformed as the result of having received a letter.

The colonel's remarks, in effect, detailed his life as a boy, his entry into the army, his privilege of serving under his hero general, his injury while serving his country and so on and on. It was an almost verbatim account of his years as explicated in minute detail to Eduardo in private.

In closing, the colonel reasoned that while the army was federally controlled and funded and even though it kept the national treasury in a constant state of monetary deficiency, it was worth every peso, nevertheless.

The after dinner oration to the sleepy-eyed audience continued when the colonel informed his guests that his use of the words "in summation" did not mean he was nearing completion. While there was unanimous disappointment that he did not say "in conclusion," his guests wisely maintained at least an appearance of interest.

Prior to concluding, and as before, he emphatically reminded everyone that between 1835 and 1855 Santa Anna had the honor of serving his country as president eleven times.

Finally, like life itself, there was an end; and in the case of the colonel's diatribe, it was about to reach a most welcome conclusion. As per custom, he proposed a toast to the tri-colored flag of the nation after which the weary guests expressed their gratefulness to their host and departed.

CHAPTER IX

THE INDOCTRINATION CONTINUES

It was soon thereafter that Don Alejandro continued his adopted son's inculcation of his numerous business interests. They subsequently visited the town dump in a distant out-lying area. There, Eduardo was astounded to see a large group of *pepenadores* (scavengers) who, on their hands and knees, dug through the town's rubbish scrounging for anything of value.

To see human beings degraded was, in itself, shocking. In addition to the deplorable sight of human degradation, the stench from the dump was overwhelming. For almost every human forager, there was an animal—horse, dog, pig or other—competing in the search for something of value. The visitor was shocked to learn that recovery of items of import was the sole source of survival of the scavenger. He was further astounded to know that the poor souls who were dedicated to this disgraceful form of livelihood were required to purchase a license from the town allowing them to scrounge for their meager existence.

Traumatized beyond belief, Eduardo, concealing his anguish, asked the colonel for his estimate of the volume of refuse that was dumped each day, the number of foragers, etc.. The calculation given was astounding. Throughout it all, he retained his composure, finally excusing himself to avoid throwing up. Regaining his equanimity, Eduardo requested the *cacique's* permission to remain at the garbage dump for a short time to explore on his own. He was told that someone would call for him in one hour.

Eduardo was anxious to meet with and speak to the *comandante* of the dump. The *comandante* was the ruling authority over his sixty-five co-workers. After a brief search, the group's leader was found. He was obviously intoxicated as were all those who toiled in this deplorable garbage heap. Eduardo quickly learned that it was only by remaining in a constant state of inebriation that the foragers could endure the stifling stench.

Eduardo was dumbfounded to witness the competition that existed between man and animal for anything of value. Each on all fours, digging, digging, digging. As they proceeded to uncover hidden "treasure', the stifling stench grew stronger to the point where he was forced to leave the immediate area of activity. He wondered how this mountain of discarded food, cans, bottles, boxes, and demolished construction waste could possibly have any value.

No longer able to tolerate the unbearable odor and wishing to speak with the *comandante*, Eduardo asked the leader to move to a less odorous area after offering him a sizeable gratification. The already astonished visitor learned that a scavenger, like his father before him, was born into this vocation. Most foragers, he discovered, began as young boys instructed by their parents in the technique of spotting items of value that would provide support for their families. It was from the dump that discarded materials were retrieved to either build or improve a simple dirt floor home.

Understandably, under such conditions of breathing impurities and contaminants during the many hours spent at the dump, there was uninterrupted coughing and wheezing by the scrounging deprived mortals. This, added to a daily habit of intoxication, was reason enough why the life of a *pepenador* was of short duration.

With the arrival of transportation, Eduardo was more than ready to leave, for he had witnessed more than enough of the depressing lifestyle for one day.

Some weeks later, Eduardo was asked to accompany Don Alejandro in order to become further acquainted with one of Soledad's few *criollos*, Don Benito Garcia, owner of the town's only newspaper, *La Universal*.

Don Benito was a tall, elderly gentleman with a full head of long, gray hair, a matching handlebar mustache and an impressive beard. He was a kind, gentle person. His high cheekbones accentuated his deep blue eyes and sun wrinkled forehead.

He was most cordial upon greeting his visitors. Together, they retired to Don Benito's living quarters where they enjoyed coffee and whole-hearted affable conversation. Eduardo was given a tour of the printing establishment where he had the opportunity to meet and greet the shop employees. This visit had been, without doubt, the most pleasant business related trip thus far.

Upon their return to the town hall, the *cacique* informed his understudy that the kindly Don Benito received a monthly check of appreciation, which allowed the *cacique* to approve of or edit questionable subject matter prior to it being printed. Where normally this form of payoff would have dismayed Eduardo, now, with all that he had witnessed to this point, this revelation did not overwhelm him.

The young engineer had now been exposed to the unremitting despotic ruthlessness of the colonel. He was unmoved to learn that even the judges in the local court system were at the disposition of the *cacique*. They would not render a judicial decision without first consulting with Don Alejandro. Eduardo did not accept, in its entirety nor at prima facie, the glowing acclaim and praise his father-in-law bestowed on his sacred cow, Santa Anna. He was determined to pursue the veracity of the facts relating to the general. As an engineer and a practitioner of certitude, he was intent on conducting in-depth research to satisfy his doubts.

Obtaining the reference books that were available from the poorly inventoried library, he attempted to pursue an unbiased characterization of the eleven-time president.

By the conclusion of his study, he had discovered that, in effect, the hero general was an astute, crafty and treacherous man who firmly believed that providence had chosen him to be the republic's savior—an ambition sustained by figments of Catholic superstition. He observed that the militarist, a young *criollo* officer, was intellectually illiterate, never dedicating time to read, and spoke a bastard Spanish enlivened by words of his own creation.

On the positive side, he was a profound judge of men with a keen insight into human character while always maintaining his finger on the public pulse. He was a born warrior. His entire political life was spent making war, raising money and plotting for his future. When out of office, he relentlessly plotted how he would return to power as evidenced by his repeated successful eleven periods as president.

Whatever else he may have been, Don Antonio Santa Anna was the politico of his era. Completely adaptable, he was everything to all factions. There was evidence of the general's love of gambling, his attraction to women, his devotion to cock fights and his unending expert dissertations that monopolized dinner conversations.

In summation, Santa Anna was a man shorn of principle, save his own ambition, who never hesitated to take charge of any military campaign believing that there were heroes in evil as well as in good. Eduardo was convinced that Santa Anna truly believed there had never been a good peace or a bad war.

One of Santa Anna's many memorable acts occurred in the port city of Veracruz where Santa Anna led his troops in an attack on the French occupiers. Wounded by a cannon ball, he lost his lower left limb. After being treated for his trauma, he ordered the severed member buried with full military honors.

In conclusion, Eduardo resolutely opined that the general was a calamity in Mexican history that plagued Mexico for three decades. He was directly responsible for Mexico's loss of one half of its territory to the United States (Arizona, New Mexico, Nevada, and part of California)—an area of 851,598 square miles. He sacrificed all of this territory for fifteen million dollars.

Now in possession of the irrefutable details of the "Age of Santa Anna," Eduardo was able to piece together the similar characteristics of the general and the colonel.

CHAPTER X

PLOTTING FOR A PRESIDENT

It was July 1876, a time when the colonel was deeply troubled with a number of problems related to his business interests. For one, the world price of silver had dropped drastically creating decision time for the future of his Santa Rosa silver mine. It was be necessary to evaluate the situation in order to determine the outlook for further development of the operation.

Added to this concern, there was a rebellious movement by the tenants of the local adobe village. These rental units were owned by the *cacique* and had fallen into serious disrepair. The tenants, a mixture of *mestizos* and Indians, primarily the latter, grumbled amongst themselves though not openly. To do so they feared grave recrimination.

Concerned with the existing situation, the *cacique* knew full well that it would be wise to resolve this type of insurgency as soon as possible.

In the midst of his many preoccupations, both governmental and private, he was not overjoyed to receive an order to meet with General Manuel Muñoz, the caudillo of the southeast region of Mexico, which included the state of Chiapas and the southern portion of the state of Oaxaca. Such an order was not subject to debate; consequently, the colonel made the necessary plans to travel to the designated meeting that would take place in the city of Tuxtla Gutiérrez, the capital of the state of Chiapas, approximately ninety miles northwest of Soledad. The directive gave no explanation as to the reason for the reunion other than specifying the date and location. While attempting to reason why, the *cacique* departed for the rendezvous.

Once in the state capital, the colonel learned that all *caciques* in the region had been ordered to attend, though he still did not know the reason for the meeting.

From the outset of the meeting, the attendees were informed that there were factions in Mexico City that were planning to incite revolt. There existed discontent throughout the nation with President Lerdo whose authority was being challenged by a growing liberal movement. The situation was exacerbated in that the president would not hesitate to intervene with federal forces against even the most minor provocation.

Without question, the general and the *caciques* present, all past militarists, were archconservatives. Together, as a unified body, they supported the president, he, also, having been a general in days past.

It was the prevailing consensus that the Lerdo administration was probably one of the most respected simply for the fact that it had now virtually endured its four year term, which had never before been accomplished.

Even so, as the president planned to complete his legal term in office, he would not leave unscathed. His liberal enemies united with the liberal press assailing him mercilessly while liberal politicians spoke out strongly against him. The rumors were vicious. One account recalled that he had studied for the priesthood and while president, as charged by the libertines, he was making up for precious time lost as a celibate.

General Munoz was determined not to allow the rebellious reformists to disrupt the status quo. He knew that the strength of the caudillos and the *caciques* throughout the nation could only survive as a trickle-down from their favorable relationship with the chief of state. To further ignite the ever-growing dilemma, Lerdo announced that he intended to seek re-election. Such a proclamation of a president in disfavor severely complicated the successful continuity of conservative power.

With loyalty now becoming a secondary concern, the group decided the hour had arrived to dump Lerdo and endorse an opposing candidate who would conscientiously follow the reactionary line. Lengthy discussion and deliberation ensued with their resolution to support someone who, like themselves, was a heroic army veteran, General Porfirio Diaz. With the selection now formulated, they initiated a plan to discredit their present chief of state.

They charged that Lerdo had repeatedly violated the sovereignty of the republic's states and municipalities, sacrificed Mexico's best interests in negotiating contracts, reduced the right of suffrage to a farce and squandered public funds. However, of greatest importance, they pursued legislation that would establish a no re-election law for the president as well as all state governors.

With mutual accord to proceed with the plan, it was further agreed that General Muñoz would be entrusted to inform other regional caudillos of their resolve. After meticulously detailing the strategy to his counterparts, the general would ask for their cognition and support. With the meeting concluded, the colonel returned to Soledad.

Four months passed since the gathering of the *caciques*. Don Alejandro learned that the agreed-upon conception had become known to Lerdo who pledged to militarily dispose of the chosen opposition candidate. It was inevitable that armed confrontation would follow.

And so it was that the forces of Lerdo engaged those of Diaz on November 16, 1876, at Tecoac in the state of Tlaxcala. Diaz carried the day with an overwhelming victory. Realizing that the route to Mexico City would be virtually unobstructed, the victorious army of Diaz entered and occupied the nation's capitol on November 21, 1876.

In retaliation, Lerdo de Tejada was exiled to the United States. While the conspiracy succeeded in removing the chief executive as he completed his prescribed term of office, a critical threshold had been crossed. For the first time in Mexico's history, a president had served out a full term. While force was employed to effect the transition, it had, to a great degree, laid a solid foundation of presidential service on which incoming governments could build.

Irrespective of the apparent intent of the caudillos nationwide, which appeared to be for the national good, and the eventual success of their decision, there could be no doubt that their motive and resolve was primarily self-serving.

As the sun rose in Soledad on June 3, 1877, little did the community know that theirs would be a town drenched in sorrow before the sun would set.

It was early morning when the colonel received the grievous news that Santa Anna had passed from this world the day earlier. Shocked by the tragic announcement, the *cacique* declared a three-day state of mourning to be observed by all. He ordered *el Toro* to have the entire town draped in black crepe. Notices were posted so that on the third day all commerce would be shut down. On this day, there would be a memorial service in the town square commencing at 9:00 A.M. with the entire populace ordered to attend.

Visibly shaken, the distressed colonel went into seclusion in his private quarters at the mansion ordering that he not be disturbed, not even by his pride and joy, Maria.

The extent of the *cacique*'s grief caused Eduardo to continue to speculate the ongoing question, "Why?". Piecing together his father-in-law's past relationship with and hero worship of his champion combined with his personal investigative study of the general, he concluded, precisely as he had before, that there existed a trenchant parallel in their lives. Eduardo was cognizant that while the year of birth of both had been established there was no recorded day of birth of either. The general arbitrarily selected February 5, the day Mexico celebrates its constitution, as his day of origin. In like fashion, the colonel chose the exact day for himself. This imagined bond was further enforced when the colonel divulged to Eduardo that in a past life he had served in the military, side-by-side with Santa Anna.

Don Alejandro remained sequestered in his quarters during the entire period of mourning until early on the third day when he prepared to attended the memorial service.

He joined his family for breakfast prior to departing for the town square where Father Agustin Diaz would participate in the ritual. From the grayish pallor and the obviously exaggerated visible pain on his face, one could readily deduce that the *cacique* was in severe anguish.

At the appointed hour, the family, as a group, proceeded to the covered grandstand. With good fortune, it was a pleasant summer day. Following the invocation by the priest, the colonel was introduced by his bodyguard and assistant, Raul Molina.

The *cacique* opened his address by explaining to the throng why they had been directed to assemble. He proceeded to relate the story of the seventeen years of his life when he served under his champion. This address was not a repetition of his annual remarks delivered on the occasion of his birthday. He had specifically crafted his comments for this specific occasion.

It was for this particular moment that he believed it to be imperative that he review, in detail, the unforgettable acts of Santa Anna, which the audience would soon learn were many—perhaps too many.

He commenced, "Mexico was gifted when the good Lord gave us such a leader, such a hero, such a liberator as Antonio Lopez de Santa Anna Pérez de Lebrón." He continued by telling the crowd, "As a young man he did not have the privilege of formal schooling. He was compelled to seek out odd jobs; and at the age of sixteen, he joined the army. He was baptized by fire in repelling an anti-government rebellion. Promoted for his bravery in combat, he was elevated to the rank of captain and for the next ten years served as a royalist cavalry officer in the army of the Crown.

"His aptitude for the military was readily recognized with the result that in 1817 he was appointed an aide to the Spanish viceroy in Mexico City. Being the true patriot that he was, he renounced his loyalty to Spain in 1820 in support of the Mexican revolution. Victorious in the conflict for independence in 1821, he continued his service to his country by volunteering to roam the countryside in order to eliminate any remaining Spanish troops. Once again, he received field promotions, first to the rank of major and shortly thereafter to colonel.

"It was at this point in Mexico's history that turmoil erupted accompanied by anarchy. We had a new nation without an understanding of self-government. Almost immediately, there were political difficulties. There was the inexperience of *Creoles* in public administration, the tendency of regional caudillos to become despots in areas where they had fought and the desire of the top caudillos to become president.

"Added to all of this strife, there was discord between the military and the civilian population, clerics versus bureaucrats, and the political extremism of the middle and lower classes.

"To resolve these many differences, a government commission was created on September 28, 1822. It was composed of thirty-eight aristocrats and loyalists, including Santa Anna, who were charged with the responsibility of selecting the national flag and its insignia."

At this point in the address the colonel vigorously waived the Mexican flag, shouting, "This is what Santa

Anna gave us! This is what our leader gave us! This is what our hero of heroes gave us!"

He went on to inform his listeners that this leader of leaders continued to serve his country in government as well as on the battlefield. He asked, "Who else would lose a leg in battle and continue to fight until he achieved victory? Who else I ask you?"

He continued, "I could go on telling you of his bravery under fire. I stood side-by-side with him in combat, and I tell you I was honored to do so."

He further remarked that Santa Anna, as the commanding general, stormed the Alamo and fought hand-to-hand in order to achieve victory.

He emphatically detailed his hero's continued service as president of the republic and went on to remind his audience that there was but one, only one and one alone, who between 1833 and 1855 occupied the office of president eleven non-consecutive times. Again he asked "Who else would return again and again and again to serve when called upon? Only one patriot would do so—General Antonio Lopez de Santa Anna Pérez de Lebrón. God bless his soul."

With the audience now completely exhausted and standing only with great effort, the priest gave the convocation and blessed the crowd. The ritual had come to an end.

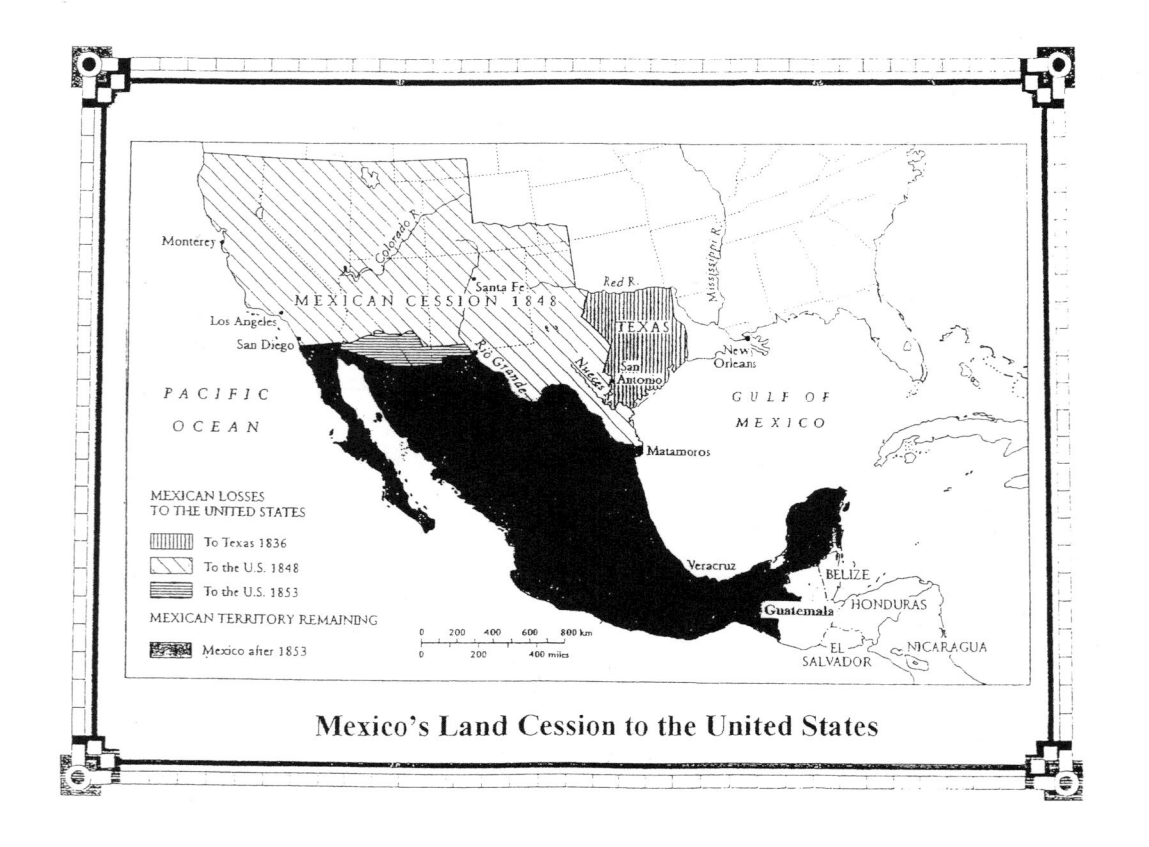

Mexico's Land Cession to the United States

CHAPTER XI

UNREST IN SOLEDAD

While harmony reigned supreme at the mansion, Eduardo could not bring himself to share the colonel's manner of conducting business. Nevertheless, the Hernandez family had bonded into a warm and loving household. Maria was a beautiful little girl and a joy to all.

While Eduardo outwardly suppressed his opposition to Don Alejandro's modus operandi, his instincts alerted him to the fact that all was not well in Soledad. By virtue of his inner sensitive perception and his upbringing by compassionate parents, he was cognizant of the prevailing simmering unrest in the town.

On the other hand, the *cacique*, by virtue of his autocratic tunnel vision, remained unaware of what was transpiring with the town populace. Unlike the *cacique*, who ruled from a position of strength, Eduardo, highly respected by the townspeople, enjoyed a sense of trust and understanding with them. It was through this relationship of cognition that he was able to investigate, with the assistance of his local confidants, and, indeed, ascertain that all was not at peace. He discovered that there was serious discord within the provincial army barracks.

This discontent was of a general nature and was related to poor food, extra long hours on guard duty, ill-fitting uniforms and inadequate pay. It was common knowledge by all military leaders that whoever controlled the army, controlled the country. This axiom was well heeded and not to be forgotten by the caudillo as well as the *caciques*.

There was yet another serious threat to peaceful existence and order. A grave situation was being orchestrated by external instigators who were attempting to incite the abused Indian populace in view of their oppressive manner of existence. Having become apprised of both potentially explosive situations, Eduardo, with great forethought and procrastination, deliberated what his next move might be – if, indeed, there was to be one. After protracted soul searching, he concluded that it was his responsibility to inform the *cacique* of the deteriorating state of affairs. With a flicker of apprehension coursing through his body, he called Don Alejandro to request an appointment.

It was not unusual to patiently wait for the *cacique* to arrive even with a pre-set appointment. In this particular instance, the boss arrived promptly and, as was usually the case, greeted his son with an *abrazo*. There existed a warm and cordial relationship between the two since they first met. However, this would be the first instance where the *cacique* would be informed of an unbeknownst potential threat to his absolute authority.

Eduardo cautiously initiated the conversation by carefully measuring his words so as to test the *cacique*'s reaction. As he continued to speak, he gathered confidence that his revelation would not create an undesirable first-ever confrontation. Surprisingly, the colonel digested Eduardo's every word listening dispassionately. Though somewhat flushed, he remained silent and did not interrupt the young man.

Once concluded, Eduardo, perspiring and exhausted as a result of nervous anxiety, sat motionless, his face resembling the withered look of a deflated balloon as he awaited the colonel's reaction.

Much to his dismay, the *cacique* reacted completely unruffled and responded by simply saying, "Thank you. I shall take care of these matters."

Problems were not new to the colonel. They merely represented a challenge requiring a solution. He maintained a conviction throughout his life, even as a youth, that the greater the dilemma, the greater the glory in resolving it. He pondered his options deciding to first attempt to resolve the situation at the local level knowing full well that in some instances the use of external force, namely federal forces, was not indicated.

His first act was to invite the senior military officer in the *cuartel* (military barracks), Major Francisco Pedraza, commonly addressed as Paco, to lunch at the mansion. He preferred to resolve such matters privately; consequently, Eduardo was not included in the meeting.

In such circumstances, it was accepted policy to employ bribery with the result being a corrupt military. Senior army officers were anxious to enrich themselves through business opportunities, gifts, sinecures and favors, which could include illegal activities such as contraband, expropriation, prostitution and land grants.

Unlike the military in the mother country, Mexico's revolutionaries had no aristocratic tradition. Its troops consisted of volunteers from the poorest sectors of the peasantry who were grateful for food, clothing and shelter.

In spite of the uncontrolled corruption, the army remained a vitally essential element in the nation's internal security system. Therefore, the government was determined to maintain a placated military hierarchy, which might, under massive unrest and persuasion, be induced to act independently.

It was for that reason that the government was completely conscious of the fact that the army, being the sum of its parts, was widely scattered throughout the country. As such, it was dependent on the combined local *cacique* system to maintain order and accord with their local army components.

The military, serving as a common bond between

the colonel and the *cuartel's* major, had an open and frank discussion of the inequitable conditions within the *cuartel*. Don Alejandro extended an offer whereby Paco would personally receive a tract of land in the region that was being cultivated by a group of Indians. Neither appeared to be moved by the actuality that the confiscation would deprive the disadvantaged of their sole meager sustenance.

In addition, the colonel committed to supply the soldiers with food products not normally included in their daily diets. The major, speaking for himself and his men, accepted the proffer and thanked the *cacique*. One problem had now been resolved.

With one problem settled, there remained the pending matter of the instigators who were attempting to organize the Indians for the explicit purpose of challenging the oppression under which they existed.

Historically, the Indian culture sought isolation. Following the Spanish conquest, they fled to the mountain and desert areas for refuge in order to maintain their independence of possessing and working their land. The land represented a vested interest in a territorial base that was an essential element of Indian life and culture. Unfortunately, as civilization expanded into developed farming areas, their isolated world was no longer isolated. Hence, the *mestizo* was identified as the intruder and the enemy. As one Indian chief approached the encroachers, he remarked, "No one can do anything against them because they are strong. They rob, they kill our people, they enslave and rape our daughters, they use our land to grow marijuana, they make us drink our firewater."

The message delivered by the agitators in an attempt to provoke rebellion was that the *cacique*'s intimidating treatment prevented the Indians from essential foodstuffs, medical treatment and basic education of their young. It was the theory of the oppressors that it was essential to control a hungry, sick and ignorant people.

Like most of the nation's deprived, they suffered from parasites, respiratory ailments and such tropical diseases as malaria, all of which were aggravated by malnutrition. Through the sale of mescal and/or pulque, the *mestizo* extracted most of the inadequate earnings of the Indians rendering them impotent against their despotic subjugators.

It was believed that there were definitely two, possibly more, provokers actively engaged in arousing the deprived to unite in order to demand not only survival but also an improved lifestyle.

To resolve this remaining bone of contention, the colonel decided to test his understudy by entrusting him with the responsibility of resolution. When advised of this unexpected duty, Eduardo sat expressionless, his face devoid of emotions. His only response was, "Yes, sir. I'll handle it." A response he had heard just days earlier.

This was the first true paramount responsibility to be placed squarely on his shoulders. He was mindful of its significance. He decided to embark on his mission by first determining how many instigators were involved and precisely how they would be identified. Unlike the *cacique*, he would benefit from a mutual relationship of confidence with the townspeople. While he was respected, he was not feared.

Having championed their cause, he was received as a friend by the local Indian leaders. It was for this reason he was graciously bid welcome by the tribe fathers. It was for this reason, as well, that the *cacique* assigned the task to him.

He immediately sought and was granted an appointment with the representative chief of the clan. There were repeated meetings and discussions—all friendly, all cordial. During this period of negotiation, Eduardo elected not to discuss the matter with the colonel.

It was two weeks after his first meeting that Eduardo met with the *cacique*. "The Indian dilemma no longer exists." With that brief summation, the colonel did not ask for further explanation nor did Eduardo offer one.

Time passed without repercussion from either perplexity. The colonel appeared to be quite satisfied that his son's grooming for the top job had progressed adequately. He felt at ease in naming Eduardo to assume the additional duties of public education and town maintenance. He further designated him manager of the soft drink bottling plant. While this particular appointment did not enthrall Eduardo in view of the devious business practices employed, he reluctantly, though graciously, accepted the position.

CHAPTER XII

THE COLONEL PASSES ON

With the transition of the presidency in 1876 long concluded, Mexico was preparing to enter the year 1878 with President Porfirio Diaz in absolute control. His predecessor, Lerdo de Tejada, was revered as much as yesterday's newspaper. Under the ironhanded rule of Diaz, the nation looked forward to a future of promise and prosperity.

Upon assuming office, the chief executive committed his regime to advances in science and technology heretofore unexplored. The so-called "good life" existed only in the larger urban centers while the people of less populated areas eked out a mere existence.

In retrospect, pursuing a well-planned program for improvement was virtually impossible inasmuch as there was a presidential change seventy-five times in the fifty-six years since independence from Spain.

As is generally the case, where there is stagnation and incompetence, there is also financial instability. With an empty treasury, accumulated foreign debt and an enormous bureaucracy whose salaries were in arrears, the government faced a dilemma of major proportions.

From a commercial standpoint, imports far exceeded exports resulting in a disastrous cash flow predicament. To add to the administration's woes, Mexico's system of governing was laughed at abroad to the extent that foreign investment was neither extended nor expected while Mexican wealth found a new home overseas.

Public services such as street cleaning, garbage collection, police and fire protection, mail delivery and the like were all in a state of turmoil. Of particular outrage was the well-founded rumor that mailmen, when wishing to curtail a day's delivery, would simply dump the mail in a local trash heap.

Unlike the efficient operations procedures of the Spaniards, the mining industry was in complete disarray. Where gold and silver once filled the Crown's coffers, production of these two metals, in demand on world markets, was severely reduced. Even the output of mercury, a vital element utilized in the processing of gold and silver, had virtually disappeared.

Nowhere was there a light on the horizon. The situation in agricultural output was similar to the catastrophic situation encountered with commerce, credit and precious metals. Agribusiness systems and equipment were either antiquated, non-operative or both.

The president was cognizant of the many ills haunting his administration requiring him to pledge that the country would progress and take its rightful place among nations of the world. He knew well that in order to do so would require an abundance of foreign investment.

With all that was wrong, there was but one glimmer of satisfaction—the railroad between Mexico City and Veracruz had been reconstructed. Nevertheless, aside from this one satisfying assessment, there remained the need for telegraph construction and the harbors on both coasts, with their unserviceable docks, sorely and urgently required dredging.

Last, though certainly not least, was the task of establishing respect for law and order. Neither the streets of the cities nor the countryside were immune from bandits and an occasional murder. The president was aware that he would face an impossible task of attracting tourists and developing a tourism industry if visitors to his country feared for their safety.

As he reviewed the nation's shortcomings, he pledged to rectify the problems by whatever means necessary. He was determined to follow the precept of "Order and Progress" no matter the cost. In view of his impeccable background, Mexicans, after so many years of stagnation, believed that with Diaz there was finally hope for a better life.

With the president in office for his first year, the period passed without incident in Soledad. The family and the town celebrated the new year in their customary fashion. The two previous bones of contention had apparently been resolved with the town functioning in routine fashion with the exception that there was a perceptible change in the colonel. He was more irritable, even less placatable when spending time with little Maria. At times, he appeared to be confused to the extent that his mind refused to register the significance of his words. Both Eduardo and Rosita begged that he be examined by the local doctor or, even better yet, go to Mexico City for a thorough checkup. He refused to entertain the thought of either.

With his inherent perception, Eduardo, observing the colonel's every move, logically concluded that his father-in-law was suffering from some form of neurological disorder. Once again, he attempted to prevail that the colonel seek medical attention. Once again, the colonel refused.

There were days when Don Alejandro's condition prevented him from attending to his local administrative duties or his business enterprises. The very capable engineer, now thoroughly familiar with both, assumed his position of responsibility tactfully without mentioning to the colonel that he was doing so.

It was just two weeks later that the seventy-seven year old warrior suffered a crippling stroke forcing him to be confined to bed. Being completely apprised of his physical condition, he did not hesitate to order his "right hand" to assume his normal responsibilities. Along with the misfortune, there was a favorable happenstance in that his speech had not been adversely affected.

In true professional fashion, Eduardo accepted his charge and was very well received as a welcome change at the town hall. As expected, being the diplomat that he was and with the exalted respectful esteem he nurtured for the *cacique*, he continued to administer from his own personal office. He regarded the *cacique*'s high-back chair as being for the exclusive use of his boss.

For the following ten days, everyone in the household, including Eduardo, Rosita and Maria, were at the beckoned call of the colonel offering every possible gesture of love and affection in an attempt to lift his spirits. During the period of illness, the colonel asked that Eduardo spend much of his days at this bedside for he had a strong affection for his adopted son.

The colonel rambled with advice on the duties and the performance expected of a *cacique,* mindful that his heir was a compassionate person. At times, he would dwell on his memoirs and statements of fact.

There was one particular story he seemed to relish relating. So much so, that during his period of illness he retold it four times. This tale seemed to invigorate the patient and put a twinkle in his eyes.

He spoke of his experience as a young man under Spanish rule. It was the custom of the Indians, as a peace offering, to give the Spaniards young girls. Among the many, was a beautiful princess, daughter of a tribal chieftain, who became the property of the Spanish General Jorge de la Vega. She proved to be a most valuable asset as she spoke Náhuatl, the language of the Aztecs and the Mayas in addition to her own dialect. Once baptized by the Spaniards, she was no longer just Marina. From that point on, she was addressed as Doña Marina.

Being smart, able and attractive, she was always at the general's side, figuratively becoming his shadow. The general traveled from pueblo to pueblo expropriating food, goods, money, girls and whatever else he wished. Doña Marina served him well as an interpreter and intimate companion. In being a truly remarkable helpmate to the Spaniards, she was derogatorily called *Malinche* by the natives—*Malinche* signifying betrayal.

At this point in the story, the colonel's eyes gleamed like glassy quartz rock, apparently very pleased with himself.

As the story continued, the general was in a small town laying plans to annihilate a large Indian commercial metropolis. As interpreter and confidant, Doña Marina was completely aware of the entire plan of attack. Speaking to the Indian *cacique* in Mayan on behalf of the general, she was able to reveal the comprehensive plan, detail by detail. Without hesitation, the informed Indian *cacique* relayed the plot to his counterpart in the targeted municipality.

Completely prepared for the planned onslaught, the Indians fought valiantly decimating the attackers and killing the general.

Doña Marina was now satisfied she had evened the score with the despotic conquistadors.

Concluding with self-satisfied sunshine breaking out across his face, he remarked, "You know, I was a friend of the Indian princess." And then with a wink of an eye he said, "Yes, I knew the princess. I knew her very, very well."

As he had done on many prior occasions, the colonel continued his never-ending stream of advice and recommendations sensing that he was gravely ill and would not recover. He was most emphatic in stressing that the political stability of the country depended on the continuity of the caudillo/*cacique* system of control. He would always complete his remarks on the subject by saying, "Never, never ever forget it." He constantly reminded his heir apparent that the structure was like the divine right of kings and the infallibility of the pope. He stressed the role of his successor by declaring, "You will be heir to the pre-Hispanic tradition of theocratic authoritarianism. You will be a unifying symbol of power and above public criticism. You will be the stronghold of security and stability, which shall not be subject to challenge.

"During your lifetime, you will be all powerful. You will control your land and its people. In the event of dispute, you will be both judge and jury. Your unlimited power will give you a king-like quality. With all of this, you will lose a treasured asset for you shall never again enjoy a private life. Compliments paid to you will not necessarily be from the heart. Beware of flattery given for personal gain.

"There is a common, oft-repeated phrase that I shall give you that is always good for a laugh. Just in case, at any given moment, you should ask an aide, or even a stranger, 'What time is it?' You can expect the reply to be, 'Whatever time you say it is, Señor *Cacique*.'"

Concluding, he reminded his adopted son, "Remember, the *cacique* system has survived because it reflects the strengths, weaknesses, virtues and defects of your people. It combines a ritualistic sense of hierarchy with an enormous capacity to enforce your will. And most importantly, the secret lies in your ability to manage internal and external interests and political factions that threaten the *cacique* system for they do not benefit from its survival."

Now exhausted, the colonel asked that Eduardo return later. It was early evening that the colonel was back in talkative form further articulating, "Many of our people are descendents of German migrants—the Hoffmans, the Meers, the Schmidts and so on. They emigrated by crossing the border from their native Guatemala to Chiapas in order to avoid military oppression. Watch them! Watch them! While they may become invaluable in your industry, they may also attempt to take what is yours.

"You must continue your close church affiliation and ask guidance from Father Agustin. We have a morals problem in Soledad which is inherent in the Mexican people—men and women alike—though more in men than women." While the colonel looked upon business as unscrupulous competition for dollars, he was a firm believer in God, devoutly religious and a regular Sunday churchgoer.

The colonel was more than aware that Soledad was suffering from a lack of morality caused, principally, by the men of the community. The spark igniting the morals problem was alcohol. The men, after being paid for their labor, would deplete their wages in drink and then proceed to humiliate and then pummel their defenseless wives. This was the means by which the male exhibited his chauvinistic prowess and control.

"My son, the male in our community thinks only of himself and his self-satisfaction. We, unfortunately, have many women who no sooner give birth to one child and are immediately pregnant again. Now, when you realize that the poor woman, with a protruding belly, has to look after her children, clean her home, cook for the family and be ready and waiting for an overly proliferous husband to come home, it is, indeed, a tragic situation. In spite of all of this, no sooner would she give birth to one, another child would follow. An absolute no win dilemma." With those words, the colonel's eyes closed with his momentarily falling asleep.

As evidence that the colonel had retained his facility of complete memory, the following day he summoned Eduardo to apologize for falling asleep the previous evening. He recalled the subject matter of his discussion remembering precisely where he concluded. With renewed vigor, he continued his dialogue by revealing that there was another problem of grave concern. He explained that the men in Soledad, traditionally, leave their wives and families moving in with other women with the deplorable result being illegitimate children born. Sadly, adultery was quite commonplace.

It was evident that the colonel's capacity to speak was noticeably diminished, whereupon Eduardo suggested that his father-in-law rest for a while. While the colonel was in accord, he insisted on first relating remarks that he believed were of significant importance. He went on to say, "Son, there are some things you must know. First, no man is without fault. I admit to wrongdoing; and I know that in many cases I have reacted harshly, perhaps too harshly. However, in so many instances the pain that resulted from unremitting acts I have committed on others was more painful to me than it was to them." With those words, whispered as he finished, the *cacique* turned to one side and dozed off.

To Eduardo, the colonel's last pronouncement appeared to be a deathbed confession. It was the case, for those were his last words. On that day, the twenty-eighth day of January, just eight days before his adopted birthday, the respected, though feared, Colonel Alejandro Fernandez Bravo passed on peacefully in his sleep.

With the demise of the colonel, Eduardo once officially installed, would ascend to the exalted position of *cacique* of the township. Under normal circumstances, the governor of the state of Chiapas would be required to extend his blessings to a successor *cacique*. However, in this particular instance, Eduardo was so highly regarded by the governor that there was no question regarding his assuming the charge. In the company of the colonel, Eduardo had enjoyed many pleasant meetings with the governor who openly expressed his high regard for the young engineer.

Eduardo's first act as *cacique* was to declare a week of mourning. He immediately ordered *el Toro* to drape the town in black. All radio broadcasting was to be exclusively martial music out of respect for the departed military hero.

The funeral, scheduled for the third day after the colonel's demise, resembled an interment befitting a monarch. All offices, stores and businesses were closed and the entire populace attended the religious service as well as the entombment in the family crypt constructed by the colonel where his loving departed wife, Rosa, was put to rest.

As planned, the funeral services were conducted by the *cacique*'s life-long friend, Father Agustin Diaz. The Hernandez family was visibly shaken. Eduardo's voice broke as he delivered the eulogy, Rosita's sense of loss was beyond tears and little Maria seemed confused by all that was transpiring.

With the rites concluded, it was customary on such an occasion for those in attendance to line up for as long as the new *cacique* would allow with the hope of exchanging an *abrazo* with the new ruler. Attempting to receive the embrace carried a degree of risk. The gesture, if extended, was considered a great honor. However, if only a handshake was offered, it was considered an embarrassing humiliation.

Rosita, as well, was a center of attention. She was consoled by handshakes from the men and kisses on the cheek from the women. No one was denied the opportunity of paying his or her respects to Don Eduardo and his lovely wife. Once the protocol was concluded, the family retired to the mansion to continue the period of lament.

Being the cultured person that he was and out of respect for the late Colonel, Don Eduardo ordered that there be no public demonstration or celebration upon his assuming the highest office in Soledad. He decided to delay his festive investiture for one year. Consequently, in a simple ceremony on the town hall steps, he was sworn in as *alcalde* (mayor), his official title of office.

With the oath administered, there were the normal congratulatory *abrazos* and/or handshakes, after which the new *cacique* retired to the mansion to be with his beloved Rosita.

CHAPTER XIII

A TIME FOR CORRECTION

On the following day, his first in the town hall as *cacique*, Eduardo called the entire staff together. In order, he praised the deceased *cacique*, thanked the staff for their past loyalty and reminded them the he would expect their cooperation to the benefit of all citizens.

After hesitating and gathering sufficient will, he finally entered the office the colonel had occupied for the past twenty-four years. Pausing for five minutes, he ultimately sat in the coveted high-back leather chair. Sitting motionless for twenty minutes, his life passed in revue, year by year and he marveled at how fortuitousness could shape one's life. He thought, "Here I sit, the absolute ruler of thousands of people, living in a mansion with a family I love very much, and all as a result of a single letter from President Lerdo De Tejada. I wonder where I would be if that letter had not been sent."

On the first week following the period of mourning, he immersed himself in the town's activities under his dictate as well as the business enterprises established by the colonel. He enthusiastically issued his first edict. As of that moment, there would be no charge nor license required of the *pepenadores* who attempted to eke out a meager existence at the local dump.

He was intensely determined, even at the risk of failure as *cacique*, to humanize the office that he now occupied. Irrespective of the consequences, he would reform the manner of rule and treatment of the citizenry.

He would exercise his authority to severely reduce,

or even eliminate, corruption within the local police force. Previously, the ruling police authority was completely aware of the ongoing depravity but excused the vice by a wink of the eye or a nod of the head. All the while corruption continued to flourish. It was more a cultural problem than a social problem.

From the most lowly uniformed policeman to the chief of police, there was deep-rooted corruption resulting from old habits of nepotism, influence peddling and the standard *mordida* (the bite or graft). In reality, the problem was self-created in as much as active duty policemen received no salary. They were merely provided with uniforms and pistols but virtually no training. It was simply a matter of survival where everything goes. The situation would be remedied in that the *cacique* would put the entire department on a payroll that would adequately cover their basic every day living expenses.

Don Eduardo, as he was now addressed, prepared a well thought-out, detailed plan of amelioration that would be directed not only to the town but to the family's businesses as well. As expected, the plight of the abused Indian was foremost in his thoughts. History had treated them badly. During the regimes of both the liberal President Benito Juárez and the conservative President Lerdo de Tejada, both more dogmatic than compassionate. Land parcels were distributed to the Indian heads of families. Transformed into a homeowner of his *parcela* (small piece of land), the Indian, generally ignorant of what private property entailed, became a victim of *hacendados* (large land owners) and ranch operators. Usurpation of their lands became a fact of life. Judges sold themselves, corrupt officials confiscated lands because taxes were not paid precisely on their due date. *Hacendados* became Shylocks and then foreclosed on the land when loans could not be repaid. And so it went.

Aware of the abuse of the well-intentioned

presidential program of land distribution, the *cacique* ordered all affluent landowners to immediately desist. He established a dictate of monetary punishment on land expropriation that would be enforced on violators. To demonstrate his seriousness on the matter, it was just one month later that he applied both a cash fine and a land confiscation to a wealthy transgressor.

Tirelessly and without let-up, Don Eduardo continued his pursuit of reform. While he experienced limited success, the effort progressed at a snail's pace, retarded by custom imbedded over time. There was, as months and years passed, a marked change in the integrity of the *cacique*. While his sympathy for the disadvantaged, particularly the Indian population, continued unabated, his desire for personal monetary gain became noticeably insatiable.

The year was 1880. Eduardo had been in office for almost three years while President Porfirio Diaz was completing his first four-year term. The president had entered office an already established hero for his military accomplishments, especially his prodigious victory over the French on May 5, 1862. It was a particularly noteworthy triumph inasmuch as the invading French forces consisted of many veterans from the glorious days of victory in the Crimea. In recognition of the victory over the French, Cinco de Mayo (Fifth of May) was added to the national calendar of holidays.

Without question, the first term of Diaz was an overwhelming success. He had accomplished all that he had wished for to the extent that his term was hailed as the Mexican miracle. The president, in just four years, had cast Mexico in an international role—an active participant in world affairs. Quite an accomplishment for a fifty-year-old divinity student and lawyer. The face of Diaz, with his impressive white, dangling moustache, had become a familiar sight in the foreign press.

The incredible accomplishments of his regime did not come without a price—the loss of personal liberty. To enforce the wishes of the president, a private police force, the *rurales*, was created and consisted of thugs who, most precisely, carried out all orders of the president irrespective of the law of the land. On the positive side, Mexico, for the first time, had become a nation free of highway holdups, street muggings and thievery in general. The country was now ready to promote tourism for its streets and roads were equally safe for both its citizens and visitors.

With discipline and order now prevailing in the nation, foreign capital was being introduced in large amounts affording incredible industrial growth. Mexico, once looked upon as the unmanageable debacle of Latin America, had now become the talked-about success of the continent.

Mexico was now a member of the family of nations—an aggressive and respected participant. Its acceptance was due, in great part, to the political professionalism of its president. Eager to participate in the booming economy of the nation, consular and business offices of representation, as well as diplomatic ties, were established.

The manufacturing sector flourished while the pride of the administration was the incredibly improved agricultural production. Notwithstanding the multitudinous gains achieved, the newly established oil industry was looked upon as king of the day.

Now, with the economy booming, the rail system appreciably expanded, and port facilities modernized, Diaz retired to his home in Veracruz to ponder the matter of re-election. He would reflect on his four years in office recalling how he vigorously campaigned on the premise of no re-election.

He was urged by influential business constituents to consider a second consecutive term, for they did not wish to see the Diaz "train of prosperity" slow down. After two weeks of deliberation, Diaz decided to step down and not seek re-election. He reasoned that by his not remaining in office he would be sending a signal to all of the world that Mexico had matured politically and that there would be a peaceful transition of the presidency. He knew that this being the first passing of the office of the Mexican chief of state in accordance with the law, he would have inscribed his legacy for all time.

While he would outwardly relinquish the power of being the nation's first citizen, he, nevertheless, wished to retain at least a portion of his past influence and exert it on the new administration. Very cleverly, he made known that he supported a close comrade in arms, the then Secretary of War, Manual Gonzalez. With the open approbation of the incumbent, Gonzalez was elected in a landslide.

With the transfer of power, a new president in office and all *caciques* serving at the pleasure of the chief of state, Don Eduardo offered his allegiance to the new chief executive with whom he had no familiarity. While he did not anticipate directly interfacing with the new first citizen, he hoped that his superiors in the presidential office, the caudillo, General Carlos Bersunza, and his one-armed aide, General Rudolfo Ramos, would speak on his behalf.

During the period of the election for a new president and the transition, Don Eduardo had now become fully acquainted with his position of *cacique* while his varied businesses continued to thrive. The bottling plant continued its production of Jumbo and Superior soft drinks under the established devious size and price offering. The potable water distribution operation carried on as before with the only change being that the price per bottle had increased.

The general store maintained its practice of selling its products at exorbitant prices and assessing outlandish charges for credit extended to purchasers. The capital of the *cacique's* bank had grown appreciably with its loan portfolio generating extortionist profits. Non-payment of a loan resulted in merciless foreclosure. Crime, an every day occurrence, remained unchanged with the jails filled to capacity and the practice of buying freedom with adequate payment. Even with the minimal salaries for the police force initiated by Don Eduardo, the uniformed enforcers of the law continued to accept *mordidas* openly and without hesitation.

Corruption continued to plague the town administration. Try as he might, the *cacique*, while feathering his own nest, attempted unsuccessfully to eliminate, or even reduce, the prevailing corruption. He even researched the historical behavior of the culture seeking the explication for its shameless propensity.

After lengthy study and analysis, he reasoned that Mexican's corruptive tendencies were inherited from their Spanish conquerors who looked upon the new land as booty to be ransacked. Government jobs were routinely sold by the viceroys and privileged appointees. "Grease of Mexico" became a Spanish euphemism for a bribe or graft. Independence from Spain offered no relief from the malady where public life could be defined as the abuse of power to achieve wealth.

The lines between honesty and dishonesty were blurred by entrenched habits. Any position of authority implied an opportunity for self-improvement. As a result, ordinary citizens learned to petition for favors rather than demand rights. Government, in particular, was a prize to be exploited, though no sector from business to church was excluded from the modus operandi. Eduardo deduced, to his amazement, that these common practices were not thought of as corruption but rather just the way things had been and would always be done. Dejected, he questioned whether there could be an honorable future for Soledad— never calling his own greed into question.

As he reviewed the overall situation in his canton, the *cacique* became a victim of his own conscience. He could no longer hide from lingering remorse. Once again, he felt the urgency to call on his treasured confidant and friend, Father Agustin Diaz, who was now semi-retired.

Always an attentive listener, the father allowed his revered friend to speak without interruption. Don Eduardo detailed the many disturbing conditions in the town placing emphasis on the prevailing crime and corruption. He went so far as to include his failure to separate himself from the intense greed that apparently possessed him. With a flushed expression and film of sweat on his face, he concluded his elucidation.

The priest responded, "My son, have you discussed this matter with Rosita?" The reply was a simple "No." With that reply, the father continued by commenting that he was completely mindful of the fact that Mexican males, insisting on preserving their self respect as macho refused to discuss personal matters with their spouses.

He counseled that his good friend would not undo what was implanted for centuries. He articulated that as long as people were willing sell their principles for money, corrective action would remain an impossibility. "It is corruption that enables the system to function. It provides the grease that allows the bureaucratic wheels to turn and the glue that seals political alliances. It is a well known certitude that all levels of civil power are virtually obliged to enrich themselves in order to enjoy creature comforts in the present and security for the future."

He culminated his remarks by repeating the key issue "As long as our people sell their integrity for money and personal gain, there will be no remedial measures." He hoped that his final remark would leave an imprint in the *cacique*'s mind.

Having expressed themselves, they prayed together and said their good byes. Prior to departing, Don Eduardo asked, "Father what do I do now?"

The priest responded, "God will guide you!"

The *cacique*'s distress remained to possess him. Over many months, Rosita had perceived a troubled expression of pain in her husband's eyes. Where his anguish was evident in days past, it was even more so now. No longer predisposed to refrain from mentioning her preoccupation, she asked her husband if he was perturbed about something. His answer, brief though respectful, was a simple "No." Knowing well what was expected of a Mexican wife, she commented, "*Muy bien. Espero que no.*" (Good. I hope not.)

As a result of his years of experience as an engineer, he had the capacity to gather facts and then proceed in order to reach a logical solution. He was determined to properly evaluate his unsatisfactory and constantly deteriorating state of mind as well as the inequities in Soledad.

Deep within the *cacique,* there was a profound sympathy for the oppressed. This deep-rooted compassion included the incarcerated who lacked legal representation.

His first act was to improve the standards heretofore employed in the treatment of prison inmates, including substantially increased exercise periods, improved meal service, additional extra curricular activities and periodic entertainment to somewhat relieve the unavoidable stress. He monitored the program constantly to insure that it did not falsely imply weakness on his part.

He next directed his attention to the problem of abandoned families and orphaned children. It was a generally accepted fact that in the *campo* (countryside) abandoned or unwanted children were sheltered and cared for by local families who made the children their own even though they were already hard pressed financially to survive.

Such children without parents were a serious

problem for the citizenry, for left to their own devices, they would either form a band of brigands or join a gang of similarly forsaken juveniles. It was his wish that such little people not become the *olvidados* (forgotten ones).

Once absorbed into such a mob, they routinely engaged in stealing and more insidious crime. To ameliorate this social conundrum, the *cacique* directed that families who adopted parentless children would be rewarded with a modest stipend—in reality, an allowance for food and clothing. The announcement was loudly applauded when made public. The *cacique* believed that now one additional imbroglio confronting Soledad had been resolved.

Being a highly religious man, Don Eduardo, as expected, was a man of high moral standards, notwithstanding his penchant for amassing huge personal wealth by whatever means. Correcting the issue of probity confronting the *cacique* would be most arduous as it was an innate cultural disposition.

The term *casa chica* was well known though not highly respected except for those proliferous males who maintained one. It was an inherited tradition from the days of the conquest that those who had the means and the desire could elevate themselves in the eyes of their fellow men by maintaining *la casa chica*, the home-away-from-home. With the wife caring for the principal home and the children and preparing food, the husband could find time for his extracurricular activity with his paramour. The wife, aside from being a ready and concordant partner, was always at her husband's beckoned call and satisfied to know that the family would join together for the traditional Sunday mid-day meal.

Pondering the complexity of this Pandora's box, he reached a vital decision. He would look to Raul Molina who retired from government when Don Alejandro died. He ordered el *Toro* to return as a town public servant. By virtue of Molina's size, temperament and reputation, *the cacique's* requests were always looked upon as something not subject to discussion.

Having formulated his plan, the *cacique* had little trouble in apprising the populace inasmuch as, like most everything in Soledad, he controlled the editorial content of Benito Garcia's local newspaper. With the complete domination of the editorial pronouncements of the newspaper, there was no need for him to own it.

By decree of the town's *cacique*, it was stipulated that once cognizant that an adulterous situation existed, there would be a three-fold course of action. First, Molina would personally confront the participants with a recommendation that the relationship cease at once. In the event there was not immediate compliance, the mistress would be counseled again by Raul while two *pistoleros* (gunmen) would pay a courtesy call on the adulterer who would be left to treat his wounds once the visitors departed. In the rare event the relationship endured, the husband would be jailed while the paramour would be exiled to *Isla de Mujeres*, the sparsely populated island off the coast of the Mexican territory of Yucatan.

Though it would be most uncommon for a husband to be jailed, on such an occasion the family of the adulterous husband would become a ward of the community during the time of the breadwinner's imprisonment. Now, with the blue print of corrective action for adultery in place, only time would determine its success.

CHAPTER XIV

THE OIL IS OURS!

As the years passed, little changed in the routine of the Hernandez family. Eduardo continued his pursuit of necessary corrective measures in the town while his many business enterprises flourished. The soft drink bottling company, the spring water distributing plant, the general stores, the bank, the farms, the combustible fuel depot and his real estate holdings were all growing like weeds. The only exception was the exploitation of his silver mine, which was on the decline as a result of a depressed world market for the product.
 Both Eduardo and Rosita were preparing to live in a lonelier mansion inasmuch as Maria, now seventeen and an excellent student, would soon be leaving for the University of Mexico in Mexico City. The *cacique* selected this particular institution for it was considered to be Mexico's finest. Its location in a cosmopolitan center and its reputedly select teaching staff were positive contributing factors. There was profound preoccupation by the parents as travel between Soledad and the capital was extremely exhausting; consequently, visitation would be infrequent. The rail line from Veracruz to the capital was the only completed rail system in the country. They would have the option of traveling over a tortuous road to the city of Veracruz, then continuing by train. The alternative means of travel from Soledad to Mexico City presented the nightmarish prospect of crossing mountains and plateaus in a horse-drawn coach over convoluted roads in complete disrepair. Eduardo vividly recalled his horrendous carriage

journey to Soledad almost twenty years aforetime.

Inasmuch as the state of Chiapas was far removed from the center of federal government and in a mountainous and non-essential location, there was virtually no appropriation of funds for development. Chiapas was commonly referred to as the "forgotten state."

The parents' fear of their daughter being alone at such a distance was somewhat diminished in that another student from Soledad would also be enrolling in the university. He was a highly intelligent, polished and handsome young man, Nicholas Garcia, nephew of the aged proprietor of the town newspaper, *La Universal*. There was a comfortable feeling that each would furnish support to the other while they were so far from home and in an unfamiliar environment.

Just prior to departing, Rosita embraced her daughter, tears streaming down her face, and repeatedly kissed her. It was at that moment that she removed the diamond encrusted St. Christopher medallion from around her neck and placed it around the neck of Maria. She explained that she had received the precious gift from her father on her tenth birthday.

Rosita went on to detail the origin of the legend of St. Christopher concluding her commentary by saying, "You shall be watched over and protected by the martyr on your forthcoming trip."

And so, it would be off to school for Maria, however, not before her father counseled her, closing his remarks by saying, "Remember, my dear, aim for the top. There's plenty of room there. There are so few at the top, its almost lonely there. God Bless!" Then, with all of the family shedding tears, Maria was on her way to a new life in a strange city.

While still mentally immersed with Maria's departure, the *cacique* became aware of a most distasteful matter. It was disclosed that there had been flagrant thievery committed related to the combustible fuel dispensing depository which was owned by the *cacique*. Even more disheartening was the fact that it was being perpetrated by a retired army major, Javier Ramos, who had served under the command of the late colonel. In view of that past cordial relationship the colonel enjoyed with Ramos, he awarded the major a concession to deliver petroleum products to combustible depositories in the region using the major's own wagons. The retired officer was apprehended and charged with grand theft. He was accused of very cleverly designing his tanks with specially constructed bottom sections that could be filled when the tank was replenished and then closed off. When the load was discharged, the fuel in the bottom section was conserved for the major. In this manner, the wagon could, by proof of its loading manifest, certify that it had taken on a specified number of gallons of combustible. However, while apparently delivering an entire load, the unscrupulous operator retained the production in the bottom portion of the tank for his personal account.

At this point, the rule of law was whatever was ordained by the *cacique*. In this particularly unusual situation, and for appearance sake, a trial was ordered to commence in two weeks as set forth by the court.

The day for the hearing arrived and the courthouse was packed to the rafters. With all seats occupied and standing room at a premium, many were obliged to stand outside near the door with ears straining to grasp at least something of what was transpiring within. The case received wide publicity being labeled "*el doble fondo ratero*" (the double bottom crook).

The presiding judge, Alonzo de Regil Mendez, a stately, dignified *criollo*, gave an air of respectability to a suspect court system. Erect, with a full head of graying hair and a well-trimmed moustache, he entered the courtroom amid the applause of all in attendance for he represented the only possible means of just and fair treatment for the townspeople.

He had been regarded by all as the judge who had more regard for justice than for men. Of course, this would exclude the wishes of the *cacique*.

Once seated in his high-back black leather chair, he gaveled the court to order and directed the bailiff to bring the accused to the courtroom.

The government prosecutor presented an ironclad case with irrefutable evidence as to the alleged criminal practice. With hard facts and figures, he demonstrated beyond doubt that the theft had been perpetrated on thirty-two retail distribution stations, of which seven were owned by the *cacique*.

At the request of Major Javier Ramos and with permission from the judge, the accused spoke on his own behalf. The charged, now a somewhat elderly, slim and balding retired military officer, stood staring with head bowed and shoulders drooping and began speaking. He commenced by referring to his impoverished boyhood, family abuse and his final escape to freedom by joining the army. He stressed his profound respect for, and close relationship with, Don Alejandro, accentuating his dedication to his country and his honorable military service. As he concluded, he asked the court for clemency in consideration of his past.

The judge listened attentively to his pleading and then asked, "Why did you go to such lengths in modifying your tanks in order to pilfer petroleum products?"

Major Ramos responded quickly, "Your honor, for years we Mexicans have been very possessive regarding the oil that is recovered from our sub-surface. We have always asserted with pride, *'El petroleo es nuestro'* (The oil is ours). Your honor, as a Mexican, I was only taking my share."

Try as he might, the judge could not refrain from

throwing back his head and releasing an outburst of laughter. The entire courtroom erupted in hilarious giggling. The judge immediately gaveled the court to order informing Ramos that he would pronounce punishment in a few days. Inasmuch as the crime involved a business interest of the *cacique*, he would, naturally, exercise extreme discretion by discussing the matter of punishment with the *cacique* prior to rendering sentence.

Accordingly, the judge met with Don Eduardo and outlined the pertinent points of the trial, expecting to reach an accord as to the punishment to be imposed. He was somewhat astonished when the *cacique* told him to hold the matter in his pending file for the time being.

After weighing the matter for several days, the *cacique* ordered that the major be brought to his private office. With Ramos seated in front of his desk, he reviewed the charges and evidence in detail. The major remained silent throughout, glum faced and tight lipped.

It was then Don Eduardo articulated, "Javier, in consideration of your camaraderie and service with the late Don Alejandro and additionally your family relationship to General Rudolfo Ramos, my friend and aide to the caudillo of Mexico, I shall offer you a proposal to close this matter. Simply, it is this. As of this moment, I shall become a fifty percent partner in your petroleum delivery business. You will continue your practice of withholding the bottom portion of the tank of combustible as before, with the exception that you will put an end to stealing product from my seven depositories. Understand, you will carry on with the other twenty-five fuel stations just as you have done in the past, but not mine. In return for your word as a military officer, I shall have the judge extend a pardon for your past transgressions. That's the offer. Yes or No."

Without the slightest hesitation, the major, briefly though to the point, exclaimed, "Agreed." And so, in rapid succession, the matter was resolved and the *cacique* had acquired a new business interest.

CHAPTER XV

TRANSFORMATION OF AN IDEALIST

It was early morning the day after the situation with Major Javier Ramos had been resolved when Don Eduardo received a visitor well known to himself as well as to the upper social strata of the community.

The caller was Doña Luisa Maria Alvarez, widow of deceased Colonel Juan José Alvarez, owner of the largest cattle ranch in the state of Chiapas. She had come to ask for help relative to a most serious problem. The ranch adjoined a vast farming enterprise that was owned by a *criollo*, Don Esteban Gurria. He was preventing the flow of water from the nearby river to her ranch. The water supply was vital for the well being of her cattle.

After a short wait, she was graciously received by Don Eduardo who, after serving his guest coffee, listened attentively, focusing on her every word. The *cacique* agreed to investigate the matter in due time; however, for the present, in addition to numerous town administrative pressures, he and his wife were still grieving over the departure of their only child.

He went on to explain, apparently looking for sympathy, that there was an emptiness at the mansion since the passing of Don Alejandro. With Maria gone, the void was amplified. There was an empty chair at the dinner table and no longer was there the routine "goodnight" to the daughter they both adored. Don Eduardo stressed that a strong link in the family bond no longer existed.

Upon concluding his account of the existing

situation, Doña Luisa Maria expressed her commiseration. He, again, assured his caller that he would research the source of her distress.

Two weeks later, he recalled his commitment to the widow and directed a messenger to her home to advise her that he would visit her the following morning. Traditionally prompt, he appeared as promised and was cordially greeted by his hostess, a strikingly beautiful, statuesque woman of fifty years of age with a seductive body and wholesome good looks.

In her normally gracious fashion, she invited her guest to the traditional morning snack of *café con leche* (cappuccino coffee with warm milk) and *orejas* (elephant ear-shaped cookies). Amplifying on her previous explanation, she articulated that during her husband's lifetime, her neighbor allowed a stream of water from a river on his property to be diverted to their ranch. The arrangement was most probably influenced by respect for, or possibly fear of, the power-wielding Colonel Alvarez, an army colleague of the late *cacique*, Don Alejandro. As a result of the unsheltered intimate relationship between the deceased *cacique* and Alvarez, many sought favor with the defunct Colonel Alvarez.

Since the death of her husband, her former friend and neighbor had curtailed the flow of water to her ranch with damaging consequences. With an intermittent glance of admiration for the striking señora, Don Eduardo agreed to speak with her adversarial neighbor and return within a few days.

The following day, the *cacique* commanded Don Esteban to visit with him at his office. There, he presented the facts of the arduous situation. After a lengthy discussion, it became apparent that the water stoppage had been affected inasmuch as Don Esteban no longer feared recrimination from his influential adjoining property owner. It was his ulterior motive to force the widow to sell him her ranch at an unrealistically low price. He reasoned well that without water her cattle would perish. The exchange had brought forth an offering price of purchase for the property.

As promised, Don Eduardo returned to visit the widow to inform her of his deliberation, which finalized in an intent by Don Esteban to acquire her property. All the while he spoke, the *cacique* riveted his eyes on her trim body mentally seducing her. He sensed an intense sensation of sexual attraction.

Once the price of purchase was revealed, the widow, without procrastination, rejected the offer, which meant that the lack of water for the livestock would persist. It was then that the *cacique*, in an attempt to ingratiate himself with the señora, offered to have his tank trucks bring sufficient water to fill the ranch reservoir. He would continue to do so until the dispute was resolved.

The sexual attraction was apparently mutual, for after a hasty lunch, they found themselves in her bedroom engaged in passionate lovemaking. Her body ached for his touch while a dizzying current raced through both. It was late in the afternoon when, with a long and affectionate embrace, the *cacique* departed having promised to pursue the problem.

Returning to the mansion, Don Eduardo asked himself how his infidelity might affect his relationship with his beloved Rosita. He pondered how a man of supposedly high moral conviction, like himself, could commit adultery after publicly decreeing the impropriety of such an act. He pledged that this would be the one and only improper act in which he would participate. Yet from deep within, he knew his transgression would be repeated.

Meanwhile, the *cacique* continued, without incident, to guide Soledad in every aspect. He ruled with an iron hand in both his administrative duties as well as his prospering businesses. The only exception to his general successes was the questionable accomplishment in his attempt to rectify existing frailties.

There appeared to be minimal reduction in the corruption within the police department or in the abuse of the Indian population. Most gratifying, while reminding him of his indecorousness, was a noted decline in reported cases of adultery. With extreme caution, the *cacique* concealed his own illicit affair. His relationship with the widow Alvarez continued to coalesce to the point that they enjoyed almost weekly trysts.

During the course of the next eighteen months, there was no disentanglement of the long-standing conflict for water nor had an agreement been reached for the sale of the ranch even though the purchase price was raised incrementally from time-to-time.

For understandable personal benefit, there was no reason to expedite the matter of selling the ranch. The ranch was being supplied with ample water, and the two lovers were satisfied with the status quo.

As is so often the case wherein a paramour is involved, something occurs that contributes to the dissolution of the immoral relationship. In this particular case, there was a two-fold provocation. The sense of electrification once enjoyed by the *cacique* had disappeared. In addition, he sensed that Rosita's female intuition perceived unusual behavior in the couple's private life. Eduardo was unsure of his wife's speculation. Was she merely suspicious or did she know? He valued his family above all.

Not wishing to risk his marriage, he reached a decision to terminate the relationship. Without a desire to continue the supply of essential water for the ranch, he developed a plan to resolve the on-going dispute. He was determined to acquire the ranch after first procuring the farm of Don Esteban Gurria through the omnipotence of his office.

With the blueprint now formulated, Don Eduardo visited Don Esteban to submit a proffer to purchase his farm. Typically, the primary consideration was price. The offering was so low that it was immediately rejected by the seller, a response anticipated by the *cacique*. He then directed the conversation away from money and straight into logic. He reasoned that the farm could only be operated with electric power from the Soledad plant; that seasonal planting could not be effected without financing from the local bank, which was owned by the *cacique;* and finally, that the movement of produce must necessarily travel over government roads. He then further implied that a substantial increase in land tax would be a disaster.

Having presented his case he asked, "Esteban, what would your property be worth if you couldn't harvest crops? What would it be worth if your taxes increased appreciably?" Gurria, well aware that the threats were not idle and without an option, accepted Don Eduardo's offer of purchase.

Once the sale was consummated, the *cacique* proceeded to the second phase of his well-orchestrated plan. He visited Doña Luisa Maria stating clearly that his intention was to discuss business and that their liaison was now a thing of the past. Patiently, and in minute detail, he stressed the fact that he, for reasons undisclosed, could no longer continue providing her water requirement. In addition, he informed the now-apprehensive widow that the neighboring farm had passed to new ownership and that the new owner refused, at any price, to allow water to flow to her ranch. In summation, he strongly recommended she sell her ranch as a distressed property at a give-away price. She agreed to consider the proposal, consenting to meet again in two days.

At the request of the widow, the two met at the ranch to pursue the suggested recommendation. When the *cacique* arrived, he found his former infatuate pale and shaken. She confessed that she had no solution to her predicament asking whether her former lover had come upon an answer. The *cacique* expressed his sorrow that he could not be of assistance regarding her dilemma, again advising that she should sell at any price.

After a short period of deliberation, she queried, "How much?" The *cacique* quoted an inconceivably low figure, which, Señora Alvarez, without hesitation or objection, though with an expression of disillusionment, accepted. Having agreed to sell, she asked, "Now, who do I deal with on the sale?"

The *cacique* responded, simply and much to her amazement, "Me."

Disappointed and astonished, she remarked, "It's strange how money separates more friends than it unites."

In just a short time, the *cacique* had augmented his farm holdings and had become the largest ranch owner in Chiapas. There had been, over time, an incredible transformation of that young utopian visionary who delivered a punctilious valedictorian address just twenty years ago.

CHAPTER XVI

THE FAMILY VISITS MARIA

The clock continued to advance at an incredulous pace. Maria was completing her second year in college. She had not been home since entering the university. There had been no contact between parents and child except for a periodic letter. During the academic year, she was completely immersed in the study of Mexico and its people. She was, as well, consumed in a torrid relationship with Nick. Other than time spent in class, they were together during the day and most particularly every night—all night.

During the summer vacation following her initial year, both she and Nick volunteered to toil at the Indian village of Las Cruces, some thirty miles from Mexico City. Unlike their relatively luxurious accommodations in the city, the two were housed in a one-room adobe hut with a leaking roof. It had neither screened windows nor indoor plumbing. Nevertheless, they had become impassioned transcendentalists; and, of even greater significance, they were together.

Eduardo and Rosita longed to see their daughter and did not wish to undergo another long period of separation. They dispatched a courier to inform Maria that her parents would travel to the capital to visit with her for two weeks prior to her annual summer service at Las Cruces.

And so, as planned, just prior to the completion of the school year, the parents departed by carriage to Veracruz and then by rail to Mexico City. Needless to say, the trip was anything but pleasurable. After an uncomfortable journey on a dusty road, the continuing junket by train was equally stressful. The train was very poorly maintained. There were broken windows, unserviceable bathrooms, uncontrolled small animals and no food service. Their only salvation was the sustenance sold by the locals at the train station stops.

Delighted to finally reach their destination they found their "little girl" waiting to exchange hugs, kisses and more hugs. In their own affectionate way, this was truly a loving family. The first order of business was to discuss what transpired during the two-year separation. The parents then retired to their hotel room for a sorely needed rest, satisfied that their daughter had enjoyed a productive two-year stay. Maria had divulged most everything that had occurred at school other than her intimate relationship with Nick.

Having been in the nation's capital after graduating from the University of Guadalajara, Eduardo was somewhat familiar with the interesting sights as was Maria. Consequently, Rosita was the lone stranger who would be shown about by two experienced tourist guides. The first three days were spent visiting historical and unusual spectacles. With Eduardo scheduling the itinerary, they visited the National Palace, the Cathedral of Mexico, Chapultepec Castle, the San Angel colonial area and the floating gardens of Xochimilco. On the third day, they continued on to the Pyramids of Tenochtitlán, the Museum of San Carlos and the Church of San Fernando. Completely exhausted, they decided it would be wise to relax so that the women could have a day for "girl talk", affording Eduardo the freedom to pursue matters of personal interest.

At the top of his "to do" list was to visit the university and speak with Maria's professors. Since she had left home and by scrutinizing her letters and now having spoken with her, he harbored a suspicion that his daughter had adopted strong socialistic beliefs. He recalled that as a young college student, he, too, was an ultra pursuer of ideals. Now, however, in that circumstances alter credence, this was no longer the case. He thought it prudent that he acquire in-depth knowledge of the school prior to meeting with the professors. Hence, his initial stop was at the institution's library. Having been a student at a highly conservative university, he was eager to become acquainted with the background and teaching attitudes of the oldest university in the nation.

His research demonstrated that the National University was created in 1551 as the Royal Pontifical University of Mexico by petition of Viceroy Mendoza of Spain. Classes commenced in 1553, making it the first university to function in the new world. Its purpose was to educate *criollos* for the clergy. However, with time, its guiding principle was modified so that by the end of the seventeenth century it produced many of New Spain's leading literary figures, scientists, lawyers, medical doctors and theologians. The school continued to grow, and by the year of Eduardo's visit, the institution had granted over thirty thousand bachelors' degrees and approximately one thousand masters and doctorates.

With this new knowledge in hand, he now moved hastily to keep an afternoon appointment with three of Maria's professors. Under normal circumstances, such a group meeting could not be arranged, however, since a *cacique* had requested this coming together it was granted.

Joining in a discussion with academic intellectuals brought back fond memories of his youth when he participated in deliberation with his professor father and other like academicians.

The meeting was most cordial, lasting over three hours, during which time the faculty members set forth their ideologies on a multitude of subjects. The discussion followed a pattern where Eduardo would initiate the discourse by asking a question and then allow the educators to answer. Upon concluding the meeting, Eduardo profoundly expressed his gratitude to the three. He departed having confirmed his suspicion that the university was a hotbed of socialistic teaching. A myriad of Maria's pronouncements had now been explained.

On the second day of Eduardo's emancipation, he was scheduled to meet at the National Palace. He had been there briefly once before when, as a young graduate, he met his benefactor, President Lerdo de Tejada. He would have enjoyed meeting the current president, General Porfirio Diaz. Unfortunately, his request was denied.

Nevertheless, he was granted an interview with the caudillo (supreme military commander) of Mexico. The office of caudillo was a presidential appointment normally granted to a retired general, in this case General Carlos Bersunza. The caudillo was all-powerful—one step below the president. It was his task to oversee the nation's regional caudillos and municipal *caciques*, which, in effect, meant that it was his responsibility to see that order in all parts of the country was maintained. His virtual absolute control included his chargeability to ascertain that taxes were punctually collected and transmitted to the National Treasury.

It was an established fact that the federal army was substantially undermanned due to lack of funding. Inasmuch as there was no threat of attack from without, the *cacique* network was an indispensable system essential in preserving internal discipline.

Upon arriving at the office of the nation's caudillo, he was greeted by his friend and superior's aide, retired General Rudolfo Ramos. General Ramos, a native of Chiapas, was an intimate friend of the colonel and had spent numerous enjoyable evenings at the mansion with the *cacique*, Eduardo and Rosita. This general was no ordinary retired general. He was a short, stocky, gray haired man with an amber flame in his eyes and a dazzling smile. He had lost his left arm in battle serving with the caudillo. He was a nationally recognized personality. In 1860, he actively campaigned for the office of president. He was memorialized for his unforgettable campaign slogan, which he proudly pronounced, "I am your only honest, principled candidate for president. I ask that you look closely and you will see I have but one arm and one hand. You can see for yourselves I have only hand with which I can steal." The catch phrase was remembered by all though it was not enough to gain a victory for him.

Without delay, Eduardo was ushered into the impressive office of the caudillo. It was an enormous room with a high ceiling and sun-bleached curtains of anemic pink. The general was a large, bald man with a hard, tendoned neck and broad chest. His once tanned, wrinkled face now had a pallor as a result of his extensive time indoors seated at his desk.

He was most cordial to Eduardo, mentioning that he had been an intimate friend of the late Colonel Alejandro Fernandez Bravo. Their conversation centered on personal and family matters for a short while before turning to business. The general, without hesitation, remarked that he was aware that there existed undercurrents of discontent in Soledad. He clearly and emphatically declared, "Discontent leading to possible chaos results when people change faster than conditions." While the conversation was amicable, it was obvious that the caudillo did not perceive that the *cacique*, not being an ex-military man, had a firm grasp on how to maintain the necessary autocratic control of his region. The caudillo counseled his visitor by forcefully articulating, "Don Eduardo, I am a much older, more experienced man by virtue of time than you are. Remember, as a leader, you must constantly look back to make certain you have followers." Then the caudillo asked, "Is there something I can do for you?"

Eduardo responded, "Yes, thank you sir." He

explained, in detail, that while in his region there were situations requiring rectification, there was an urgent need for a high volume, deep well pumping installation. He stressed that potable drinking water was vitally necessary for Soledad, pointing out that such an installation would certainly have a calming effect on the town's people.

As the discussion continued, the inevitable matter of cost was broached. Eduardo proposed that the federal government, the town and private initiative in Soledad each share in one-third of the anticipated expenditure. The caudillo reviewed all that had been discussed regarding the water supply matter and agreed to support the request. He directed Eduardo to visit the Department of Hydraulic Resources in order to formalize the proposal.

Prior to departing, Eduardo met with General Ramos to thank him for his courtesies and shake his famous hand.

Having completed his personal business, Eduardo rejoined the ladies for their daily activities. They had been told of the nearby city of Cuernevaca, famous for its eternal spring season. And so, for their final days together, the three enjoyed the city's incredible beauty and climate.

As is the case in all such visits, this trip was coming to an end. There were tearful good-byes for they did not know, in view of the distance involved, when they might again be together. It was not until her parents were leaving that Maria informed them of her infatuation with Nick Garcia, although she made no mention of their intimacy. After *abrazos* and tears, the parents began their exhausting trip home as Maria prepared to leave for the Indian village of Las Cruces.

Eduardo was now satisfied that his marital relationship was not in peril. As he thought back to his regular rendezvous with Señora Alvarez, he was proud of his inner strength to terminate the relationship. As an intellectual, he believed that he who overcomes his passion, overcomes his greatest enemy.

The *cacique* had not forgotten the words of wisdom of the caudillo, General Bersunza. While it was expected that he await the government's approval to initiate the projected deep well water system, he was determined to do something to assuage the prevailing unrest. He would announce the major restoration of the road from Soledad to the state capital, Tuxtla Gutierrez. The existing road was irregular in width and fraught with potholes. The improvement would consist of leveling the route, covering it with crushed rock and then blanketing the rock base with pulverized limestone. Once in place, the application of water to the surface would securely bond the components. It was estimated the project could be completed in one year.

Publicizing the road improvement project was a simple matter. After ordering Benito Garcia to his office, Eduardo explained the undertaking and directed the editor to announce the road effort in his newspaper and then follow up with stories regarding the public works effort.

Having the authority to tax at will, the *cacique* levied a tribute on all business in his region to pay for the twenty-three mile road undertaking. With the public being consistently reminded of the planned reformation and the funds for construction levied, though not yet collected, the engineering projection was initiated.

It was just five months since the *cacique* returned to Soledad from Mexico City and one month after starting the road venture that he received full government approval to proceed with his proposal regarding the water system. With the authorization now issued, it would be incumbent on the town to levy yet another assessment on the local private initiative as stipulated in the request by the *cacique*.

Now there would be two public works undertakings for the civic good underway simultaneously. The local press was ordered, as before, to publicize this new project.

With a direct mandate to provide a constant reminder of both projects in every edition of the local newspaper, there remained little space for other matters of interest.

The year 1893 would be remembered as that period in time when Soledad was engrossed in a road rehabilitation project and the urgently required installation of a potable water system. The *cacique* chose to personally award all contracts for work to be performed in lieu of selecting general contractors. He preferred to utilize his own in-depth engineering expertise. Obviously, by controlling the selection of those performing their trade specialties, he alone would control all funds for both projects. Understandably, the inducement and the temptation for personal gain were without restraint.

The *cacique* was completely absorbed in his civic duties, his vast entrepreneurial enterprises and the ongoing public works projects.

CHAPTER XVII

ABOUT THE FAMILY

With President Porfirio Diaz in absolute control, the once secure position of the nation's *caciques* was no longer inviolable, particularly for those who were not retired military officers. Nevertheless, the former honor student valedictorian had been transposed into an astute politician. As a form of preventative insurance and as a gesture of friendship and support, the *cacique* placed numerous intimate friends of both Bersunza and Ramos in illusionary, lucrative town positions. Such employees were commonly referred to as *pajaros* (birds), for they would appear at their phantom offices twice a month, on payday. The *pajaros* collected their bi-monthly checks and would quickly "fly" away not be seen or heard from until the next payday. This was characteristically normal behavior for government officials in high positions. Mexico, as a nation, was deeply embedded in a system of quid pro quo, which was practiced daily by all in positions of authority.

Eduardo was completely aware that his attempt to improve the agricultural production of his region had been a dismal failure. He was reminded of this by his good friend and confidant General Ramos. It was imperative that the *cacique* maintain order and tranquility in all areas of public life. Non-fulfillment in the farming sector could lead to discontent, dormant unrest and potential insurrection.

This distressful situation was brought to the attention of Mexico City in that wealthy *hacendados* could obtain bank support by mortgaging their cultivated lands.

On the other hand, the provincial peasants, when refused bank assistance, were obliged to appeal to the federal government for financial facilitation. Consequently, the sheer number of requests for government aid indicated the existence of a serious problem.

In a concentrated effort to justify the reason for the inefficacy, Eduardo, in a letter to the caudillo, explained that his state was plagued by three mountain ranges and tropical jungle with top soil so thin that cultivation for farming was most laborious. The shortage of water was particularly acute. The supply that existed was harnessed by the wealthy, powerful landowners. Consequently, the powerless peasants had no alternative but to pray for rain.

Sadly, he continued to convey, his state suffered from a land area that was 52% arid, with excessive humidity and 65% too steep for tilling. In general, those plots designated for agricultural development were normally too dry, too rocky or too eroded for cropping.

In view of these adversities, the peasantry was obliged to grow corn and bean crops in infertile soils. Because these were staples of their daily lives, they were destined for survival and not income producers such as vegetables, fruits and flowers. It was, therefore, understandable that the prayers of the peasant farmers to the rain god Tlaloc were never ending.

He strongly stressed the fact that he was, meanwhile, immersed in two public works projects, namely the road reconstruction and the installation of the potable water system.

He was quick to remind Generals Bersunza and Ramos of his recent generous consideration of their friends by investing them as *pajaros*.

It was a beautiful morning on March 21 and the city had prepared for the annual celebration of the birthday of Benito Juárez, Mexico's president who had served as the country's liberal-minded head of state from 1858 to 1867.

As president-in-exile from 1867 to 1872, he was, indeed, a national hero, particularly to the *cacique*. As a college student, Eduardo looked upon Juárez as his idol in view of the president's transcendentalism. He was heralded as the founder and leader of the nation's liberal movement whose legacy was compared to that of Abraham Lincoln. While a student, Eduardo had attempted to emulate Juárez in both thought and action.

Precisely at 10:00 A.M., the traditional parade began. It consisted of soldiers, policemen, firemen, town employees and the school band, all carrying banners of respect for President Juárez. They passed in review of the *cacique* who proudly stood erect on an elevated platform.

Once the procession was concluded, it was time for the expected, though not welcome, address by the community's lord and master. Recalling how the past *cacique* was infamous for his lengthy, repetitive and wearisome orations, Eduardo was determined to outdo the late Don Alejandro; consequently, his discourse went on endlessly before a captive audience.

On this particular occasion, Eduardo chose to speak on the subject of the Mexican family. He explained, "In Mexico, the home is all important. It is the bonding agent that ties each to the other—children, parents, grandparents, as well as all relatives living under the same roof. The makeup of the family is one of dependence, support, and a strong devotion to religious beliefs, which affords a solid national foundation. There exists a firm belief in sharing love and whatever money there might be available. It is a common belief that by producing many offspring, the parents were providing for a secure future in old age. It was not uncommon for a family to allow aged and feeble family members to share their modest home and the meager funds they might possess.

"Unfortunately, a change has occurred. That once-enjoyed togetherness is rapidly being pulled apart as the result of circumstances and so-called progress. While the family youths were, in the past, content to accept menial jobs in their home towns or villages, they were no longer content to remain at home as before. Perhaps it was the lure of the big city or the availability of better-paying jobs. The young left their homesteads for a new life.

"The consequence of their departure was that the elderly within the household were left without the previously available assistance from the young. Too, where the departed were parents with young children, the elderly being left to care for themselves assumed an additional obligation to care for the children left behind.

"Now we must reason, 'Why do our children leave their homes and their families? What is the great attraction that lures them to parts unknown?' The answer is reasonably simple. The magnet that provides the allure is money and the yearning for a better life. As you know, jobs in the provinces are not only scarce but the work is laborious, particularly farming, and the hours wearisome. The effect on the family is adversely profound.

"Having our children leave home is a most serious problem. So, what is the solution? We must create work for them here in Soledad."

While he covered a multitude of family oriented topics, the *cacique* stressed the fact that his people were not devout and were delinquent in their church attendance. He stressed that their *padrecito* (local priest) was their God-sent counsel who could bring them closer to God.

He went on lecturing that families must join together on weekends, birthdays, saints' days and vacation periods.

Speaking endlessly to a now exhausted, standing audience, he continued, "I'm now going to talk to you, the parents, the parents of our children. You are the models for your children. As examples, you must serve each other and go through life in harmony.

"I am profoundly aware of the arduous task that the man in the family has in providing for his family. His work is difficult and strenuous. He must, necessarily, have a caring wife. Nevertheless, he must treat his wife respectfully. Never forget, in years past in our violent history, our women accompanied our men into battle, cooked for them, cared for them and even buried them. So, I ask that each husband lavish his wife with love and reverence. Always remember, she is the mother of your children."

Apparently not tiring, he continued, "I know life is difficult, nevertheless and with it all, we are strong and we are united; therefore, we can overcome any adversity."

And so it went, on and on, for two hours forty minutes on a sweltering, humid day to a completely fatigued audience. Exchanging *abrazos* with his perspiration soaked hierarchy and intimate friends, and now completely dog-tired, the monocrat returned to the mansion and his beloved Rosita who, at her husband's request, did not join him on this festive day.

Upon greeting his wife, he quickly observed a strange, nervous, uneasiness about her. Without prodding, she promptly informed him that she had received a long letter from Maria in Mexico City informing them that she had been hospitalized for one week in order to treat an acute attack of dysentery. While startled by the news of his daughter's illness, he was shocked to learn that the treatment administered consisted of arsenic tablets. He immediately summoned his doctor to question the treatment employed only to learn that this was the normally prescribed treatment for the illness.

Being an inquisitive engineer, he was curious as to the possible source causing the infection. He learned that the capital's water supply flowed from the Lerma and Cutzamala rivers some one hundred miles distant. He recalled that the city was founded and developed on a dry lake. Over time, the massive, enormously weighty buildings constructed on the site were slowly sinking in the soft sub-soil. As a result of this gravitating phenomenon, underground water mains would fracture allowing accumulated sewage and farm waste to enter the potable water system. While he was neither pleased nor satisfied with his findings, he was assured from Maria's letter that his daughter was now cured and well.

With this affirmation in hand, there existed yet another concern for this protective father. The letter from his treasured little girl elaborated extensively on her growing friendship with and affection for Nick Garcia. With such seeds planted in a highly active mind, the father attempted to envision to what degree the friendship had progressed. Unknown to the *cacique*, Maria and Nick had shared living quarters during the past two years.

In her letter, Maria recounted a confrontation between Nick and the corrupt police force in the capital.

A minor theft was committed by someone unknown to Nick. Being in the immediate vicinity, Nick was approached by a police officer who informed him that he would be an attestant to the crime and that he would be compelled to accompany the officer to the police station. However, if he wished to extend a slight monetary consideration to the policeman, going to the police station would be unnecessary. The suggestion was immediately rejected by the utopian college student. Unruffled, Nick expressed his sympathy for the plight of the underpaid men in uniform. He understood why it was necessary for the law enforcers to seek economic salvation by whatever means. After a brief exchange and a warm *abrazo*, they parted.

Maria described the incident involving her paramour like a proud mother speaking about her son. The proud and affectionate tone of her account of Nick's accomplishment troubled her overly suspicious father.

CHAPTER XVIII

A PROBLEM RESOLVED

It was April 1894, and there was excitement aplenty in Soledad. While construction continued on the potable water pumping system, the reconstruction of the twenty-three mile road to Tuxtla Gutiérrez was nearing completion.

There was an additional occurrence that added to the high degree of exultation in the air. There was a new and unusual feeling that perhaps this modest town, hidden in the mountains of Chiapas, would soon possibly be the center of the nation's attention. Oil had been discovered in the most southerly area of the state. It was high drama, for the right to Mexico's sub-soil was strictly protected as national property.

A highly emotional relationship existed between Mexicans and that which was found in their sub-soil. This protective sentiment could be traced to their long and bloody struggle for independence.

Since the days of President Santa Anna, the passion for guarding and protecting that which the nation possessed below the earth's surface reigned supreme. The thought of foreign involvement was totally rejected, for it was feared that such participation could result in foreign domination. Consequently, it was an extremely bold and courageous act by President Porfirio Diaz, late 1891, to surrender the state's ownership of the sub-soil and open the door to foreign oil companies and investment. By his unilateral declaration, the way had been cleared for oil exploration and mining exploitation by foreigners.

Quite naturally, the discovery of oil in Chiapas translated to jobs and money in the minds of the populace. Within a matter of months, in rapid succession, there were indications of interest in exploration from the world's major oil producers such as Gulf, Standard Oil, Texaco, Sinclair Oil and others. The race for liquid gold had begun.

On the local scene, the day to inaugurate the new road had arrived. The celebration would be quite simple with all town employees and others assembled at the point where the road commenced.

It was announced that the *cacique* would speak at 11:00 A.M.; and, as expected, the attendees were on site and waiting for their leader. The *cacique*'s words were surprisingly brief and to the point. He declared that the improved road to the state capital would be as good as any road in the state. With that, he cut the ribbon opening the road to public use. After an abbreviated exchange of pleasantries, he returned to his office in town hall.

Once back in his spacious, unattractive office with its slightly frayed upholstery and frilly, homemade-looking curtains, the *cacique* knew well why he chose to have the road dedication of unusually short duration.

The unrealized fact to those attending the inauguration was that the road had been reconstructed only as far as the eye could see. Little improvement had been made beyond that point. Undoubtedly, a major portion of the budget allocation for the road improvement had found its way into the pockets of privileged individuals.

Anticipating there most assuredly would be repercussions once the fraud committed on the project would became public knowledge, the *cacique* decided that he would dispose of the issue in any way possible. He knew that there was continued public exuberance in anticipation of the introduction of the potable water plant. Wisely, he directed all propaganda to the awaited water system and away from the road.

Unbeknownst to the *cacique*, he was about to be confronted by a monumental problem that would disrupt his tranquility.

The communal leader, a farmer named Dario Quintero, was charged by the local police chief for inciting an uprising—an extremely grave crime. The accused was imprisoned and the members of the collectivity had congregated and were demonstrating in the town's *zocalo*.

Dario Quintero was the identical twin of Alvaro Quintero, murdered six months past in the town of Santa Clara, state of Chiapas—a rather small municipality southeast of Soledad near the border of Guatemala. During a protest, Alvaro was gunned down by government *pistoleros*. With Dario now in command, the remonstrators moved thirty-five miles north to Soledad to pursue their cause, resulting in Dario's arrest.

The Quinteros were descendents of a long line of Guatemaltecos who migrated to Mexico from Guatemala when the latter gained its independence from Spain in the early 1800's. With this independence, Chiapas, which had been a part of Guatemala, chose to be annexed to Mexico.

Alvaro, a dynamic leader who, through his revolutionary rhetoric, could incite and unite his fellow *campesinos* (peasants), protested the invasion of the communal lands by wealthy, government protected land barons.

Even with the absolute power exercised by the *cacique*, such a situation had the potential of aggrandizing to the point where the *cacique's* ability to control would be brought into question by the caudillo in Mexico City. Since the days of the conquest, the *cacique* system was a means of maintaining order irrespective of an existing or developing situation. Therefore, it was in the *cacique's* unfaltering interest to resolve the matter without displaying even the most remote sign of weakness. This particularly perceptive leader was cognizant of the fact that it was imperative that he be kept in high esteem.

Eduardo's first reaction was to have a member of the local legal establishment counsel the prisoner in obtaining a *writ of amparo* (court issued protective order). The *amparo*, unique in Mexico, was a constitutionally created defense mechanism for disadvantaged citizens and was, in effect, a form of a restraining order against the judicial authorities. Under the law, any individual could seek a *writ of amparo* from a state court or a national tribunal. It was customary that such a mandate be requested when a municipal, state or federal action might have violated the individual's constitutional rights. In the event the writ was granted, it afforded the individual protection against detention or arrest. The appointed counsel was quick to point out to Dario that such an application was time consuming and involved a complex procedure. The *cacique* was well aware of the difficulties involved.

As was normally the case, there was an option for a speedy resolution of such matters through a simple order from the *cacique* to his *pistoleros*. Such would be swift and without testification for, professionally performed, there would be no corpus delicti. After serious consideration, this alternative was rejected.

With the passing of time, Eduardo had been transformed. He was now an accomplished, shrewd, unrelenting and astute politician capable of reaching a sound solution. He decided to employ these newly acquired talents as monocrat in resolving the matter.

He further pondered the predicament before deciding it would not be wise to have Dario pursue the *amparo* route inasmuch as he knew a long delay in resolving the incident could be disastrous, for time was not on his side.

Violence and the suppression of the *campesino's* human rights were not uncommon in Chiapas. There was a long-standing clash between the privileged *mestizo* and the underprivileged Indian who remained ignorant of his right to life. There were those who argued that the Indian was a burden on Mexico while others contended that they should be left alone to assimilate in a natural way respecting their unique culture. Irrespective of one's position, there was one fact generally accepted by all *mestizos* and that was that they were all delighted by the fact that they were not Indian.

The existing quandary was the prefiguration of unrest that would be viewed with disfavor by the caudillo. A rapid and placid resolution was of the utmost magnitude, for the *cacique* knew full well that the simplest demonstration could overflow into mob violence. Eduardo was determined that there be no further manifestations of unrest. Continued degenerating mob violence could result in a profoundly damaging threat to the *cacique*'s reputation and must necessarily be avoided at any cost.

The day following his arrest, Dario was brought to the *cacique*'s office. The all-powerful leader was seated behind his enormous desk; and from his high-back chair, he observed the pint-sized peasant on the opposite side. A David versus Goliath situation.

Dario was not without a trump card. Unfortunately, being an illiterate and uneducated peon with no understanding of the political power game, he was unaware that continued harassing by the farmers could have a disastrous effect on the town administration.

On the other hand, Eduardo had, over the past three days, researched the matter and was completely informed as to the plight of Alvaro's widow, Rosenda. She was a diminutive woman with skin hardened and tanned by years of working in the fields. With the loss of Alvaro, she was the nominal head of an prodigious brood of children, grandchildren and aged relatives all sharing a dirt floor, two room adobe structure and a thatched roof hut adjoining the principal abode. While there was electric lighting in the two-room abode, there was no indoor plumbing. Water for drinking, bathing and laundering had to be hauled from a town well some five hundred yards distant. Although cramped, it was home for Rosenda and her family.

Eduardo was apprised of Dario's intense concern for the widow's support and welfare. Mindful of the preponderant circumstances, the *cacique* had prepared a proffer for the arrested peasant with Rosenda in mind.

The proposal stipulated that, in exchange for the complete desistance of further manifestations by the communal *campesinos* and their agreement to return to their farming activity, the *cacique* would accommodate Rosenda with a three room, furnished brick home, complete with interior plumbing, in addition to a job as a domestic in the town hall.

As always, an offer extended by the *cacique* was non-negotiable. Without procrastinating, Dario accepted the offer further promising the *cacique* that, as the communal leader, he would, henceforth, be an obedient servant to him.

An expeditious and beneficial outcome of the matter was never in doubt by the ironhanded ruler who knew that every man had his price. As he had so successfully prevailed in a multitude of similar occurrences, he resolved the problem by purchasing Dario—just as he would acquire a commodity.

CHAPTER XIX

MARIA'S THESIS

With the previous summer's short-lived insurrection now history, Eduardo could, on this first day of May 1895, look forward to more satisfying matters. This being the national Dia de Trabajo (Labor Day), there would be the traditional parade with the inhabitants of the region coming from as far away as fifty miles for the festivities, which would include a free barbeque for everyone.

Inasmuch as this day of celebration was labor related, the *cacique* chose to ignore the observance of the closely following national holiday, Cinco de Mayo. This day commemorated Mexico's victory, the Batalla de Puebla (Battle of Puebla), normally commemorated only in Mexico City and the city of Puebla.

At the conclusion of the observance, and pre-planned for maximum public consumption, the *cacique* would initiate the functioning of the potable water installation. For many months, the *cacique* had prepared for this memorable day. Resplendent in his finest attire, his massive shoulders filling his jacket and proudly donning the sash of his office, he was in a particularly good mood.

At the designated hour of 11:00 A.M., the signal was given for the parade to start on its long procession, passing in review of the grandstand and the town's dignitaries. The parade consisted of a hodgepodge of workers, policemen, firemen, soldiers, bakers, security guards, domestics, butchers, etc.—all in their traditional work attire. Included, as well, were farmers, office employees, store clerks, laborers and just about anyone who was somehow gainfully employed, wearing their work garb. The procession was as far removed from a military review as is possible. It was rag-tag from beginning to end.

As expected, there was obvious extreme boredom by all in the reviewing stand. Nevertheless, visible acclaim was required; otherwise, they would be subject to disfavor by the *cacique*. After almost two hours, the parade was finally over and the long awaited feast was about to begin. This gratuitously offered barbeque was probably the reason that the streets were lined with the region's peasantry.

There was barbequed lamb and pork, tubs of rice and beans, stacks of tortillas, red and green pepper sauce, guacamole, fried onion strips and more. Such a celebration would not be complete without the typically essential tequila, pulque, beer and soft drinks. The venerated *mariachis* (vocal and string musicians) were, of course, present. Each such annual cookout was discussed for months while the citizenry awaited the next year's event.

With the shadows of evening approaching and the festivities still going strong, the *cacique* decided to temporarily suspend the commemorative and gala day so that he could introduce the new water system while he still had a sizeable audience.

Determined to start the water flowing while there was still daylight, the celebrants were directed to the site where the *cacique* would throw the switch and start the water streaming. Being somewhat exhausted, Eduardo's words were brief, praising his own efforts in order to bring Soledad its first potable water system. With water gushing, the exhausted *cacique* ordered that the party continue, after which he returned to the mansion.

Rosita, who did not attend the traditional Labor Day festivities, had prepared her husband's favorite meal— chicken fajitas, fried black beans and oversized blue corn tortillas. Prior to dining, she relaxed her beloved Eduardo with a prodigious margarita.

While enjoying their pre-dinner cocktail, Rosita informed her spouse that she had received a letter from Maria informing her of the date of their daughter's graduation in Mexico City. Additionally, her letter included a copy of her final dissertation as well as that of her friend, Nick. The *cacique* suggested that in view of the extremely long and tiring day and the lengthy enclosures, he would digest her letter on Saturday, his next day free from his administrative duties in town.

As per custom, he was up at 7:00 A.M. on Saturday even though this was his day to rest and he could do as he wished. Following established procedure, he informed Rosita of his plan for the day.

Sitting in the dining room, he observed the cloudless sky and sun-filled day through the arched window. He addressed Rosita, "This day is my day to do as I wish. My dear, look over there to the east. You can see the sun rising. It is a remarkably beautiful day—a truly enchanting day!"

After a breakfast of *huevos rancheros* (fried eggs ranch style) with *salsa picante* (hot pepper sauce), he visited his ranch and soft drink bottling plant. He assumed that his bottled drinking water enterprise would pass into history now that there was a potable water system in the town. He anticipated that he would return to the mansion for lunch and then meticulously read the letter from his daughter. Having now returned home and after lunch followed by a short catnap, he retired to his favorite overstuffed chair to review his daughter's missive. He learned that his treasured Maria, now a young lady, would be graduating from the nation's foremost university "with distinction." He could not be more proud. He was also aware that she had not volunteered to work in the Indian village of Las Cruces during the summer as she had done for the past three years. He sensed that she had profound utopian tendencies and tenets, probably inherited from her father.

The *cacique* learned that graduation would take place on June 20. This particular day, being a Thursday, would afford him the opportunity to visit Generals Ramos and Bersunza either prior to or after the graduation ceremonies.

The moment had arrived to begin scrutinizing Maria's treatise. As he expected, the subject matter related to the deprived Indians in Mexico.

A History of an Honorable Past—an
Inequitable Present

Since the arrival of Cortés and his conquering armies, there has been one race enslaved beyond one's imagination—the Indians. The repayment for the long hours spent in factories and farms has been their subjugation and oppression. To view the result of their forced drudgery, one must only stroll down any avenue in our capital to marvel at the magnificent structures that line the thoroughfare. The local markets evidence their handicraft in the production of jewelry, pottery, and artifacts of every description.

The Indian population, in an effort to free themselves from enslavement, attempted to obtain freedom by escaping to the surrounding mountains. Their endeavor was without positive result and was only partially successful. A limited number succeeded in establishing a new life even though they survived on the most meager necessities required to maintain their existence. Sadly, for those who wished to retain their communal identity, they were involuntarily obliged, for lack of food, water and other essentials, to return to the haciendas of the all-powerful landowners to once again work the land from daybreak to sunset in order to keep body and soul together.

While the Indians had for centuries worshiped their gods, their forced conversion to Christianity was tedious and painful. Finally, after a long, concentrated effort, the Indian finally, reluctantly accepted Christianity in his own unorthodox way acknowledging the Virgin of Guadalupe as his goddess.

By inscribing the Indian populace into the Christian religion, the church inherited a newfound force to implement its domination over its disciples. To further the church's control, it exerted an ongoing effort of dispatching missionaries throughout the nation to become fluent in the multitude of dialects and tongues. While not physically challenged, the emissaries were energetically rebuffed. No longer permitted to worship their gods, the vanquished Indians molded small images of their Spanish conquistadors, which were substituted for their former idols. While some adopted the Virgin of Guadalupe as their icon, others secretly directed their glorification to a clay effigy while others accepted neither continuing their veneration of their gods as they had done for generations prior to their domination.

The rarest of expectations occurred

in 1855 when Benito Juárez, a full-blooded Indian, became the first to ascend by election to the presidency of the republic. Heretofore, the Indian race, during this period, had been degraded and ordered by the federal government into designated areas for the purpose of isolation. And so it was that the deprived Indian had been relegated to work arid, mountainous land producing only enough to barely survive. At long last, in 1862, President Juárez decreed that the Indian population could best serve the nation and themselves through their complete integration on an equal footing into the *mestizo* work force.

As a first act of implementation, the president commanded that where heretofore the Indian had been allowed the use of government-owned communal land for farming, they would, in the future, be free to compete on the open market with the *mestizo* population. While well intentioned, the plan was a dismal failure for the Indian had neither the know-how nor the financial wherewithal to compete with the *mestizo*. Unfortunately, a well-preconceived plan had gone awry.

Through the years of their existence, the subjugated Indians had been debased, dishonored and maltreated to the point that they had to withstand a constant effort to expunge the culture in its entirety. It was only through the Indians profound belief in their heritage and devotion to their civilization that they were capable of surviving. They shall survive. Their culture shall survive.

After a detailed perusal of the dissertation, the *cacique* could only deduce that his cherished child was, indeed, a true pursuer of ideals. His mind bulged with unanswered questions while his powerful definiteness was hounded by the lack of answers. Adding to his quandary, there was yet another puzzling thought of concern. He was not at ease with the very affectionate praise of Nick Garcia by his daughter and her extolment and support of his final thesis. With great anticipation and unsure of what to expect, he commenced a scrupulous review of Nick's treatise.

CHAPTER XX

NICK'S THESIS

Proceeding with caution relative to the unknown, the *cacique* started a critical evaluation of Nick's thesis.

A People Betrayed

My name is Nicholas Garcia from the town of Soledad in the state of Chiapas. I am twenty-three years of age, and I attend the University of Mexico in order to pursue a course in journalism. Upon graduating, I intend to return to my hometown to become manager and editor of our municipality's lone newspaper, which, today, is operated by my uncle.

In our township, we are subjected to authoritarian rule by virtue of a *cacique* who rules by fiat. The *cacique* is normally the principal landowner in the region and dictates who buys what and at what price. He controls all aspects of commerce. In an Indian dominated region, it is the *cacique* who purchases their crops at a price he, alone, establishes. These disadvantaged souls are forever in debt to the *cacique* who controls them by the power of armed hired guns. Until I arrived in the capital of our nation, I assumed that in Soledad we experienced the highest degree of corruption. How wrong I was.

During the past four years of my residence in Mexico City, I have witnessed an unbelievable magnitude of villainous depravity. Sadly, I have concluded that this sinfulness is, in fact, the means by which our political system survives.

I have attempted to piece together the reasons why we continue to exist as a people. We live day-to-day, always attempting to reason who we are, only to discover that we are neither Spanish nor Indian.

We live in a culture that not only accepts and welcomes corruption, but also thrives on it. It is a tradition inherited from the conquest in 1519, which found receptive partners in our Indian and *mestizo* population.

This combination of a confusing heritage and the willingness to practice depravity in our daily lives has resulted in a system of government that rewards greed by whatever means achieved. Our governing structure closely resembles the mountains of our nation. There is one single opportunist at the peak who benefits personally. As we proceed down the incline, the number of benefactors increases at each level of descent. Eventually, multitudes have filled their pockets ensuring themselves and their heirs of a comfortable lifestyle. Incredibly, with each change of administration, new mercenaries with outstretched hands come into being and enter the scene to personally partake of our nation's wealth.

And so, my loyal and dedicated patriots, while we strive to exist not knowing who we truly are, we do so in a corrupt society governed by avaricious compatriots who superficially pledge loyalty to our flag with one hand with the other hand extended for the spoils of their positions. I'll set forth the facts.

I was appalled to discover that in the recent past our government had imported a large quantity of engines and pumps that were distributed to our laboring farmers to be employed in the pumping of underground water for the irrigation of their crops. Perhaps it was for lack of education or understanding or insufficient funds, the equipment was not maintained properly and eventually was rendered permanently inoperative.

The supplier's agent, upon learning of the dilemma, approached our government's purchasing agent to suggest that the farmers be properly instructed in the use and maintenance of the equipment, even volunteering to personally offer the guidance and inculcation. The agent, shocked beyond belief, was told by the government employee, "Don't worry about it. If the engines get burned out, we'll just buy some more." Obviously, more engines, more graft.

Yes, corruption is like an epidemic. It requires people who work together in order that the disease spreads from one to another. The plague flourishes on government controls and disbursements when administered by a network of dishonorable individuals who have mastered the rules of how the game is played. Their common motto is greed, sharing, on occasion, their ill-gotten wealth with subordinates within the system.

It matters not where we look for we encounter similar shameless practices. For a small gratification, a clerk in our bureaucracy can be purchased. Permits for construction or the importation of goods may be obtained well in advance of the normal waiting period for a small bribe. While the payoff may seem to be insignificant, the volume of such incidents is enormous resulting in a modest fortune for the public servant.

Such incidents of payment for preferential services confront us in every walk of life every day. There is the policeman on the corner who manufactures an offense in order to extract the customary *mordida*. His superiors, many of whom are in the prison system, amass fortunes by selling state property to inmates and others. This does not preclude food items, cigarettes, items of clothing, and all forms of intoxicants.

Within the system, the advantaged who have the means enjoy privileges not normally extended. It is common knowledge that one of our renowned politicians, imprisoned for a capital crime, enjoyed an uncharacteristic lifestyle of an elegantly furnished suite of cells and the visitation of his infatuate. The "residence" was replete with a furnished kitchen where a well-paid inmate prepared meals as well as cleaned the makeshift apartment.

In contrast, poor prisoners, who can spend years and years merely awaiting trial, are condemned to overcrowded conditions and grossly inadequate food. It is a nation-wide tragedy that money purchases the grease that makes the wheels turn and delivers privileges. It is a mournful catastrophe for those who cannot afford to purchase the vitally critical grease.

And so it continues. To this point, I have only discussed the petty, dishonorable, underhanded, bribable mercenaries that function within the system. I shall now lay bare those of a respected profession.

During my years at the university, I have made a concentrated effort to meet and interview local journalists. Inasmuch as I shall initiate my career in just a few months, I hoped to discover seasoned newspapermen to be honorable and free of contamination by the system.

I was absolutely shocked to learn that professionals in the field of journalism, like so many others, are on the take. They, however, are not alone, for their publishers are equally, if not more so, corrupt. It is the norm that these publishing magnets, in exchange for government benefits, cater to the whims of the politicians. Nothing is printed that is derogatory to the government.

The profession has become corrupt. The watchdog of the public's interest has become non-existent. With the reporters contaminated and the publishers a purchased commodity, who is safeguarding the public's interest?

Politics and politicians control our minds through the collaborating printed media. We have become robots who comply with their wishes as a result of our brainwashing by newsprint.

It is shameful that such a noble profession, journalism in all its aspects, has been shamed. We are helpless when editors, reporters, columnists and publishers all sell their honor. What we read is not the professionals speaking, but money talking—the money that wields enormous power.

How disillusioned and disappointed I am in the industry of which I shall become a part. I am repelled by the flagrant misbehavior of members of the press corps.

Ironically, the foundation of our governing structure is based on shameless corruption without which our present system could not function. Hopefully, at some future time, our leaders will abolish the means by which individuals serving all of us can enrich themselves, and they will be stripped of their uncontrolled power.

I anticipate that I shall graduate with honors on June 20 and will have the distinction of giving the valedictorian's address. At that time, I shall, without restriction, set forth my code of morality for government; business in general, and the newspaper industry, in particular; and our conduct as individuals.

In closing, we are a nation with an

elected central government that allows oppressive regional despots to reign so that there will be no pulling of the central binding thread that might unravel the cloth that intertwines the government structure. There must be clarification of the relationship between central and regional control of our country. I will awaken all Mexicans to the doctrine of our beloved President Benito Juárez that stipulated that we must build a nation with a central authority that will observe the rights of the individual whoever or wherever he may be. The age of regional despotism must come to an end.

Now having digested the thinking of Maria and Nick, Eduardo sat quietly attempting to evaluate the contents of the letter and the two dissertations. He was not disturbed by Maria's sympathy for the impoverished Indians and their threatened culture. Her sentiments had been discernable since childhood. Nick's thesis was, of course, another story, particularly in view of the obvious ongoing relationship between Maria and Nick. The concern was so great that Eduardo decided to once again scrupulously review Nick's thesis.

Unhurried, he analytically re-examined the work attempting to assess the depth of Nick's conviction. Completing his perusing of the composition, he sat motionless and silent in a state of deliberation. The silence was broken when Rosita entered his study to ask that he join her for dinner.

He responded, "My dear wife, I have carefully read Maria's letter and enclosure, and I can clearly see the writing on the wall. I fear that at some time after June 20 we could have new problems in Soledad. I anticipate that we might have a perplexity to which there will be no simple solution. Incidentally, I shall never again declare that a day is beautiful until after the sun has set. Let's go eat."

CHAPTER XXI

MARIA'S GRADUATION

It was but six weeks before the trip to Mexico City for Maria's graduation. In addition to seeing his daughter graduate, the *cacique* would attempt to mend any official fences that required mending.

For the moment, all was right with the world. The *cacique*'s business enterprises were operating trouble free. The soft drink bottling plant, the farms, the ranch, the banks and the others were all reporting increased profits. The newly inaugurated potable water pumping system was functioning as hoped, creating a decline in the demand for bottled "spring" water.

The disquieting incident with Dario Quintero and his supporters had been satisfactorily resolved. The widow of the co-conspirator, Alvaro Quintero, was settled in the new home provided by the *cacique* and was gainfully employed in the town's administration building.

With no pending problems, Eduardo felt secure in planning his forthcoming trip to the capital without fear of a civil uprising or disruptive occurrence. He believed that all was peaceful and under control. Nevertheless, through his unique perceptive ability, he sensed that there was, indeed, a storm on the horizon.

And so, on a bright Friday morning on June 14, 1895, Eduardo and his beloved wife, Rosita, boarded a private carriage for Veracruz. There, they would embark on the anticipated exhausting train trip to Mexico City. Seated in the first class section, they were isolated from the peasants traveling with chickens and small animals.

Unfortunately, the trip far exceeded their most feared expectations. The train departed four hours late and, en route, a malfunctioning engine caused an additional five-hour delay. In addition to the unscheduled delays, the train stopped at every town en route. The Pullman seats were in complete disrepair, windows were broken or missing and the rest rooms were inoperative—somewhat the same conditions encountered on their last train adventure. The trip was an unforgettable nightmare.

After a tortuous thirty hours and arriving at 4:00 A.M., the two exhausted voyagers were overjoyed to at last retire in their hotel room.

It was 3:30 P.M. when they finally arose from a deep sleep. Despite enjoying a long and well-deserved rest, they were experiencing the effects of the journey. Feeling that he was not ready to return to a daily pursuit, Eduardo decided that Monday would not be a "work" day. Consequently, they agreed to spend their first evening and the following days with Maria. Meanwhile, Eduardo contacted General Rudolfo Ramos to arrange an appointment for the morning following commencement ceremonies.

Their private time with Maria passed quickly. Eduardo avoided mentioning Nick's name hoping that Maria would perceive that her father was not particularly interested in her lover.

Even though June was the first month of the rainy season, with good fortune, the morning of the outdoor graduation was cloudless with a welcome gentle breeze.

As each graduate's name was announced, the recipient passed to the dais to receive his or her diploma. The proud parents applauded enthusiastically as their daughter was honored as graduating with distinction.

It was now time for the introduction and presentation of the valedictorian, Nicholas Garcia. The *cacique* waited intently for Nick's address. He was prepared for almost anything after having diligently digested the young man's thesis.

The honored student proceeded to the dais. He was a large, ascetic looking, raw-boned man with an ingeniously appealing face. He stood tall and erect like a towering spruce. All the while, thoughts of his own graduation and valedictorian address raced through Eduardo's mind.

The *cacique* was expecting Nick's attack on the system under which all Mexican's lived. In a matter of minutes, the theme of his address would become apparent to all.

After recognizing the university and visiting dignitaries, he greeted his fellow students and welcomed the guests. With his voice strong and firm, the speaker proclaimed, "Like each and every one of you, I am a Mexican who is living under a theocratic, authoritative system. There is a fantasy under which we live and that is that the president of our nation is all-powerful, king-like and infallible. Now, the weakness in all of us is our submission to this assumed power, which is immune to criticism. There is one law for the powerful with another law for all others.

"And so, as each chief of state assumes power, we yield and accept the tradition inherited potentness. While you probably assume that I decry the system, I do not. It is only through this deplorable system that our nation continues to exist. This is a system that wraps the president in an imperial aura and he, in turn, rules through the appointment of regional and local *caciques*.

"During his four years in office, our president reigns over the congress, the judiciary, our state administrators, our bureaucracy and our public life—yours, mine and everyone's.

"The system is a bureaucratic machine whose mechanism must constantly be lubricated. This lubricant takes the form of your hard earned pesos or personal patronage that, traditionally, rewards loyal and unquestioned service.

"The ritual of providing continuity of our government is vital to the survival of the system. The ruling elite is obsessed with the unwavering requisite that power be perpetuated. Is all of this legal? Unfortunately, yes.

"Our constitution does not set forth the rules that control our daily lives. It merely stipulates the social-political objectives of our system of government. A system that is unscrupulous, bribal and immoral.

"And so, my friends, do we accept the status quo? I say No! I say Never! So what do we do? The people must let their voices be heard and, more importantly, we must inform those who are not aware of our corrupted system.

"I shall exert all of my energy to creating disarray within the political bureaucracy, and I implore you to join me. Let me tell you something, and I plead that you do not forget it. When our government officials feel protected by the system and have no opposition, we, the people, have no choice. The people's voice shall be heard. The foundation for a better tomorrow must be laid today. We cannot delay. We must act today. Thank you."

At the conclusion of the address, the *cacique* whispered to Rosita, "I had anticipated that we might have an insurmountable problem in Soledad in the near future. Now, my dear, I am absolutely assured of it."

The evening was spent with Maria celebrating her successful college effort. Again, there was no mention of Nick. As a precaution, Nick moved his possessions to the living quarters of a friend in the event that Maria's parents visited her apartment.

It was a warm Friday morning when Eduardo presented himself at the National Palace. General Ramos was waiting to greet him. He was quick to express his profound thanks to Eduardo for having given gainful employment to his designated friends. In a joking manner he said, "You have been a good friend and achieved much as *cacique*. I salute your accomplishments. In recognition of your successes, I would so like to applaud you, however, as you can readily see that is impossible do that with but one hand." They both enjoyed a good laugh before exchanging *abrazos*.

After a brief exchange, the *cacique* was ushered into the chambers of General Bersunza. Eduardo had come well prepared with a detailed account of his efforts on behalf of his citizenry. He falsely described the reconstructed road as an improved thoroughfare from Soledad to Tuxtla Gutiérrez. He assumed credit for resolving a peasant insurrection and vividly expounded on his bold accomplishment of the newly installed potable water system. Their warm and conciliatory meeting lasted two hours. "My son," the caudillo said, "again I remind you to continue looking back to make sure you have followers. May God be with you." With that, they embraced and Eduardo took his leave.

The family spent the remainder of the week together enjoying the fine cuisine of the capital city and shopping. As before, there was no mention of Nick. The *cacique* did not care to display interest in furthering a liaison between Maria and Nick. He wished for a more cosmopolitan suitor for this daughter. Little did the parents know that when Maria returned to her apartment each evening, Nick was waiting for his paramour.

It was time for the family of three to return to Soledad. The trip by rail was surprisingly uneventful and completed on schedule. By reason of experience, the *cacique* was concerned that the pre-arranged coach would not be waiting for their arrival. His fears were justified for the transport to continue their trip home was nowhere to be found. While he was a powerful *cacique* in his small region, he impressed no one in the relatively large port city of Veracruz. With good fortune, he was able to communicate with the *cacique* of the Veracruz district who graciously and immediately provided transport to Soledad for his colleague. As always, returning home was most welcome.

It was just a matter of days when the first episode of the *cacique*'s prognostication occurred. It became readily apparent that Maria was not the adolescent who left for the university four years bygone. She asked for a meeting with her parents. With the customary twinkle in her eyes, her eyebrows arched mischievously and a suspicious line at the corners of her mouth, her father surmised that the discussion would be of a significant nature. In a matter of minutes, and without equivocating, Maria emphatically voiced her intent to have her own home away from the mansion. She maintained that she had enjoyed the privacy of her own apartment in the capital. Not said was the fact that she wanted to have her own place where she could continue to bed down with Nick who would be arriving in a matter of weeks and who would live with his uncle Benito.

Her parents, after recovering from shock, sat motionless without any response. A cold, cold, congested expression settled on Eduardo's face while Rosita's demeanor was one of pained tolerance.

The ultra conservative traditions of the Mexican upper class were particularly strong in the smaller provincial communities where the weight of public opinion was respected and where the appearance of propriety was paramount. The education of girls was not of vital concern and normally neglected. It was a generally accepted fact that girls were brought up to be wives and mothers. Additionally, the courting of a marriageable young lady was generally a long and protracted romantic ritual. It was an accepted tradition that she would reside with her parents. A young suitor, on his best behavior, would court his intended, always accompanied by a chaperone when the couple was together. Among the provincial bourgeoisie, virginity until marriage was sacrosanct.

Having been confronted by Maria's decision, which she stressed was irreversible, the parents were left to debate the matter. To deviate from a deep-rooted tradition was particularly troubling in that Maria was the daughter of the *cacique*.

Unable to reach a mutually agreeable decision, Eduardo turned to the one person who had given guidance for over twenty years, the parish priest.

After a sleepless night, the *cacique* met with his ecclesiastical friend early the following morning. Greeting the *cacique*, the cleric remarked, "My son, I see a touch of sadness in your face. What's wrong?"

For a few moments, the visitor did not respond though his expression spoke for him. He embraced the father saying, "My protector, I have a most serious problem." He went to explicate, in minute detail, the entire matter confronting him as relates to Maria.

For a man who was normally calm and collected, on this occasion he was ruffled and confused, frowning intensely, his eyes squinting under drawn brows. A cold dignity created a visibly stony mask on his face. For ten minutes the two sat, heads bowed without an utterance.

The priest spoke first telling his parishioner that he did, indeed, understand why his friend had a grievous problem. Nevertheless, he advised his long-time friend not to fear the complexity of any situation, amplifying his advice by stating, "When God shuts one door, he opens another." After an extended period of questioning Eduardo, the father reasoned, "For you to prohibit Maria, a very determined young lady, from living as she wishes would, most probably, result in her carrying out her choice of lifestyle and you losing a daughter. On the other hand, there will be much gossip among the townspeople, for such a lifestyle is contrary to the regressive traditions of our people. However, don't overlook the fact that you are the *cacique*, therefore, any gossip mongering will be subdued and behind closed doors. Remember, my son, you may feel disheartened now; however, I ask that you keep your faith, for faith will move mountains. We are merely attempting to move a small hill." Accepting the advice of the man of God, Eduardo received the priest's blessings. They embraced warmly and Eduardo departed.

It was now mid-day and the *cacique* was in no mood to attend to his official duties or think of his business enterprises. He found it difficult to accept the dictate of his own daughter, which was completely incompatible to his own wishes.

Once at home, ensconced in his favorite chair, he summoned Rosita to inform her of his meeting. He hoped they could mutually reach a decision on how they would superintend the resolution. After a lengthy discussion, they agreed to rent and furnish a small bungalow, distant from the mansion, and allow Maria to establish herself in her new home with no explanation to anyone. They concurred that their daughter's privacy would be respected.

To ease the disconcertment on the people's leader, they decided that Rosita, alone, would very subtly undertake all of the details involved in the preparation and execution of this unwanted relocation. During the two-week period of transition, the exchange between parents and daughter was polite though not affectionate. The *cacique* had observed the transformation of Maria over the past four years away from home. He perceived her intense passion regarding the travail of the underprivileged and how it caused her to frown on her father's tyrannical methods of governing and his business involvements.

With much heartache, the move was implemented. Maria was particularly pleased for she had learned that Nick, after spending three weeks in Mexico City being briefed on modern techniques of publishing a newspaper, would be returning to Soledad momentarily.

CHAPTER XXII

START OF A CONFRONTATION

It was now early September 1895 and the town was preparing for its annual celebration of Mexico's Independence Day on the sixteenth day of the month with festivities commencing one day earlier.

Maria was now settled in her new home and visited her parents for dinner three evenings each week, which allowed her several nights each week with her inamorato. While there were hushed rumors and mumblings about Maria's private life, there were no public pronouncements. Maria had obtained a position teaching in a catholic private school for girls while Nick was preparing to assume his position as editor of *La Universal* from his uncle Benito.

The two young lovers had now developed a most intimate relationship. She loved him for the light that glinted behind his dark brown eyes, his gaze focusing on her lips with her femininity responding completely to his masculinity. She couldn't resist his potent brand of sensuality. He would look at her with something deeper than mere masculine interest while exuding a reckless passion. She was, indeed, at peace and satisfied with her life.

It was announced in the newspaper that Benito would pass control of the post of editor to Nick at noon on September 16, 1895. There would be a by-invitation-only reception at the newspaper's office followed by a public barbeque, which was being offered by the paper in conjunction with the day's festive program.

The fall evening of September 15 was ideal. All

preparations were completed for an impressive and well-rehearsed reenactment of the declaration of independence. As had been done each year since 1810, at precisely 11:00 P.M., the *cacique*, from the balcony of town hall, waved a large Mexican flag attached to a long pole and three times recited the words of Father Miguel Hidalgo y Castillo in the city of Dolores Hidalgo eighty-five years ago. The assembled throng enthusiastically shouted, *"Viva Mexico"* (Long Live Mexico).

Looking down on the crowd from the balcony, Eduardo spotted Maria with Nick. His brow wrinkled with contemptuous indignation. With eyes fixed, he asked himself, "Could it be that in the not too distant future that man standing with my daughter will become my sanguinary enemy?" At the conclusion of the ceremony, there was an impressive fireworks display.

In view of the existing circumstances, there would not be the usual extravaganza celebrating Maria's twenty-first birthday. She was, however, showered with gifts from her parents.

The next day at noon, the local newspaper was the town's focal point for a limited number of special guests who assembled at the offices of the newspaper to greet the new editor. Although Señor and Señora Hernandez were invited, they did not attend. Once the guests had consumed a variety of drinks and trays of hors d'oeuvres, they moved to the town center to partake of the barbeque hosted by *La Universal*. While the *cacique* was not present, everyone knew his bottling plant had contributed all of the soft drinks. The partying continued until early evening, with Nick remaining until the last celebrant had departed. The following day the fledgling journalist would be on the job as editor.

Meanwhile, Maria enthusiastically lectured her young students on issues such as the need for and right to an education for young ladies, which was normally reserved for boys. She stressed that the ultra-conservative tradition that teaches that girls are brought up solely to be wives and mothers was pure fallacy. Even though the mother superior objected to such teaching, she dared not openly oppose the expositor. After all, Maria was the *cacique*'s daughter.

Meanwhile, another insurgent was preparing his first issue of the local paper. True to form, he was prepared to go on the attack against the system without fear of retaliation. In deference to the wishes of his amorist, he agreed to initiate his career with a condemnation of the privileged against the deprived Indians.

His editorial delineated how Indians were enslaved working on the large estates, living in miserable huts, permanently indebted to the hacienda store and merely surviving by growing crops on tiny plots of land for which they paid excessive rent to the landowner.

Continuing, he clarified that as the gold and silver mining industries grew in importance as well as output by utilizing the cheap Indian labor, they gave birth to prosperous mining communities that benefited the advantaged. As a result, while work brought the Indians to the thriving work centers, they continued to live in their traditional style, many far from the haciendas or mines, speaking their inherited dialect, wearing traditional dress, ruled by their bosses and worshiping their gods – Quetzalcóatl, Tenoch, Huitzilopochtli, Tlaloc and others. The advancements of a prospering society did not trickle down to the deprived. The declaration stressed that the increased national production and wealth did nothing to improve the lot of the Indian population.

There was no obvious pointed attack on the local authority. The *cacique* patiently waited for the other shoe to drop.

The weeks passed quickly and soon there was yet another holiday. Of the many holidays celebrated, the *Dia de los Muertos* (Day of the Dead) was certainly the most solemn and impressive. All business activity would come to a halt on this most sensitive holy day. The observance was celebrated on the first day of November. In cemeteries throughout the land, both children and adults tidied up grave plots, cleaned headstones and placed tons of flowers on the burial sites.

It was the rule rather than the exception for relatives to prepare the favorite dishes of the departed and place the prepared meals on the grave believing that the deceased would actually join them in partaking of the repast. Of particular note was the offering of specially prepared bread known as *pan de los muertos* (bread of the dead) along with wine, tequila, beer, papier-mâché skulls and cardboard skeletons. While the entire ritual was somber in nature, it was by no means morbid. To the contrary, it was a satisfying day for the living to communicate with their departed. Such interlocution with the dead was widespread, not in a psychic or spiritualistic sense or as a function of a Christian faith in the afterlife, but simply as an outgrowth of the knowledge that the past was not dead. For Mexicans, neither birth nor death was seen to interrupt the continuity of life.

The day following the reverential observance of the deceased, groups formed to protest the lack of potable water from the recently installed plant. The intended beneficiaries of this precious commodity were compelled, once again, to purchase bottled water from the *cacique*'s bottled water distribution facility. As complaints of the shortage mounted, it was only natural that Nick became aware of the problem. As an investigative journalist, he was determined to seek out the cause.

He first visited the town hall hoping to obtain an answer or uncover a lead. Upon arriving and posing questions to those administration-trusted servants in the water department, it was immediately apparent that he was person non-grata. He was more than percipient that he was not held in great favor by the *cacique*. However, the fact that he had apparently been blacklisted only intensified his desire to seek out the reason for the water shortage.

He next visited the structure housing the water pumping equipment. Again, he was instantly rebuffed without the opportunity to ask questions. The total rejection he encountered only added to his insistence to pursue his inquisition.

The next week was spent by Nick inquiring and exploring every available source that might provide an answer. The important disclosure he so diligently sought came about in an unexpected manner. While seated in his office preparing the weekly edition of *La Universal*, a most fortuitous visitor appeared. The unexpected caller identified himself as José Vasquez, an unemployed foreman who had worked on the ranch of Señora Luisa Maria Alvarez. Well dressed, his open shirt revealed the muscular chest of a big and powerful man. His first words were to excuse himself for intruding and to request a few moments with Nick who was obviously extremely occupied. He went on to explain that he had been a loyal servant to Señor Alvarez for twenty years prior to his passing and then to his widow. He continued by saying that he was completely apprised as to how the *cacique*, by unscrupulous entrapment, acquired the ranch of his boss and that thievery should not go unpunished. Vasquez went on to say that he knew of the protest against the potable water shortage currently being vented by outraged citizens. Nick sat and listened patiently while his visitant spoke. He leaned forward, elbows on his desk, as José proceeded to speak. "Señor," he remarked, "I know why there is so little drinking water in the pueblo. The water we treasure in order to survive is being diverted to the ranch the *cacique* swindled from the widow Alvarez. He is taking our water for his cattle and to irrigate his farm."

Needless to say, Nick, in absorbing and digesting every word, sat stunned. He continued the conversation to assure himself that José was speaking fact. Once satisfied, he thanked his visitor rewarding him with a sizeable sum for his invaluable service, which would eventually benefit the populace.

It was now "stop the presses," for Nick would dedicate his paper's editorial to revealing the scandalous act of the *cacique*. And so, the hastily modified weekly revealed the corruptive use of the public's water supply. To emphasize his disgust for the community's leader, he pointedly advanced his suspicion that by diverting the town's water the inhabitants would be compelled to purchase the *cacique*'s bottled water. He closed his editorial by condemning the despotic control over the populace, for if it was not unlawful, it certainly was immoral. He reiterated his alarming advice that unless the people oppose the autocrat, he is secure and the people are without a voice. The other shoe had dropped! There was little doubt the war had begun.

With the public's outcry and denunciation of the *cacique*, Nick wondered what the effect might be on his lover. Much to his surprise and satisfaction, he was pleasantly shocked to learn that she completely supported his critical disclosure of her father. As gratifying as her empathy was for Nick, it was earth shattering to her family. Eduardo's face became a marble effigy of contempt upon learning of her public sanctioning of Nick's editorial. He fell ill and required hospitalization. Visibly shaken, he continually asked himself, "How could she do this to me, her father? How could she?" Upon examination, it was determined that Eduardo had suffered a mild cardiac arrest that would require him to remain under a doctor's care for approximately one week. Rosita was at his bedside from early morning to late evening every day. Her faint smile could not conceal her profound torment. Together, sharing their grief, they attempted to console one another. They did not know how they would react when they next confronted Maria.

The day following Eduardo's admission to the hospital, Maria joined her mother for dinner in her father's room. While the meeting was cordial, the reunion lacked fervor. There was no mention of Nick's editorial or Maria's concurrence. After dinner, they exchanged their customary kiss. Eight days after internment, the *cacique* was released for normal activity.

Nick was without fear and fiercely resolved to continue his attack on the integrity of the system. With no opposition from his infatuate, he proceeded to reveal the depravity of the structure under which Mexicans lived. The banner of the paper quoted the German intellect, who, on visiting the country said, "Mexico is a nation of inequities where there is no equality in the distribution of wealth and culture." The body of the editorial went on to quote the German as saying, "The war of independence has caused your governing *criollos*, priests, *peninsulares*, academics and liberal thinkers to reevaluate the Indians and *mestizos*, even though nothing has been enacted to improve their lot." To this commentary, Nick added, "Beloved compatriots, fate has placed freedom in your hands. If you do not shake off the yoke you wear, you will indeed be wretched." This position declaration was made with the clear intent to incite the dissidents.

And so it went, week after week, Nick unrelentingly attacked everything and everyone directly or indirectly related to the government.

As time passed, there was little change in Soledad other than an increase of twenty thousand additional inhabitants and the recognition that Soledad was a city and no longer a town. The *cacique* continued to carry the title of mayor and to serve as administrator of the new mini-metropolis. All of the businesses of the *cacique*, less the bottled water distribution enterprise, continued to flourish. The disclosure by Nick forced the *cacique* to restore the entire output of the potable water plant for consumption by the city's residents.

The relationship between Maria and her family remained strained causing her father's physical condition to deteriorate. It was now a well-known and accepted fact that Nick and Maria were enjoying an intimate relationship. The *cacique* had openly decreed that he would never approve their marriage. He continued to look upon Nick as his mortal enemy and would have jailed him if it were not that such an action would most certainly cause a public demonstration and possibly a revolt. In view of the obvious close association with Maria, the *cacique* rejected the thought of having Nick silenced by a hired gun.

With all that was transpiring, Rosita continued to be well balanced, endurant and conciliatory. She insisted that she and Eduardo regularly attend church. Additionally, she constantly affectionately stroked him and heaped unlimited praise and support on him as often as possible. As a result of her persistent appeal, the *cacique* agreed to work half days and to nap each afternoon.

CHAPTER XXIII

A REQUEST IS GRANTED

It was a pleasant fall day in November 1896. Once again, the presidential term of General Porfirio Diaz was coming to an end and, once again, having been re-elected, he was to commence yet another four-year period as chief of state.

Diaz was more than mindful of the fact that he had served as the nation's leader since 1876 with the exception of the period 1880-1884, during which time Manuel Gonzalez wore the sash of office.

As a self-serving measure, Diaz was responsible for installing Gonzalez as a puppet one-term interim president. While campaigning for the highest office in the land in 1876, Diaz forcefully raised the banner of "Effective Suffrage—No Re-election." A condition set forth in the Mexican constitution. Consequently, upon completion of his first term, he judged it prudent to step down in order to demonstrate to the world that Mexico had matured to the point that a peaceful, orderly succession of the presidency was the order of the day in compliance with the law.

Now, preparing to once again take the oath of office, he questioned whether the citizenry had tired of him after eighteen years of service or whether his disregard of the principle of "no re-election" would plague his future. He was more than aware that as his party's leader, there existed well-organized opposition forces.

He recalled the merciless treatment heaped on Manuel Gonzalez prior to his leaving office in 1884 and feared the possibility of similar recriminations. He vividly remembered the vicious assault from all quarters on his controversial predecessor.

He dwelled on the past when Gonzalez had boasted of his successes—the highest national income ever, the expansion of the railroads, development of the steamship lines, improved systems of communications and an expanded program of education. All were true. Nevertheless, the hostile opposition was "out for blood." There were those willing to forget but not forgive.

Supported by the media, they condemned Gonzalez for his costly development projects, bills left unpaid, government civil servants demanding their salaries, international debt unresolved and a substantial budget deficit.

Diaz was acutely preoccupied that at some future date iniquitous condemnation could be directed at him by a vengeful critical proletariat. He was extraordinarily sensitive regarding the vilification of an individual's character.

In that regard, he vividly recalled how the opposition press levied accusations of graft, corruption and immorality against the Gonzalez administration. They charged Gonzalez with accepting illegal contributions, kickbacks, disposing illegally of government property and the hideous shame of actually stealing from the national treasury.

Diaz had reached the pinnacle of respectability and honor—a military hero frequently referred to as the savior of the nation's ills. He meticulously weighed the circumstances and conditions surrounding this particular period of time in his nation's history. After profound deliberation, he determined that it was the will of the Almighty that even at the risk of jeopardizing his legacy that he continue to pursue the "Mexican miracle" which he started in 1876.

Content that the prevailing administration of

Porfirio Diaz would persevere, the cacique enjoyed a perception of national stability and enduring prosperity.

The *cacique* was surprised to find Father Agustin waiting for him when he arrived at city hall, the former town hall. Eduardo apologized for not being available when the priest showed up. Since his illness, Eduardo did not appear at his office until 10:30 A.M. each day and returned home at 2:00 P.M. for lunch and his afternoon nap.

After an *abrazo* and a blessing by the priest, the two went directly to the *cacique*'s private office. Eduardo spoke first. "Father, it's customary that I come to the church to see you when I have a problem. Now that you've come to see me, do you have a problem? To what do I owe this honor?"

The priest responded, "A problem, my son? No, but I am here to ask for a favor."

Eduardo was quick to state, "Anything, anything without restriction or limitation. Anything you ask shall be done."

The cleric went on to explain that for the past ten years he had traveled to the village of San José Marti some twenty miles distant. "The village is poverty stricken, a collection of thatched roof adobe huts. The village's only solid structure is a whitewashed one room church eighteen feet high with a domed bell tower. The sun's reflection on this tower is the only brightness one can find in the village. My son, the village has nothing—only conviction. There's no piped-in water, there's no sewer, lamps are scarce and when they have no kerosene for their lamps and there's no moon, they are in complete darkness.

"Pigs, chickens and raw-boned dogs roam the unpaved streets at will, leaving a mess. No home in San José Marti has a sink or a bathroom; consequently, people bathe themselves outdoors and relieve themselves outdoors as do the animals. No one has an icebox and with no ice, perishable food cannot be preserved. There are but two dilapidated wagons that serve as their basic source of communication and supply." At this point, the *cacique* was wondering just what it was that the man of God would ask. Anxiously, with his hand stroking his chin, he asked that his friend continue.

The priest resumed his account in a quiet, though firm, voice. "The village is so poor it has but a one room adobe hut for a school. Its church is without a priest and, therefore, every other week I travel to the village to say mass and hear confessions."

Somewhat losing his patience, Eduardo interrupted, "What is it that I can do?"

The father, responding in a forceful manner, retorted, "Please my son, patience, patience." He went on to reveal that the villagers accept the Virgin of Guadalupe as the patron saint of the nation. The father then asked Eduardo, "Do you know the genesis of the Virgin?"

Eduardo replied, "I do not."

"In 1531," the cleric explained, "Juan Diego, a mere peasant at the time, was on a hill just outside of Mexico City when the Virgin appeared to him. When he went back and reported what he had seen, the bishops did not believe him. So he went back to the hill and she appeared to him again, this time telling him to go look for roses at a certain spot. He did and found them, oddly enough, growing in the frozen ground. When Juan Diego opened his cloak before the priests back in Mexico City, the roses fell out, revealing a perfect image of the Virgin stamped on the cloth. His cloak now hangs in the Guadalupe Basilica for all to see. At least that's what we are told.

"I can assure you that ninety percent of all Mexicans—*criollos*, *mestizos* and Indians alike—believe in the Virgin of Guadalupe. You've seen the display of their faith in all places—on walls, restaurants, in homes, in stores, on necklaces and rings. Our Virgin is everywhere.

"Inasmuch as extreme poverty exists on all sides,

there is a movement afoot by socialistic organized missionaries, or better yet, proselytizers, who are advocating conversion from Catholicism to bible reading. Their beliefs prohibit the use of alcohol and require telling the truth and an absolute ban on adultery. While all are virtues, there would be no threat from this attempt at proselytism was it not that the crusade is lead by capable and dynamic leaders.

"My son, there are two issues involved here so let me start with the first. It is a fact that most Mexicans are Catholic even though they may practice Catholicism in their own way. They cling to their own polytheistic universe regarding themselves as good Christians while not grasping the Christian abstractions of sin or virtue. The community of martyrs, those intermediaries between God and Karl Marx, are accepted begrudgingly. While they pay homage to the symbol of the crucifixion, they see it as a reluctant act of sacrifice. The Indian thinks of God as powerful but neither omnipotent nor exclusory. To them, heaven and hell are merely places. While they no longer practice human sacrifice, they ascribe souls to animals and inanimate objects. You can readily see how the Indian embraces Catholicism in his fashion. Nevertheless, they are Catholic.

"The villagers who are dedicated, practicing Catholics are as poor as poor can be. By lacking every creature comfort, they are vulnerable to turn to any source that offers them hope for a better life.

"Now, let's talk about the second part of the problem in San José Marti. There is an overwhelming desire by the villagers that they have a local patron saint to watch over them. It is their belief that with their own patron saint their luck and lives will improve through a miracle. What I am asking, my son, is that you provide the good people with a life-like image of a patron saint they can call their own.

"Since their futile days of suppression starting with the conquest, there has been no improvement in their lives in over 350 years. On one hand, I am fighting for their lives; while on the other hand, I'm fighting for their souls. I ask that you seek out, by whatever means, a way to improve the meager existence of the pauperized inhabitants of San José Marti and consider gifting a patron saint to the village. I bless you, my son, by saying that when you are good to others you are best to yourself."

The *cacique*, in his normal commanding manner and with an air of authority, advised his friend that he would somehow comply with his wishes though he would need several days to ponder the matter. After their customary embrace and prayer, the priest took his leave. Eduardo, somewhat exhausted, decided to leave his office at an early hour and cogitate during his afternoon of leisure.

Two weeks passed since the parish priest asked for Eduardo's help. The *cacique* was clearly showing emotional distress as a result of his strained relationship with his daughter and the continuing journalistic attacks by Nick. Eduardo, now immensely wealthy, ailing and fatigued, hired Armando Vilas, a young, local attorney-turned-businessman to administer his many enterprises. The ferocious attacks on the system and the *cacique* continued to flow from the pestiferous pen of his reportorial antagonist.

One of Nick's editorials discussed the subject of infidelity and the insecurity of the Mexican male. It detailed how the mating of Spanish men and Indian women produced the now common *mestizo*. This union caused the men to surmise that their women would betray them even though the men dominated them by force and even rape. Just as the *cacique* could never put complete trust in the conquered, there existed a lack of good faith in the subdued female. As the writer pointed out, the male looked upon his wife as a sex object subject to humiliation and unworthy of the husband's fidelity and respect.

In another edition, the editor viciously attacked the *cacique* for his lack of attention to the improvement of the local public school structure. Nick recapitulated the educatory process dating back to the conquest when education was completely controlled by the Roman Catholic Church with priests and nuns providing sophisticated teaching methods. He unrelentingly stressed the present day social responsibility for the elimination of all illiteracy. He emphasized the fact that it was the absolute accountability of the city's regent to ascertain a proper program for the preparation of the Mexican youth for the challenge of developing the nation's economy and safeguarding its national identity. The *cacique* was irrefutably accused of the improper tutelage of Soledad's school children as a result of teachers who were neither qualified nor properly paid.

Eduardo had explored, without success, every possible avenue to either jail Nick or close down *La Universal* in retaliation for the never-ending attacks by his adversary. He vowed that somehow, someday, he would come upon the manner by which he would destroy his enemy.

After deliberating for almost three weeks, the *cacique* arranged for a meeting with the parish priest to further discuss his respected compatriot's solicitation. He had meticulously weighed all aspects of the appeal and had arrived at what he thought would be a fruitful resolution for all concerned.

With the priest in his office, and after their normal exchange, the *cacique* opened the conversation, "Father, I believe I can now respond to your twofold request. I shall commence by addressing the matter of a patron saint for the village of San José Marti.

"I have determined that the prevailing situations at the village are desperate and demand an expeditious solution. With distinct honor, I shall provide an icon as you requested, with the understanding that the effigy be that of *San Eduardo el Martir* (Saint Edward the Martyr). I have obtained a one-half life size figure of *San Eduardo* and shall have a proper oratory constructed in the village church, *Iglesia de Nuestra Madre* (Church of Our Mother). There will be a bronze plaque at the base of the saint that will be inscribed as follows:

San Eduardo el Martir

Eduardo was the eldest son of King Edgar of England and his first wife, Ethelfleda who died shortly after her son's birth. He was baptized by St. Dunstan who helped Eduardo become king in A.D. 975 after his father's death. Eduardo's stepmother, Queen Elfrida, wished the throne for her son Ethelred. Eduardo ruled only three years when he was murdered on March 18 while hunting near Corfe Dastle, reportedly by adherents of Ethelred; though William of Malmesbury, the English historian of the twelfth century, said Elfrida was the actual murderer. In the end, Elfrida was seized with remorse for her crime and, retiring from the world, she built the monasteries of Amesbury and Wherwell, in the latter of which she died. Eduardo was a martyr only in the broad sense of one who suffers an unjust death, but his cultus was considerable, encouraged by the miracles reported from his tomb at Shaftesbury.

"With this, you can start saving souls.

"Now, let's get on to the matter of hope and improving the lives of the poor, destitute inhabitants of the village. I promise you that their situation will be rectified once the saint is installed which should be within thirty days. You have my word and my hand on this." Whereupon he shook the cleric's hand and they embraced.

The clergyman placed his hand on Eduardo's shoulder and after a brief prayer said, "In the name of God and *San Eduardo*, may you be blessed for your generosity and understanding. In their names, I accept that which you have offered. Bless you, my son."

With every passing day, the *cacique* dwelled on the unresolved business of admonishing Nick. While perhaps not naming the culprit of the wrong doing to be the *cacique*, each week there was always the indirect or veiled censure of the mayor in the local paper. With Armando Vilas now caring for the daily management of his business interests, Eduardo had even more time to mull over some means of quieting his unrelenting antagonist.

It seemed as though lightning had struck early one morning while the mayor was seated in the city's barbershop being shaved. Without any warning, he cast aside the large white cloth that covered his upper body from neck to knees with one movement. With the vein in his forehead swelled like a thick black snake, he hastily left the barbershop without a word of explanation. The stunned barber stood motionless wondering what he had done to cause such a hurried and unexplicated departure.

Once in his office, he ordered his trusted "right hand," Raul Molina, to immediately telegraph General Ramos in Mexico City. He wished to know the name of the individual who controlled the distribution of newsprint for the state owned news print monopoly. Included in the request, he asked if the general enjoyed a personal relationship with the individual.

Minutes later, there was a response in the

affirmative to both queries. Self-satisfied and glowing like the cat who ate the canary, Eduardo asked his general friend to approach the indicated individual and ask that all shipments of newsprint to *La Universal* in Soledad, Chiapas, be discontinued immediately. In an addendum, the amount of the *mordida* offered as the expected and accepted form of service fee was stipulated.

Within a matter of hours, there was a continuous exchange of telegraphic messages including an acceptance of the *mordida*. The *cacique* knew without a doubt that only a few editorials of attack remained to be published in the local paper. He had vowed that he would even the score, which he had now accomplished. The *cacique* was in a state of extreme high-spirited jubilation. He calculated that in just a few weeks the supply of newsprint of *La Universal* would be exhausted.

Almost a month had passed since he was last with the parish priest. With the new saint installed in the prepared niche in the Church of Our Mother, he was now ready to meet with his old friend. Eduardo preferred meeting in the sanctuary of the cleric's house of prayer. Once together, they embraced, prayed and commenced their interlocution. The *cacique*, with lines of concentration deepening along his brow and under his eyes remarked, "Father, I have devised a plan that I shall delineate most precisely. However, first, I wish to tell you something of a very personal nature. Here in our fair city there are many who claim friendship with me. Despite those claims, I want you to know that aside from my beloved wife and daughter, you are my only intimate friend."

With a grin that spread across his countenance and warmed the room, the priest grabbed his friend's hand saying, "My son, you have demonstrated that you understand the true meaning of friendship. It is love with understanding. As for my request for help, you have proven that when a friend asks for a favor, there is no tomorrow. May God bless you." Eduardo went on by asking the cleric if he was acquainted with the Alberto Fonseca hacienda that bordered the village of San José Marti. The clergyman replied, "Yes, though I know little about it."

The *cacique* spelled out that the hacienda consisted of twelve hundred acres on which there were a few cows and only eighty acres under cultivation. He continued by saying, "My plan is as follows. I have bought the Fonseca hacienda, and I shall annex the village to it. It is my intention to have Raul Molina, who so loyally served the late colonel and myself, retire from public service. While I shall own the hacienda, he shall manage all of the lands, which hereafter shall be called Hacienda *San Eduardo*. I plan to increase the herd and cultivate the entire property. As you can readily see, such an ambitious undertaking will provide employment for all, yes all, of the inhabitants of the village, including the women and children at harvest time. What do you think?"

Too startled to respond, the father hesitated before asking, "What do you intend to do regarding the farmers who are growing crops on communal land assigned to them by the government?"

There was no hesitation on the part of the *cacique* to clarify that the farmers would clearly benefit by working for the *hacendado* and went on to illustrate his point. "Peonage will be the salvation for the impoverished Indians of the village, who, by simply becoming part of the hacienda, will gain a high degree of protection. They will acquire improved living conditions and have a secure job. I have instructed Raul to become the defender of the villagers and to care for them in emergencies. They will be protected from voracious labor contractors. We will ascertain that the workers have food, clothing and shelter. I can trust Raul to carry out his mission. Oh, yes, father, they shall also have a young priest assigned to the village church. He will baptize their young, marry their offspring, bury their dead and say mass."

Excusing himself for interrupting, the priest cited past efforts of *hacendados* to create similar operations that would improve the lot of the working class. "My son, as you know, we men of the cloth meet annually. In our discussions, we talk over having heard such promises before. Unfortunately, that sort of golden assurance results in hollow pledges.

"Are you aware that over the past four decades the worker in the field has been nothing more than a human machine toiling for survival? His essential food costs have multiplied three fold while his slave wages have remained unchanged for forty years. The *hacendado* has, from year to year, promised to improve the lot of the *peon* (unskilled worker). As you know, these have been empty promises.

"As for the *hacendado*, he reaps the benefit of negligible taxes and virtually gratuitous labor, for the minimal wage he pays comes back from the exorbitant profits he derives from the hacienda store where the worker pays dearly for his purchases of essentials.

"How can you not pity the overworked and underfed *peon* who does not have the freedom to leave the hacienda and, in effect, is 'owned' by the *hacendado*? The poor sole is prevented from seeking an improved way of life for, as you know, he is eternally in debt to the *hacendado*; and consequently, by law, he cannot be hired by anyone else until he is debt free.

"My son, I do not doubt your good intentions. You are a good and honest man. If I seem skeptical, I have reason, for I have heard of similar offerings without positive results. It has always been more of the same— words, words, words."

Interposing, the *cacique* forcefully articulated, "Perhaps you are thinking of the *hacendado* Jaime Silva who worked his peons to the bone, flogging them while stealing the virginity of their daughters, jailing them for petty violations and then forcing them to work in chains. I can assure you, I pledge to you, this will never happen. You have my word on this."

With a twinkle in his eyes and a smile displaying approval, the cleric walked over and embraced Eduardo while reciting a meaningful poem:

> "You sought to hear the voice of God,
> and climbed the topmost steeple.
> But God declared, Go down again
> and dwell among the people."

Then he added, "My son, you have heard God!"

As they concluded the meeting with their customary ritual, Eduardo abruptly turned and with a wink of the eye remarked, "Father, when you present this plan for a new life to the villagers, could you suggest that this miracle occurred specifically as a result of their adopting *San Eduardo el Martir* as their patron saint?" The father stood motionless for a moment. Feeling assured that Eduardo would keep his promise, he responded with a wink of the eye and an affirmative nod. With that, the mayor returned to his office a placated leader.

CHAPTER XXIV

A FAMILY TRAGEDY

While haciendas were considered the pinnacle of the social structure, there were untold facts about them and their *hacendados*. While the law of the land prescribed a separation of church and state, there existed an even greater separation of those of wealth and poverty. At this particular period in Mexico's history, that disengagement of the two classes was most apparent.

As a norm, the main hacienda residence was sumptuous, externally and internally, even though the *hacendado* spent a scant few months in his home. Most often, he had several haciendas to oversee or other businesses to manage in the city, or both. Then there was the time consumed in traveling to visit his children enrolled in the institutions of learning in Mexico City, the United States or Europe. It was, therefore, that the hacienda provided the *hacendado* with substantial income in addition to serving as a vacation home and a symbol of social status. The *hacendado's* children, beneficiaries of almost unlimited funds, used the hacienda to impress their contemporaries.

Irrespective of the family size, the hacienda would accommodate all of the occasional gatherings of the clan. On such get-togethers, it was customary for the young boys to don *charro* costumes, mount carefully bred and well-groomed horses, and fancy themselves as country squires.

Birthdays, saints' days, feast days and special days for celebration provided sufficient reason to move the family from their city home to the hacienda for jollification.

It was not unusual that entire train cars would be reserved to carry guests, musicians, local dignitaries and domestics to the hacienda when there was an announced engagement, a wedding or a significant anniversary.

The contradiction between the *hacendado* and those who toiled in every aspect of the hacienda's operation was gargantuan.

Inasmuch as all justice was administered by the hacienda manager, the peon had no legal right or recourse. There was no accountability for over-punishment of a real or concocted offense.

At close proximity (normally within a mile) to the grand residence was the miserable one-room, floorless, windowless adobe shack of the worker. Water had to be carried a great distance from a central hand pump. The subjugated worker was compelled to develop his own allotted parcel of land only after his prescribed work for the day had been completed. While the *hacendado's* family feasted on delicacies, the enslaved workman was allocated a few minutes twice a day to eat tortillas wrapped around beans, rice and chile, which would be washed down with a cup of black coffee or water. Meat, fish and fowl were never on the daily bill of fare. They were enjoyed only on rare special occasions. The diet of the peon was virtually without protein.

Diversion for the worker was a rarity. It was reserved for a local fiesta which, with good fortune, would come to pass two or three times a year. As a detraction from his impoverished lifestyle, he would try his hand, as an amateur aficionado, fighting a half-grown bull that appeared larger as it got closer. Saturated with mescal or pulque, the semi-inebriated novice toreador would find momentary gratification from the monotony of every day life. A broken bone or two or a light puncture from the horns was considered a small price to pay for escape from daily boredom—even for a few hours.

Six months had passed since the *cacique* disclosed his plan to develop the Hacienda *San Eduardo*. The project was proceeding as planned with Raul Molina enthusiastically propelling the undertaking forward. The herd of cattle had been augmented considerably, and the entire land tract was being prepared for seeding. All able bodied men in the village were now gainfully employed.

In addition to the business-related amelioration, the *cacique*, was working with a local architect to build living quarters for all employees, which would include a small house for Raul. He would then proceed to construct the grandest residence in the entire southern region of the state. It would be more than double the size of the mansion—50,000 square feet—and would incorporate the latest home improvements available in the United States and Europe. It was his intention that this home would be the envy of all. He would name the palatial residence *Casa* Rosita (Rosita's home).

The *cacique* was a glowing portrayal of self-satisfaction. Since the government-owned newsprint monopoly had curtailed shipment of newsprint to Nick, *La Universal* was no longer being published. It appeared as though the publication had ceased to exist. The downside of the discontinuance was the divide between Eduardo and his daughter, which had widened appreciably. Her sympathy for Nick was public knowledge. Her routine of joining her parents for dinner was a thing of the past. She saw her father on rare occasions, although she continued to visit her mother privately. As for Nick, he was now unemployed.

In spite of the family conflict, Hacienda *San Eduardo* continued to progress at an accelerated rate, much to the delight of the *cacique*.

Similarly, the *cacique*'s enterprises, under the guidance of Armando Vilas, flourished. Eduardo grew increasingly prosperous with each passing day. Rosita was distressed by the deteriorating father-daughter relationship; but as a typically obedient Mexican wife who respected her husband as the master of the home, she voiced no antipathy to the distasteful situation.

Time marched on. With each visit to the hacienda, the *cacique* became more personally involved. While the parental rapport remained stressful and continued to wane, he appeared to gain fortitude and contentment in witnessing the advances ameliorated at the developing estate. Nick accepted a teaching position at the city's secondary school. Newspapers for local consumption were delivered from the nearby town of El Jacote. The fact that the reading public received the tabloids a day after publication did not seem to bother anyone.

With all the good that was occurring, there was the customary inevitable bad. Eduardo was provoked by an incident involving a trusted agent. Javier Sanchez, a food inspector on whom Eduardo had long relied, was ordered to survey each of the city's curbside food dispensing stalls. He was directed to inform the operators that, henceforth, they were required to have the means to boil water in order to sterilize cups, glasses, plates, utensils and the like after each serving. The requirement was of the greatest urgency. Communicable diseases were being passed from one user to another by implements employed in serving food that were being washed in buckets of cold water.

After a protracted period of time, it became evident that only a few vendors had complied with the order. As is quite natural, there was the question of "why?" The *cacique*, in conducting his own investigation, learned that the sidewalk food providers who had not complied found a more convenient way to resolve the costly problem involved in making provisions for boiling water. The vendors and Sanchez had come upon a mutually beneficial resolution through the *mordida*. The food dispensers were spared the cost of investing in the required equipment,

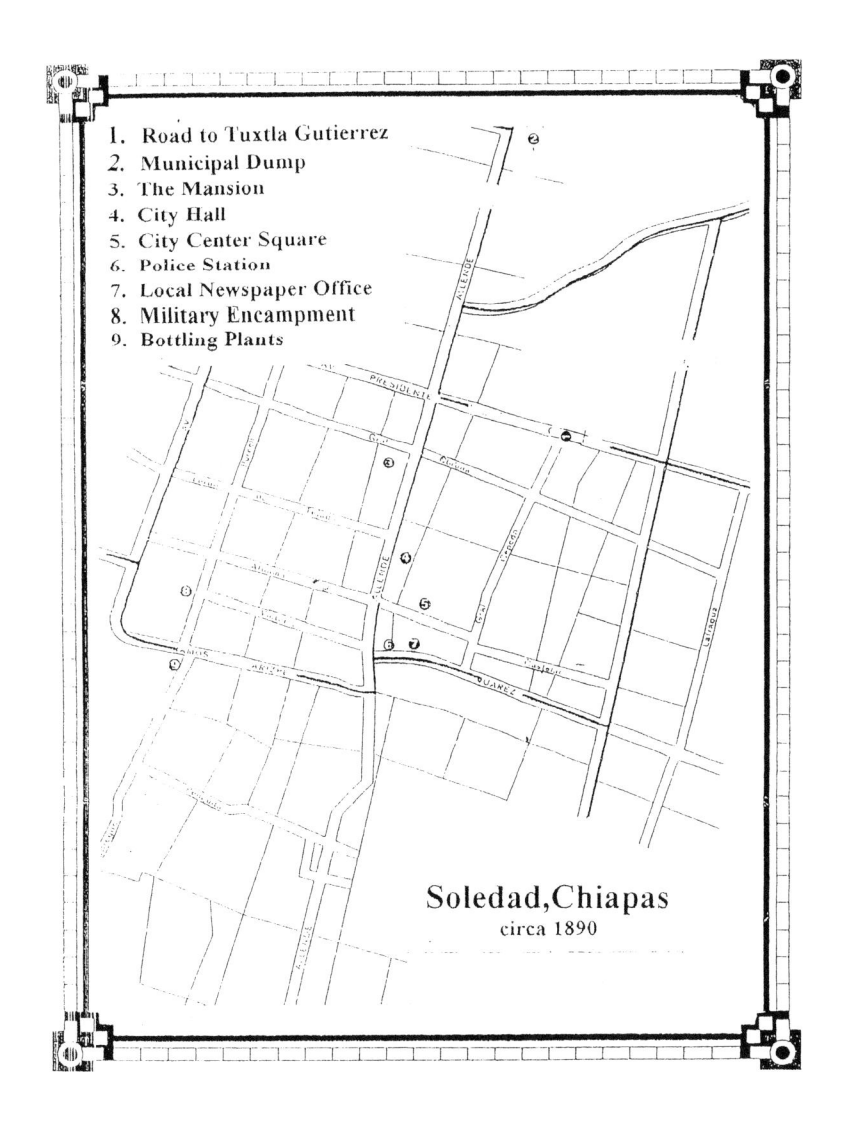

1. Road to Tuxtla Gutierrez
2. Municipal Dump
3. The Mansion
4. City Hall
5. City Center Square
6. Police Station
7. Local Newspaper Office
8. Military Encampment
9. Bottling Plants

Soledad, Chiapas
circa 1890

while the inspector generated a steady cash flow with each visit to inquire as to whether or not there was compliance.

Under normal circumstances involving a friend, the *cacique* would admonish the individual involved with a tongue-lashing and then some form of menial sentence. It was Javier's misfortune that Eduardo was not the Eduardo of the past. Time and circumstances had embittered him perceptibly. Without deliberation, he ordered his old friend jailed without any indication as to for how long.

In the growing city of Soledad, the season had changed. It was some months following the incident with Javier Sanchez that Eduardo was comfortably seated in his favorite overstuffed chair when Rosita entered the room. She initiated the conversation with idle chatter, causing her husband to suspect that she wished to discuss something without knowing just how to go about it. After exhausting his patience and with a warning cloud settling on his face, he impatiently inquired, "Dear wife, what is it you wish to tell me?"

Taking a deep breath and attempting to force a smile, she carefully and very slowly informed her husband that their daughter was pregnant and would give birth in seven months. Without responding, Eduardo sat motionless. He failed in an attempt to smile while digesting the astonishing pronouncement. He just sat with his head bowed and his arms folded across his chest, obviously in profound anguish. No longer capable of seeing her husband suffer, Rosita left the room. It was very early the following morning when Rosita became aware that Eduardo had not gone to bed. Hurriedly, she went to the room where she had left him and found him still in the chair in a dazed condition.

Semi-panicked, she dispatched a servant to seek out and return with the family physician. Thirty minutes later that the doctor was examining the *cacique* who had been moved to his bed. After meticulously examining his patient, the doctor announced that his patient had, indeed, suffered a mild heart attack. He recommended that the *cacique* remain at home with a nurse in attendance, day and night, who could administer oxygen and medication as prescribed.

After four days of recovery, during which time there were daily visits by the doctor, Eduardo insisted that he resume normal activity. It was only after pleading by the doctor and his wife that he agreed to remain under observation for three additional days. After one week of care and with no reversal of condition, the patient was permitted to resume activity on a somewhat restricted schedule.

During his lifetime, Eduardo had encountered a multitude of challenges of every type and description. He was always capable of effecting a sound evaluation and decision. However, never had any predicament approached the significance of his present dilemma.

For days, the *cacique* went to his office but ordered that, under no circumstance, was he to be disturbed. On other days, he would retire to his den, close the door, and remain there in isolation until bedtime. During such periods of solitary, the only interruptions to his meditation were his meals served on a tray. He spoke only to Rosita saying only "Good morning, good night or thank you." All of his reclusion and confusion had become welded together. His sense of pride concealed his inner turmoil. Rosita was unable to face him directly; and on the rare occasion that she would disturb his privacy, she would ask forgiveness for her intrusion then hurriedly depart. Profound intense grief prevailed in the Hernandez household.

There had been no contact between Maria and her parents since her pregnancy was revealed. The *cacique* had been withdrawn from everyone for over five days when, in early evening of the sixth day, he informed his wife that he would join her for dinner. While dining, he made no mention of that which had dominated him for almost a week. Finally, with a sense of conviction that was part of his character he remarked, "My dear wife, you have suffered much as have I. We have agonized. Our family name has been dishonored. We are a proud community where there are few secrets. This is not Mexico City where premarital sex and divorce are accepted. Here, the family remains a powerful authoritarian institution governed by our traditions and young ladies remain with their parents until a marriage is arranged between 'known' families." His dark eyes dazzled with fury and his voice was inflamed and belligerent. He announced, "Our daughter must be severely punished. God will forgive me for she shall not disgrace us in Soledad by giving birth to an illegitimate child. I shall banish her to *Isla de Mujeres*." Rosita wept aloud rocking back and forth, yielding to convulsive sobs that caused her to shake uncontrollably. No longer capable of remaining with Eduardo, she tore herself away with a choking cry. In a strange twist of fate, Rosita's daughter would suffer the same punishment as her loving caretaker had many years ago.

In a matter of days, Rosita, alone, embraced her daughter prior to Maria's boarding the carriage that would carry her to *Isla de Mujeres*, her new island home.

Once the conveyance was out of sight, she returned to the mansion to discover her husband in his favorite chair, tears streaming down his cheeks. At first sight of her husband, she swallowed hard, biting her lip to hold back tears. Unable to restrain herself, she hurried to Eduardo, embracing him. Together they sobbed impassionedly. Eduardo regained his composure somewhat though he was still ashen. With tears blinding his eyes and gulping hard in order to speak over the lump that lingered in his throat, he declared, "My dear wife, we have lost our baby. She is gone, gone, gone! This is not the way it was meant to be."

Even though the *cacique* and Rosita had seen little of their daughter while she resided apart in Soledad, the fact that she was now in a distant, isolated place left both inexplicably alone.

From time-to-time when together, the parents would reminisce; but as much as they would try to keep their self-control, they always experienced complete emotional collapse accompanied by intractable weeping. On occasion, the *cacique* would philosophize saying, "We gave her our love and our thoughts. We provided for her every material need. For whatever reason, we could not comprehend her psyche, her inner being, in the world of tomorrow." The parents, on occasion, re-read Maria's letters from the university attempting to better understand why. Eduardo often consoled Rosita by reminding her that her gift to her daughter was a gift that could never be equaled—the gift of life. Each offered compassion to the other, assuming that time would eventually heal their wounds.

Although Maria's gestation had been successfully withheld for weeks, the topic of gossip in the city's street and central plaza was focused on the why and where regarding the abrupt departure of Maria Hernandez. Weeks passed when word spread quickly throughout the city that Nick had not reported for work and was nowhere to be found. When his uncle Benito was questioned, he unequivocally declared that he had no knowledge of his nephew's whereabouts. Eduardo, upon learning of Nick's disappearance, almost instantaneously concluded that the young man had learned of his daughter's emplacement and was, most probably, at her side.

With the expectation that Nick would not be returning to Soledad, the *cacique* grasped on the opportunity to visit Benito Garcia to discuss the purchase of the newspaper's premises. Eduardo was certain that by his publishing the local paper, he could control the minds and thinking of his people.

No one could better seize on the possibility of a potentially profitable business venture and cash in on it. With the power of his office as a weapon, the *cacique* realized that this was, indeed, a golden opportunity that should not be overlooked. Once with Benito, he offered his compassion for Nick's disappearance and then reminded him that a newspaper plant without newsprint was worthless. The *cacique* suggested that they exercise a trade of the real estate and printing equipment for a tract of land, owned by the *cacique*, on the outskirts of the city. Although Benito had been a loyal journalistic servant to the *cacique* for many years, he resented the action that suspended the delivery of newsprint to Nick. Yet, poor Benito was aware of the *cacique*'s unlimited power to force the exchange. He accepted the offer, for he knew full well that whatever his visitor wanted, he would get one way or another.

CHAPTER XXV

THE CACIQUE BECOMES A PUBLISHER

It was a dreary evening and the Hernandez family had just completed their evening meal. They retired to the den in the mansion. Something said brought on another of their oft-occurring joint crying sessions. Sobbing trenchantly, they embraced, as always, imparting a degree of consolation, one to the other. Once the tears were wiped away, they attempted to regain their composure.

With a faint tremor in his voice, Eduardo told Rosita that he had found a treatise he had written while a second year student at the University of Guadalajara in a file box stored at his office. He believed Rosita might enjoy its contents. Voicing her accord, she asked her husband to read the dissertation.

Eduardo, his voice tender, just above a murmur and shakier than he would have liked, began reading the paper.

The Mexican Family

My name is Eduardo Hernandez Gonzalez. I am a Mexican citizen of Spanish immigrant parents. I am a student at this university in the same city where my family resides. I hope that when I meet my future wife she will also be from the community, and together we will be fortunate to have our children continue to live here as well.

What I wish for has been the tradition of my parents and their parents. It is a well-accepted factuality that the family is the natural and fundamental base of society. There are those who commonly believe that if a custom is old, it is a sign that it is meant to endure. Therefore, old families, old customs and old styles have survived through time for they are meant to survive. It is further believed that the guarantee of continuity is conventionalism. Subdued, the old, in a flood of the new and the old, may or may not survive. It is my conviction that the new has subdued the old, which shall never return as our way of life.

From my observation of my fellow students, male and female, I fear the respected practices of the past may be just that—past. Students from all areas of our republic attend this institution. For economic reasons, employment or personal relationships, they will not return to their homes. It is my opinion that the family bond of yesterday no longer exists.

It is with certainty that I opine that there are two adversaries that may cause a child to be perverted. One is to be born rich. The other is to be an only child. If born rich, money will spoil him. As an only child, the family will spoil him. It is naturally the normal convention of every generation to be apprehensive regarding the decline of the family. It is most probable that we will experience the unlawful union of unmarried couples having children together giving rise to the many powerful social influences that compete with parental control of teenagers and young adults. With all of this is increased mobility of our young people to leave their families even before they go off to college or in search of careers.

I foresee a trend to smaller families resulting in the decline in the number of uncles, aunts, cousins, sisters and brothers who, in the past, have embodied the family structure. On the other hand, there is a somewhat greater indication that all is not lost.

In my discussion with members of the faculty in our school of medicine, I am informed that it is anticipated that there will be longer life expectancy in the future. Be this the case, longer life gives hope that more young people will know their grandparents longer and even the elderly may have their elders live on as well.

Unfortunately, the practices of family life today and in days to come represent the immorality of the future. The family is the great conservator of national virtue and strength. Its pillars are being tested and challenged.

After Eduardo concluded reading the discourse, Rosita excused herself, still wiping tears from her eyes, now swollen, misty and wistful. The *cacique* remained seated in his favorite lounge chair to contemplate the past and the present. He asked himself, "Where did I go wrong? Where is the happy family life I so wanted? What would my life be like if it were not for one letter?" Emotionally exhausted, he retired to his bedroom hoping that with good fortune, he might have a peaceful night's sleep.

The *cacique* escaped from his grief by making frequent visits to the hacienda. There, he reviewed the accounting statements, chatted with Raul and the workers, inspected the construction and discussed the future work program. In consideration of his wife's deteriorating health, he encouraged the architect to expedite the completion of *Casa* Rosita. He wished to insure that his beloved wife would enjoy the completed magnificent structure.

With his hacienda, farm and ranch venture, the *cacique* was, to a great extent, distracted from his deep-rooted lament about Maria. In addition, he was most enthusiastically planning for his future as a publisher. He contacted a long-time friend, the director of the Mexico City daily, *Las Noticias* (The News). He asked his friend to search for an experienced editor who would agree to relocate to Soledad for the purpose of organizing a local newspaper. Eduardo had decided that Soledad, now a city, should have its own daily.

After only three weeks, Julio Botas arrived ready to initiate publication of *Las Noticias de Soledad* as its editor-in-chief. Arranging for the renewed delivery of newsprint from the government distribution center was negotiated quickly and without difficulty.

After a short period of preparation, the first issue of the city's daily would soon be ready for distribution. The new owner would certainly not allow such an event to go unnoticed. He would insure that the initial publication receive the maximum regional recognition.

Having set the date for the grand day of introducing the new publication, invitations were extended to the press corps in Mexico City, state and regional journalists, as well as dignitaries in the states of Veracruz and Chiapas. Special invitations were directed to General Bersunza and General Ramos. To facilitate travel to Soledad, he engaged a rail car from the capital to the city of Veracruz and then a carriage to Soledad. He further commandeered the local hotel to accommodate his guests.

The invited guests arrived and settled comfortably into their lodging. On the very special day, the festivities began with the expected parade in the morning. The visitors, as honored guests, were on the reviewing stand. Marching were all civil servants, the entire police force, firemen and the city's student body plus the male workers from Hacienda *San Eduardo* carrying identifying implements—the farmers, a shovel, the ranch hands, a pitch fork. The band was a combination of amateur musicians of all ages from all walks of life. While well intentioned, their prime virtue was that they began playing in unison and ended in concord; what was produced in between could, only liberally, be called music.

After the parade, it was time for speech making. The governor of the state of Chiapas was introduced by the *cacique*. The state's number one politician fancied himself a stand-up comic. Intermixed with the normal politico's statements of achievement were more than an appreciated number of non-humorous jokes at which the audience howled. With a smile on his face, the *cacique* thought, "It's strange how a politician's jokes are always funny."

Once the speeches had come to a most welcome end, copies of the initial issue of *Las Noticias de Soledad* were distributed to all. It was then on to a convivial, spirited barbeque with the standard fare of tacos, empanados, beans, rice, hot sauce and all kinds of alcoholic and non-alcoholic drinks. Mariachis were in abundance.

The reception in the evening was restricted to visiting guests. In the true tradition of such a gathering of persons of high position, each expected, and received, time to orate to his heart's content. Regardless of the speaker, every one, whether dignitary, journalist or guest, was bored beyond imagination to hear a constant repetition of self-praise. Once again, the *cacique*, with a smile on his face, facetiously thought, "I like to hear a politician speak about himself for I hear only that which is incredibly good." Finally, in the very late hours of the evening the dinner came to an end. The following day, the guests were returned to their homes courtesy of the *cacique* and the Hernandez family's grieving continued.

Time passed. The days passed into weeks, the weeks into months and the months into years. It would soon be the turn of the century.

The many enterprises owned and operated by the *cacique* flourished as a result of the population explosion in the city and the region. Armando Vilas continued to administer the *cacique*'s business conglomerate. Hacienda *San Eduardo* prospered beyond expectation with Raul Molina carrying out, to the letter, every commitment made by Eduardo to Father Diaz. Both the ranch and the farm were producing more than anticipated profits. *Las Noticias de Soledad* expanded its area of distribution to include all towns and villages within a one hundred mile radius.

On the lamentable side of the *cacique*'s ledger, neither Eduardo nor Rosita had received or exchanged one word, written or spoken, with Maria since her departure. While the *cacique* suffered within, he successfully concealed his excruciating grief. On the other hand, it was openly evident that Rosita was being emotionally destroyed as a result of the ongoing separation. The struggle within her was causing physical problems in the form of elevated blood pressure and an irregular heart beat. She masterfully avoided having her husband cognizant of her worsening illness.

CHAPTER XXVI

THE PORFIRIATO ERA

Since the re-election of General Porfirio Diaz to a second term in office, Mexico had continued to flourish under his dictatorial rule. With a rapidly expanding population, the need for public services and goods likewise expanded. To satisfy an essential requirement for aggrandizement, there was a concentrated effort to develop a greatly expanded railroad system whereby regional markets were converted to national in scope giving birth to an industrial revolution.

With the advent of a hurriedly developing nation, it was necessary to supplement local know-how with advanced engineering talent from abroad. This was costly and created a serious drain on the treasury.

Mexico was, at last, demonstrating the rapid progress of a developing nation. With its high-priced technicians and imported experts, it had developed into a manufacturing nation hoping to establish a thriving export market. Unfortunately, their hopes would be shattered— their effort a dismal failure.

Effecting flawed theories and assumptions, they quickly realized that which was successful in the United States and Europe could not successfully be imitated in Mexico. The Mexican worker was stubborn and refused to accept advanced technology. He had neither the education nor the inclination. The end result was a produced product that was inferior in quality and lacking in uniformity. The consequence of the well-intentioned effort was that national production was more costly than competitive imports.

Regrettably, while there were hordes of unskilled laborers, there was a dire shortage of skilled labor.

The result of the failed attempt to convert Mexico to a nation of manufactured exports was a treasury that lacked foreign exchange. The all-powerful commercial sector negotiated to purchase imported equipment duty free, which depleted the country's hard currency while dampening the initiative of national production.

The situation presented a dilemma for President Diaz that he was determined to resolve. After long and profound deliberation, he ordered a cease and desist regarding the government's attempt at national production as it, in itself, was proving to be overly costly. By allowing the union of Mexico's most powerful entrepreneurs to form alliances, a program of monopolies was instituted affording the merged capitalists the ability to completely control industrial output. While Diaz envisioned this as a means to lower prices for the masses, once again, his well-intentioned plan backfired. The result was increased suffering by the already-impoverished public as the newly formed conglomerates could fix prices at will for there was no competition.

While it is true that the strategy had, to a modest degree, conserved the treasury's hard currency, new fortunes were amassed by the already wealthy with the working class consumer paying the price.

With the numerous failures of the Porfiriato era, there were, as well, successes. Prior to the administration of Porfirio Diaz, Mexico was reputedly a lawless land where crime was the order of the day. The president was determined to establish law and order, which he accomplished, most notably, through his employment of the unrestricted force of the army, the municipal police and his own handpicked private police force of thugs, the *rurales*.

With Mexico now a land of tranquility and serene

beauty, a new industry came into being. Tourists from the United States, Europe and South America converged on this scenic nation with its electrifying mountain ranges and endless miles of pristine white sand beaches. Mexico was aware that the burgeoning tourist industry could provide its depleted treasury with the foreign exchange it so sorely required. It was ordered that all foreign visitors should receive every attention and courtesy possible inasmuch as the foreigners' dollars were sacrosanct.

Diaz was cognizant of the fact that with law and discipline established in combination with the influx of foreign tourists, the next order of the day was to establish cordial relations with other nations in order to attract foreign investment. By means of an orderly and well-orchestrated plan, relations were established leading to the exchange of ambassadorial posts, which, in turn, resulted in unexpected substantial sums being deposited in Mexican banks.

Dollars were made available at a faster pace than the government could accommodate the multitude of investors. These funds were instrumental in effecting major improvements in the railroad system, electric generating plants, communication transmission, and agricultural production. Previously, farming required costly support by the government; however, with the acquisition of the most up-to-date machinery and fertilizers, cultivated crops, which were now sold for export, became a most welcome vital source of dollars.

With this newfound prosperity, Diaz had, through sound judgment, silenced the critics of his past failures. With the advent of this thriving economy, there emerged a new class of citizen unlike any in the past. In years gone by, there were but two classes of Mexicans—the rich and the poor. Unfortunately, as time passed, the rich grew richer while the poor remained poverty stricken.

Now, a so-called middle class surfaced. This new

stratum of citizen harbored an intense desire to climb the social ladder so much so that they abandoned the traditional Mexican way of life for the more impressive French demeanor. Stylish imported furniture, home furnishing, food and wine, as well as attire, was in vogue. In this period of transformation, the blaring of trumpets of the traditional mariachis was gone, replaced by the soothing strings of violins playing "*Je t'aimerai toujours.*"

Life was good for some. While the wealthy and the new middle class enjoyed the fruits of prosperity, the disadvantaged remained as before—the new wealth had by-passed them completely. The Diaz plan for economic recovery had been only somewhat successful. While the nation's prosperity had created a new class with new wealth, there still remained the poverty stricken who continued to toil from dawn to dusk, undernourished, all the while becoming more restless by the day for a better life.

It was October 12, 1901. The country was celebrating *Dia de la Raza* (Day of the Race), in observance of the discovery of America by Columbus, and it was Eduardo's fiftieth birthday. There would be no public acknowledgement in Soledad of either as Rosita's condition continued to worsen even though there was no visible evidence of her fragile state. She continued to grieve with her emotions knotted within.

The multiple interests of the *cacique* occupied his working hours allowing him little free time to recall his despondency over Maria. His business enterprises, under the administration of Armando Vilas, continued to thrive as a result of the burgeoning Mexican economy where the general populace was awash in newfound wealth.

As a standout addition to Soledad, now a growing, prosperous city, the *cacique* had constructed the first high-rise office building. The structure, of Spanish colonial design with arched windows, was a stately six-story building that attracted visitors from miles around. Leased by the city from the *cacique* at a handsome rental, it was the first building in the area to have elevators, of which there were two.

The elevators, themselves, presented no problem. It was the endless lines of peons from every area town and village who would line up and wait for hours for the opportunity to merely ride up and down repeatedly for the thrill of traveling vertically that wrecked havoc. The huge crowds wishing to experience the free excitation were so overwhelming, it was necessary to post local police to control them. As a special consideration to the workers of Hacienda *San Eduardo*, the *cacique* issued special passes of privilege where the bearer of such a pass could advance to the head of the line in order to avoid a lengthy wait.

Like the despots before him, Diaz had his successes and failures. While he brought prosperity to the nation and the beneficiaries of the economic boom, his complete disregard of the majority, the Indian, and the impecunious *mestizo* population would, at some future date, result in a national calamity. It was said by the intellectual community that the president governed by "little politics, much administration." In time, it would become, in the *cacique*'s opinion, "zero politics, one hundred percent administration." The Diaz strategy, though questioned by many, was accepted and tolerated inasmuch as the populace was exhausted by years of economic failure and lawlessness. The president's overall package was accepted for it provided that which was lacking—opulence, abundance, and law and order. He was, indeed, the despot of his era.

It was Eduardo's belief that the objective of the privileged class of the Porfiriato was to, "achieve a good bank account, a good cook and a good digestive system." Even though he was living the good life, he was astute enough to know that it was essential to throw a few "crumbs" to the masses in order to insure one's assets from unlawful seizure.

The *cacique* was quick to recognize the achievement of the Porfiriato Era. There were industrial benefits derived from a railroad once just 287 miles long and now a national system covering 12,000 miles. During the same period, he would note that postal, telegraph and even telephone connected the reaches of the nation. With the railroad to transport national production and improved port facilities in Veracruz, Tampico and Salina Cruz, the equation was complete allowing export-import with the United States and the western world.

Like others of the advantaged stratum, the *cacique* benefited immensely from commercial financing with newly created banks making possible the expansion of agriculture, mining, commerce and industry. With the *cacique's* hacienda producing cacao, henequen, citrus, sugar, sheep and cattle, all in demand in foreign markets, the export from Hacienda *San Eduardo* became extremely profitable.

Eduardo was soon to learn that even progress and success could demand a staggering consequential cost. As he expected, and to his utter disappointment, the spoiled, rich and affluent did not share their cornucopia with others, and so, as befalls all things of man, the era of plenty would be derailed as would the era of peace, order and expansion. Its repercussions affected everyone in all walks of life.

Eduardo, brilliant in achieving the highest grades ever in a Mexican university, was quick to recognize that economic growth, despite its rewards, would exact a price. With the building of the railroads, the advent of industrialization, and the other trappings of a capitalist economy, the traditional way of life clashed with new ambitions and needs and, in turn, fed fears for the future. Similarly, if industry were to prosper, a domestic market would have to grow posthaste or new foreign markets discovered. Alarmingly, there were signs that the buying power of the national consumer had failed to stay abreast with the ability of the manufacturer to produce. Consequently, and in due time, only industries with export buyers could survive. Those unable to acquire foreign sales would stagnate.

Progress, capitalist by design and always welcome, had come to a screeching halt. Its collapse, complex though the logical result of Porfirio's successes and failures, caught both Mexicans and foreigners by surprise. Being of a profound analytical mind, the *cacique* spent extended periods of time in deep thought analyzing the problems of state.

After lengthy analysis, it was his conclusion that the problems of the day brought on by a multitude of causes were both grave and numerous. From the distant, prosperous mining operations to the close-at-hand farms, workers had money and lots of it. These laborers, plus those at the distant oil exploration site, would converge on Soledad en masse on weekends where whores, gamblers and criminals of varying hues would await their arrival. The workers' two days and nights were spent getting drunk, fighting with each other, getting fleeced, engaging in love-making and generally raising hell.

It was unavoidable that such activity would warrant untold arrests. Soon the *cacique* discovered that he did not possess enough jail cells for all and, therefore, would incarcerate as many as the jail cells would hold and then be obliged to release all others.

A problem arose within the *cacique*'s three banks in Soledad. With prosperity filling the pockets of virtually all working people, many banks in Mexico, including those of the *cacique*, implemented checking accounts for anyone who could prove his ability to write sufficiently. With the necessary initial deposit and the opening of a checking account, the account holder, as expected, was given a book of checks.

While it was clearly explained, a dilemma came to light when checks by the droves were presented for payment when there were insufficient funds to cover the remittances. Upon investigation, it was discovered that the account holder, in good faith, believed that as long as he had checks available, he could continue issuing them for payment. After lengthy consideration, the *cacique* resolved that such an advance in banking was pre-mature and checking accounts were discontinued.

Much to the dismay of the now-entrenched middle class, there were indications that the bubble of prosperity was about to burst. Frustration among the noveau riche was leading to social problems as they had now become accustomed to the good life and rebuffed any downward change.

As the economy commenced to falter, there were demonstrations in the larger industrial centers as the decline in business profitability translated into reduced salaries, unemployment, and, consequently, a diminished lifestyle. As to the "haves", their manner of being was unaffected except for the fact that their fortunes were somewhat reduced.

In the capital itself, there were demonstrations by the nation's new professionals condemning the administration for their languishing top echelon and the deteriorating pecuniary situation. In examining the ills of the nation, the *cacique* observed that there was a rotation of the same men in office in the positions most desired in government, both federal and provincial. Opportunity was denied to the younger, ambitious white-collar workers.

He noted that even with a flourishing economy, the demographic explosion created a basic problem of more people entering the job market than industry's ability to create new jobs. Job hunters were from all walks of endeavor—lawyers, engineers, architects, agronomists, writers and poets. Schoolteachers, whose ranks multiplied dramatically in the twentieth century, were an especially troubled lot. Poorly paid, they eked out a paltry existence.

The dilemma with the highly educated could be traced to the fact that the Diaz regime had made available learning facilities to the lower middle class. In itself a noble gesture. Unwisely, the offer of an education without an equal opportunity for the future was an invitation to protest.

Those who had studiously pursued their prescribed courses could not, upon successfully completing their curriculum, find employment. They vigorously protested claiming that all positions in government were being retained by elderly political appointees. They demanded that government placements be open in a fair and competitive arrangement.

Complaints were heard from others in addition to students. Farmers across the land were loudly voicing their grievance against the administration for invading their property while expanding the rail service. Their complaints were not expressed while crop prices were elevated. However, now that market prices were depressed they were laying claim for reimbursement for the transgression by the government. With the farmers acting jointly, numbering in the thousands, their dissatisfaction was not taken lightly. Within weeks, they had organized into a bonded group of twelve thousand joining in street demonstrations throughout the country. The government was aware of the public sympathy to their cause and feared the consequences.

While the many ongoing bones of contention did not directly affect Soledad, some did, with all having deteriorating effect on the morale of its inhabitants.

The economic decline was well underway although the eventual resulting adverse fall-out had not yet reached its full effect. The *cacique* visualized the potential danger to the nation, and he felt compelled to express his thinking in a letter to his superior in Mexico City.

>General Carlos Bersunza
>Caudillo de Mexico
>Palacio Nacional
>Mexico, D. F.

My respected General Bersunza,

I request that you permit me to present my impression of what is transpiring in our beloved Mexico as relates to our social structure. As we know, all nations experience a society that consists of a limited few extremely wealthy individuals on the top rung of the ladder with an expanding middle class below and then the great masses at the bottom. The configuration resembles one of the many mountains found in our country.

The theory of those on top is that there is a trickle down process that benefits everyone on the way down. They further submit that all below the top have the opportunity to climb the ladder for a better life. This is a self-satisfying theory of the privileged.

In reality, Mexico's ladder for a more fruitful life, unlike other developed countries, has such a steep incline, ascending it is a nightmarish experience with but a limited few able to climb to the next level.

For one to improve socially and

financially in our system is as difficult, painful and hopeless as walking barefoot on broken glass. It is astonishing that Benito Juárez, an illiterate Indian, could have achieved incredible success as president of our nation. Miraculously, he conquered all political obstacles that he encountered.

Being cognizant of the multitude of impediments that one confronts in an attempt to improve oneself, I must make mention of a potential social problem that I envision in the offing. We have a new generation of college graduates—doctors, lawyer, dentists, engineers, etc.—who wish to climb that ladder for a better life. They look to their government for employment only to find that all lucrative positions are filled by old men who have enjoyed the beneficial enrichment of their positions for decades.

Alarmingly, these young and vibrant graduates cannot accept the status quo. They are extremely energetic and believe that there is stagnation in the bureaucratic system. They wish to become active participants in government service and are determined to achieve their goal by whatever means. Should they find the door closed for entry, I fear they shall employ rebellious activity. My general, it is essential that we encounter a solution to this potentially grave situation and prevent, at all costs, the possible devastation of our body politic.

We cannot fashion our system after others even though their methodology has proven successful. Our ladder is almost vertical while their ladder is subtly inclined. That which serves them well will not necessarily serve us the same way. We differ, for we are a poor, under developed nation born of insurrection with a distinct heritage and culture.

My chief, I am a loyal and patriotic Mexican. I envision clouds on the horizon that shall become storm-like at some later date. We, alone, are the prime movers of our destiny and, therefore, positive action must be taken. Together we must optimistically look upon the present enthusiastically as the past of our future. We must act today.

There must be programmed redistribution of our nation's land and wealth, however insignificant, to those who toil daily for a meager subsistence. I trust you will give this opinion your consideration.

Respectfully,

Eduardo Hernandez Gonzalez

With his communiqué now on its way, the *cacique* would patiently await a reply.

Having conveyed his message to his superior, the *cacique* returned to his daily responsibilities. Soledad continued to be a weekend merry-making center of bars, illegal gambling, prostitutes and con men. Each week brought forth new violations and problems. Disturbances increased to the point that the police chief was compelled to double the size of his force.

As an offshoot of the merriment, many workers were regularly not reporting for work on Monday morning. This, inevitably, had an adverse effect on the many enterprises of the *cacique,* including Hacienda *San Eduardo*. The worker, when asked why he did not report for work after the weekend, answered surprisingly that he was observing a saint's day, *San Lunes* (Saint Monday), an invented saint, hence, an invented saint's day. The worker was penalized one day's pay, which further diminished his already difficult ability to provide for his family. With the rapidly languishing economy, any such loss of income only added to the already brewing discontent of a populace spoiled by past fructuous years when the laborer enjoyed income as never before.

The petulant citizenry was voicing its displeasure as jobs, one by one, were lost. Of great concern was that mass meetings were held in an attempt to select a leader to represent the dissidents and voice their grievances. The *cacique* was more than aware that it would only be through a leader that any coalescence of the splintered groups could become a social peril. He, therefore, was determined to prevent the masses from selecting such a person.

The chief of police created a charge and imprisoned each potential leader in the local jail. When that was full, he utilized the lockable rooms in the local hospital ward that were normally reserved for violently ill psychiatric cases.

Over a period of six months, nine potential selectees were incarcerated without a court hearing or the benefit of legal counsel. Unable to successfully organize, the querulous assemblage accepted defeat and abandoned any further attempt at unanimity.

All editorials in the daily paper were directed to the advantage of the *cacique* while undermining the cause of the workers. Printed leaflets attacking the newspaper were without success, for the power of the press was not to be questioned.

As an escape from the many diverse pressures of his office, the *cacique* found solace by spending days on end at the hacienda. He was most at peace when Father Agustin accompanied him. Rosita rarely left the mansion due to her continued failing health. On occasion, she would gather all her strength to be by his side when he visited the hacienda to observe the operation of the ranch and farm as well as to inspect the ongoing construction.

As an astute businessman, he masterfully protected his export relationships. While other producers suffered depressed overseas sales in this period of economic recession, he continued to enjoy undisturbed sales abroad. Meanwhile, the hacienda employees, unlike others, continued to prosper.

CHAPTER XXVII

INAUGURATION OF *CASA* ROSITA

Soon it would be Rosita's birthday and the *cacique* would celebrate with a gigantean fiesta. As to the principal residence and other construction, the *cacique* was delighted that all was progressing as per plan. He was determined that the residence would be a showplace—virtually all furniture and furnishings were imported from Europe with incidentals acquired in Mexico City.

He estimated that in just a short time, everything would be completed and ready to be put on display for all to admire. Already, *Casa* Rosita was the topic of conversation for miles around with the upper crust anxiously waiting to see the property. It was his intention to give the super privileged the opportunity to inspect his dream-come-true by offering an extravaganza never before experienced in the region.

Invitations were sent to all *hacendados* and key politicians in the states of Chiapas and Veracruz as well as Mexico City. Armando Vilas was entrusted with preparation of the guest list to ensure that no one of importance was omitted. It was estimated that four hundred people would be invited.

While Eduardo anguished that his only child would not be present, his burden was somewhat diminished inasmuch as he dedicated himself completely to the details involved in the forthcoming birthday celebration and the inaugural festivities of *Casa* Rosita.

Everyone became involved in the minutiae of the

arrangements. The city's civil servants, employees from the *cacique's* enterprises, trades people and paid consultants from the nation's capital were all involved to some degree. Following good engineering procedure, Eduardo prepared a work progress schedule and a check-off list that he, himself, would oversee. The day before the long-awaited event, he received a letter that, for the moment, dampened his enthusiastic approach to the prodigious production.

In or near the center square of all cities and towns throughout Mexico, were those individuals known as street writers. In view of the nation's staggering illiteracy, the street writers, some with antiquated typewriters, others scripting in long hand, offered their services to the unlearned by writing the spoken word. This afforded the illiterate a means by which they could communicate with loved ones and friends not in the area. They extended a complete service by suggesting thoughts, words and expressions for written missives. In addition, they provided the necessary envelopes and postage stamps, all included for a charge for out-of-pocket expenses plus a small gratification. It was this type of letter that was hand delivered to the *cacique* sent from the *Isla de Mujeres*.

Through the years, the inhabitants of the island survived by farming and charity. However, during the last decade, fishermen had converted the island to a fishing village—a cornucopia of fish and willing female partners.

Señor Alcalde Eduardo Hernandez Gonzalez
Soledad, Chiapas

Mi estimado y respetable jefe (My esteemed and respected chief),

Inasmuch as I do not know how to write, I am having this letter prepared by a street writer. He has helped me with many words that I do not use in my daily speech. Please forgive me for my lack of education.

While I believe I am a complete stranger to you, it is possible you may have heard of me. I was employed by the honorable Colonel Alejandro Fernandez Bravo, may he rest in peace, the father of your beloved wife, Doña Rosita de Hernandez, whose mother died in childbirth.

I was honored to care for her from shortly after her birth until she was twelve years old, at which time I was exiled to this Island of Women where I continue to live to this day. I was exiled to this forgotten island in the year 1867 and am now seventy-four years old.

I recall so clearly how, on Doña Rosita's tenth birthday, my chief, Colonel Alejandro Fernandez Bravo, presented his daughter with a Saint Christopher medallion on a gold neck chain. It was the most beautiful medallion I had ever seen. It was so beautiful I knew I would never forget it. It was gold, oval in shape with diamonds completely around the figure of Saint Christopher. I remember how thrilled my little girl was when she first wore it. She vowed to always wear it in memory of the father she adored. I know she treasured the medallion. It was when she was twelve years old I was sent away.

I hope you will forgive me for writing to you on a matter that haunts me day and night. Some months ago, I saw a young lady, here, on this deserted outpost, wearing Doña Rosita's gold neckpiece. I could not help myself from asking who she was and where she had gotten it. She told me her name was Maria de Garcia and that she was your daughter. Both she and her husband, Nick, are employed teaching at the island's only school. They have a young son whose name is Eduardo. My chief, please know they are all well. I could not keep myself from writing this letter. Please forgive me if I have done something wrong.

Atentamente y respetuosamente
(Yours sincerely and respectfully),

Marta Moreno

As energetically as the *cacique* was moving in preparation for Rosita's birthday celebration, the letter stopped him in his tracks and renewed the most tragic moment in his life. He returned to the mansion to sit and ponder in his favorite chair. Upon entering the room, Rosita noticed her husband's hands trembling. Without hesitation, she reached out, clutched his hands and inquired, "My darling, what is it?"

Smiling so as not to betray his inner torment, he replied, "Thinking, just thinking."

As crushing as the shocking letter had been, the *cacique* knew that guests would be arriving the next day. Gathering his inner strength, he continued to pursue all pending matters. After meticulously checking each item on his list, he finally turned to Vilas and proclaimed, "We're ready, bring them on."

The following day, commencing at 3:00 P.M., the guests began arriving. They were first greeted by the *cacique* and his lovely wife who was confined to a large, overstuffed chaise covered with French tapestry. A memorable sight awaited them. In small groups, with drinks in hand, they were taken on a room-by-room inspection of *Casa* Rosita accompanied by a well-rehearsed guide. At floor level, they marveled at the monstrous living room with its artfully hand carved and molded ceiling, the wood-beamed main dining room capable of seating thirty-six, the more intimate family dining room, den, game room, kitchen, butler's pantry, servants dining room, and wine storage for two thousand bottles of France's finest wine.

From there, it was up an elaborate wrought iron staircase to the second floor and its twelve bedrooms, each with a private bath. Throughout the home, all walls were paneled with imported oak, as were the floors, which were covered with expensive, hand-woven rugs purchased in Europe. From each bedroom, there was a magnificent view of the manicured formal gardens.

The windows were covered with French lace curtains. For purposes of effect, the den, game room and several bedrooms were furnished in Spanish colonial décor. However, all other rooms were furnished in traditional eighteenth century Louis XIV style of the finest quality. Every room in the residence had a fireplace, a noteworthy feature that set this stately home apart from all other luxurious residences in the state.

Adjoining the main house were servant's quarters, a guest bungalow and a massive carriage house with connecting stables.

After all guests had been escorted through the premises, the tents erected on the lawns became the focal point of the evening. In one pavilion, there were two alternating mariachi groups. The food tables offered every imaginable Mexican dish in addition to the essential tequila, pulque, beer and soft drinks. The Mexican delicacies included barbeque beef, grilled steak, chicken, fried pork, and the staples—tortillas, rice, beans, avocado, spicy sauces and salad. The shrimp and octopus cocktail was boasted to be the best ever.

Some fifty feet away, the environment was French. There were two groups of musicians, a string quartet and a roving group of twelve violinists, who played in concert as an assembled body or as strolling individuals. In view of the status recognition at stake and the desire to be seen favorably, it was not surprising that almost everyone congregated under this tent to enjoy the French ambrosial cuisine.

To effect authenticity, the chef and all employees, resplendent in their white uniforms, were imported from the city of Veracruz's only authentic French restaurant. The *cacique* was determined that he would be outdone by no one, regardless of when another super gala might be offered by someone else.

Appetizers included an egg-aspic combination, gratin of hard-boiled eggs, split pea soup with bacon, creamy pumpkin bisque and shrimp and lobster cocktails. The table on which the main course was elegantly presented resembled a gourmet's dream. There were salmon croquettes, salmon combined with crayfish in red wine sauce, veal with pickling onions and mushrooms, rabbit stew in red wine, and Provence braised beef casserole topped off with stuffed vegetables.

There were but a few hardy souls that could continue to the desert section. For those who did muster an appetite, there was chocolate mousse with hazelnuts, cantaloupe sorbet, fruit gratin with maraschino liquor and chocolate meringue cake.

A banquet of this category would not be complete without a selection of red and white French wines along with an endless supply of champagne.

Not surprisingly, after such a meal, few could remain standing with chairs being in great demand. For those who were fortunate enough to be seated, staying awake was a great effort as the abundance of food and drink combined to produce sleepiness.

As per custom, during the course of the evening, the men conversed in small select groups while the ladies gathered in like fashion. The men's topic of conversation varied from discussions of the recent highly fruitful days, now a thing of the past, to the declining economy and the resulting social problems.

Of a more regional pertinence, was the local worker related disturbances and diatribes. The conversation quickly shifted to national concern, which was the preoccupation of the elite, which related to announced government decisions that could adversely affect the nation's entrepreneurs and industrialists.

In an effort to conserve the treasury's foreign reserves, the government intended to educate and prepare its own people to replace the previously imported technical experts. The program to groom their own citizens as engineers, architects, scientists and the like had been in place for the past five years. Upon completion of the prescribed courses, the graduate, with a sense of prominence, expected to find a prestigious position as well as a tastefully decorated office, a large mahogany desk and, of course, a beautiful, trim-figured secretary. Much to his dismay, and as a result of a faltering economy added to a mediocre education, there was no prestigious job, no office, no mahogany desk, and no secretary. There was no employment, period.

This disappointing and frustrating situation resulted in weekly demonstrations, principally in Mexico City, where the ever-growing coalescence of protesters was gaining support, particularly from the trade unions.

Eduardo, being a student of history, informed his colleagues that the situation was, indeed, explosive and critical. He explained that history had demonstrated that when there existed profound dissidence wherein students and trade unions protested, there lacked but one ingredient to bring down the government—a manifestation of support by the church. The situation was extremely grave for the privileged not easily brushed aside for they did not know to what degree the dissident groups would unite.

At one point, the *cacique* was questioned as to how he reacted when disaffected workers distributed leaflets attacking him and his newspaper. He was quick to respond, "I taught them a lesson. I taught them one very important fact of life and that is that you never, ever, attack a newspaper unless you own it." His statement brought laughter and applause from his guests.

Then asking for attention, Eduardo, with Rosita seated by his side, launched into the inevitable diatribe so typical when politicians assemble. His words were both humbling and trumpeting self-praise.

He commenced, "I should like to present the administrator of Hacienda *San Eduardo*, Señor Raul Molina, without whose guidance this ranch and beautiful home would not be here for all of us to enjoy." With those kind words, Raul stepped forward to acknowledge his boss' praise. He was particularly flattered to be addressed as "señor."

Eduardo continued, "I welcome all of you, my friends, to 'your' home, *Casa* Rosita. Thirty-five years ago, I was an energetic young graduate engineer starting my first job in Soledad, when, by a strange quirk of coincidence, I was blessed with my beloved wife, Rosita. You are all prominent men in your communities with great mental aptitude. We have demonstrated that we, who have labored with our minds, rule, while those who labor with their bodies are ruled. That God-given capability demands that we be compassionate while being successful.

"My domain consists of banks, cattle, real estate, farming, fuel and water distributing stations, mining interests, food stores and a newspaper. With all of these assets, I measure my true wealth and success right here at Hacienda *San Eduardo*. It is here that I have created a thriving community where my people live in peace and harmony and want for little. This is my crown jewel. Now, having had the pleasure to address you, I should like to present our revered parish priest, Father Agustin Diaz, who taught me, and only after great persistence, that prayer alone will not change things. He made me a believer that prayer will change people and that they, in turn, will change things."

The father, having been briefed by the *cacique*, began, "It was some years ago that I respectfully approached Don Eduardo Hernandez requesting that he lend assistance to the impoverished people of San José Marti. When I was promised a helping hand, I reminded my benefactor that in the eyes of God a promise is a debt to be paid. While I had reason to be skeptical remembering similar promises made by the privileged, I can now tell you our God-sent angel has paid his debt in full."

Observing that much of the audience was about to collapse or drowse off into deep sleep, the man of God gave the benediction, blessing everyone. The *cacique* then thanked all for attending, wished them a most pleasant evening and bid them goodbye, for the long awaited day had come to an end.

CHAPTER XXVIII

A STARTLING REVELATION

The *cacique*'s hacienda was the talk of the town. Needless to say, the non-stop effort in preparing for the gala culminated with Eduardo being completely exhausted. He used the following week as period in which to recover and weigh his options as to what action he might pursue relative to the letter received from Marta Moreno. After a profound and soul-searching deliberation, he determined it best to take no action, at least for the moment.

With his many businesses flourishing under the guidance of his trusted administrator and with the previous concern of worker discontent now a past issue, he adopted a relaxed program for himself and his beloved Rosita. They spent four days a week in Soledad, retiring to the hacienda Friday through Sunday where they often entertained intimate friends. It seemed as though the days spent at the hacienda served as a stimulant for both. His hours at the office in Soledad grew shorter and shorter. He virtually ignored his business interests other than an occasional review of the monthly reports prepared by his accountant.

He derived intense inner satisfaction by merely walking through the manicured grounds of the hacienda. There was yet another form of idealistic fulfillment when he mingled with the workers and their families who lived in tranquility, and of great importance, prosperity.

While their continued grieving over Maria was no longer apparent, it was very much alive and carried deep within themselves. They were never completely free of their heartbreak. In recent years, their daughter's name was virtually never mentioned. During their thirty-five years of life together, the Hernandez family, except for the ongoing agonizing over their daughter, enjoyed life at its best. There was concern over Rosita's condition, which remained dormant, while the *cacique*'s heart condition seemed to remain in status quo. Together, they spent their long weekends at their treasured hacienda where almost all was at peace with themselves and the world.

However, unlike their placid routine, Mexico was undergoing critical change causing profound concern to the *cacique*. Of all the *caciques* in Mexico, Eduardo was, without question, the best educated, the most literate, and the most sophisticated. To this date, over three decades after his day as a valedictorian graduate, no one else had achieved a perfect score at a university. He possessed the perception to comprehend that which was transpiring in his country. It was not to his liking and potentially perilous, as he had previously expressed in a letter to his superior.

He reasoned that the national *cacique* structure, established in 1570 and now almost 340 years old in the year 1908, had justified its mission believing that all that was done, even when illicit, was done in the sincere assuredness that it benefited the nation. However, he was convinced that when an established system had long existed committing malfeasance, it should be old enough to do right as well once its erroneousness was recognized.

As the years passed, President Diaz continued to rule which an iron hand, in true autocratic fashion, disregarding the advice of his inner council or the censure of his adversaries. Hew was now seventy-seven years old and had served as president since 1876 with the exception of the years 1880-1884, during which time his appointed puppet wore the sash of office. Diaz was not one to reveal matters of confidentiality, even to his closest associates. Nor did he foresee the day when he would abandon the office as chief executive; hence, there was no understudy. Even after serving for twenty-eight years, he was preparing his campaign for re-election and to serve yet another four years.

The president was the toast of foreign nations. While monocratic government was not the desired form of governing, Diaz's authoritarian control and apparent continuing successes were respected. As a result, vast sums of foreign capital poured into Mexico for investment. Little were the investing entrepreneurs aware that under the ostensible economic calm there was an undercurrent of economic downturn and civic unrest by the masses. Any vocal expression of displeasure was immediately quieted by the president's private police force, his *rurales*.

The *cacique* had, in recapitulation, arrived at a frightening conclusion. He was cognizant that everything for which he had labored so long and so diligently could, like a tent in a strong wind, come tumbling down. He was positive that all the rebellious masses lacked was the necessary component for insurrection—a doctrinaire leader. Someone who would ignite the movement.

Being a master of perception and sensing the prevailing unrest in the region and the nation, he concluded it best to host a lavish, typical Mexican barbeque at the hacienda twice a month for the workers in his many enterprises as well as the employees of the city administration. At each, he made a pointed remark thanking the hacienda's work force for their support in preparing the barbeque. It was his hope that such a display of goodwill would serve as a pacifier and calm a potentially perilous local situation.

The tranquility in the adopted life style of the *cacique* was dampened by a telephone call over the newly inaugurated telephone system from General Ramos, who continued to serve the caudillo of Mexico. "Eduardo, we are in a calm before the storm, and I mean a big storm. Our failing economy and the power of the foreign interests in our country are creating havoc in our system."

Agonized, Eduardo was slow to respond. Finally, in a slow though composed voice, he replied, "My chief, please continue, explain why."

"Eduardo, in your letter to the caudillo, which was delivered to the president, you foresaw the oncoming situation. I do not have time now to elaborate. A wire will be sent to all *caciques*. Stay well and may God protect us."

The anticipated and anxiously awaited telegraphic message from General Bersunza arrived the following day. Extensive in scope, it detailed how the present *hacendado* economic system, suffering financially from the loss of a major portion of the export market, was not providing adequately for the needs of the people. The communiqué stated, in part, "Demonstrations in all sections of the nation are growing with dissenters forming alliances. There is a unifying cry of 'Mexico for the Mexicans', which evolved as a result of the administration's catering to foreign investors. Adding to the government's woes is the fact that labor is unionizing under the influence of established labor unions from the United States. They are actively propagandizing on our soil. I have no simple solution to the avalanche of problems that may lead to an ungovernable state of affairs. Each *cacique* is instructed to review and evaluate his local situation and act accordingly."

While there was no immediate urgency in Soledad, the *cacique* was aware that such insurrections could easily spread to all parts of the nation. He was hopeful that his many efforts of compassion to his employees plus his bi-monthly outings for all workers in his enterprises as well as the city employees would ensure tranquility as well as loyalty and a peaceful existence in his region.

During the months that followed, there was turmoil and social revolt in most of the country, but nothing out of the ordinary occurred in Soledad. Eduardo kept the caudillo informed of the local situation on a monthly basis. He happily advised that all was serene in his city. On the other hand, the caudillo reported monthly to all *caciques* of any disturbances nationwide.

The *cacique* maintained his routine of work, rest and programmed attention to his workers. He declared that there would be a gigantic party at the hacienda on March 18—the feast day of *San Eduardo el Martir*, the adopted patron saint of Eduardo as well as the village of San José Marti. Everyone would be invited for prayer, food, drink and festivities. The thought of hosting yet another extravaganza seemed to instill new energy in the *cacique*.

As before, he assumed command of all planning and execution including the assignment of detail to his subordinates. He was so engrossed in the observance of his saint's day that he and Rosita abandoned their days at the mansion and remained full time at the hacienda. This second home became a retreat for which the *cacique* developed a particularly revered attachment. His duties at city hall were delegated to an assistant.

Once again, he meticulously reviewed his check-off list, feeling relieved that all was in readiness for the day of prayer and partying.

As per plan, no visitor or resident of the village could partake of food or beverage without first attending prayer services at the village chapel housing the figure of *San Eduardo el Martir*. Upon departing the chapel after prayer, each individual received an indelible stamp on the top of his right hand whereupon he became an eligible and welcome guest to partake of the food and drink.

By noon, a sea of bodies numbering in the thousands was streaming into the hacienda to enjoy unlimited fare. Strolling among the throng were groups of mariachi bands. Inasmuch as there was a religious connotation attached to the feast day, no alcoholic beverages were available. To everyone's delight, there were no speeches.

While Rosita remained seated on the terrace, the *cacique*, feeling extremely spiritual, and joined by the new young parish priest of the village, roamed the grounds chatting with the attendees. The guests, gratified in having the grand honor of speaking with the two, expressed their appreciation by kissing the hand of each.

It was now evening and the crowds began to disperse. By 8:00 P.M., the *cacique* and his wife were alone in *Casa* Rosita, the home they so loved. Exhausted, they decided to remain at the hacienda for an additional week.

The *cacique* opined that that which could not be avoided must necessarily be endured. As in the past, on so many occasions, when Eduardo was somewhat at peace with himself, he would receive disturbing news. It was during this week of recuperation that he received unsettling news that shattered his peace. While it was his fervent belief that his plan for employee assuagement would have a calming effect, it was an earth-shattering revelation to be informed otherwise.

In a shocking development, he learned through a total stranger that workers in regional businesses and industry had experienced new and serious grievances. There were serious repercussions when Mexicans were paid less than their non-national counterparts for the same work in plants owned and operated by foreign interests. Secondly, the Mexican was delegated to undesirable posts while the technical and managerial positions were staffed by foreigners, namely Americans. The end product was work stoppages in many parts of the republic with management closing and locking the gates to the plant sites. Without government support, the disgruntled and unarmed workers attempted to force their way through the locked gates at which point the plant manager ordered high-pressure water hoses turned on them.

In isolated instances when the gates buckled and workers swarmed into the company's yard, they were greeted with volley after volley of rifle fire. Such chaos resulted in the death of both Mexicans and Americans. Those Mexicans not wounded would proceed to ignite the factory site. Still aggrieved, some forced their way into stores selling guns and ammunition returning to the site of the confrontation to fire on the foreign management.

Such confrontations occurred at mining operations, textile plants, food processing centers and the like. The *cacique* soon learned that such a showdown had transpired in the oil exploitation area in south Chiapas, within striking distance of his own city.

This electrifying disclosure was brought to him by a nervous, slight balding, bespectacled man of approximately fifty years of age who identified himself as Luis Rada. His face was grim and his brow furrowed. While speaking in a disquieted manner, he looked from side to side as though he was fearful of having been followed.

In precise detail, he explained that he was one of a group of *mestizo* partners who owned and operated the Rio Negro textile mill in the nearby state of Veracruz. He went on to say that he had made the trip to convey a message of urgency that could dramatically adversely affect the *cacique* whose reputation as a compassionate proprietor of many enterprises was known far and wide. He was, as well, respected throughout the southeast region of the country.

Continuing in a shaking and fragile voice, Rada asked for the *cacique*'s indulgence while he presented his message of great importance. In a forceful and resonant voice, the *cacique* remarked, "Go on, man, go on. I want to hear what you have to say after your long journey."

Now somewhat calmer, he revealed that the Rio Negro plant, with 140 employees, was successfully producing and selling sheet material of nationally produced cotton. Over a year ago, a union organizer had infiltrated his work force and deliberately created discontent among the workers. Just weeks later, the workers voted to form a union and unacceptable demands were made on management. With the rejection of labor's attempted extortion, a strike was called and the plant closed. Tearfully, he remarked, "Our plant was closed for two months, Señor Hernandez. As you know, when operations are renewed, Mexican law requires the plant owners to pay the workers their back salaries plus penalties. Even as a group of partners, we did not have the funds necessary to reopen. As a result, the *lider* (union boss) suggested we sell our plant to American investors who had sufficient funding, which we did at a great loss."

In a voice that was stern and with no semblance of sympathy in its firmness, the *cacique* interjected, "I'm sorry to hear of your problem, but what does this have to do with me?"

"Please sir, give me but a few minutes and you shall see." The *cacique* agreed. "This entire plan to seize a plant where *mestizos* worked for fellow *mestizos* was an act against mankind. The Americans have learned of the power of the *mordida*. It is clear as can be that the *lider* was not only trained but also planted by the Americans with the sole objective of stealing our plant.

"Now," trembling as he spoke, "what has befallen me does not compare to the suffering of my fellow *mestizos*. Once the Americans took control of Rio Negro, working conditions at the plant became more than horrible. Workdays were twelve hours, wages were cut thirty percent and children were employed for a pittance. If workers attempted to discuss working conditions, they were immediately dismissed by the union boss who was on management's payroll."

Once again, the *cacique* interrupted to ask how he was affected by the misfortune; and once again, Rada begged for patience and a little time to which the *cacique* gave his accord.

With permission to proceed, the visitor revealed, "Rage turned to violent insurrection when credit was denied by the plant's store. Uncontrolled, the infuriated searched for any means possible to extract their revenge on their dictatorial employers. Not capable of controlling their anger, they set fire to the store where they encountered volleys of rifle fire from federal troops. A woeful day when Mexicans fired on Mexicans.

As demanded by the families of the deceased as well as the public, an investigation was conducted by a team of government-selected bureaucrats. After giving the inquest the appearance of validity and the accompanying lip service, the finding was a declaration that the incident was worker instigated. Once announced, the outrage by one and all, for fear of retribution ceased to exist.

"Señor Hernandez, I will now give you the principal reason for my being here and why this should be of vital concern to you. I overhead, at a plant meeting between the union boss and the American *patrons* (plant owners), that you are next. Your successful businesses are the envy of the American capitalist, and he is determined to destroy you. I can assure you that at this moment, by employment of the *mordida*, one of your operations is infiltrated or shall be very soon."

By now, the *cacique* had heard enough. He thanked Luis, asking him to spend several days at the hacienda to recover physically and emotionally.

Alone, he pondered the situation in an attempt to determine his options. He concluded that there was a possibility of perilous problems ahead, not only in the nation, but also in his own domain. He was distressed that law and order was being guaranteed at the expense of personal liberty and social justice. He brooded, "My God, first it was the Indians, now it's the *mestizos*. Will the races never learn to co-exist? I fear that perhaps the only true equality is in the cemetery."

Not one to take such serious accusations lightly, he was determined to investigate the validity of Luis Rada's uncorroborated warning. He knew he had one completely trustworthy subordinate of proven loyalty, Raul Molina. The three met at the hacienda so that his guest could repeat the story. With that done, Raul was ordered to seek out anything related to a possible infiltration of a union agitator or any act of provocation in any of the *cacique*'s enterprises. Though it was unnecessary to remind his man of confidence that the use of force was off limits, the *cacique* did so anyway. Shortly thereafter, the informer, well compensated for his effort, returned to his native Veracruz. Meanwhile, the *cacique* awaited the result of Raul's investigation.

CHAPTER XXIX

THE HERNANDEZ FAMILY UNITES

In the interim, Eduardo continued his relaxed schedule of ever-shortened days at the office and long weekends at his cherished retreat. Father Agustin joined him often, affording them the opportunity of discussing the decline in the Mexican family, the economy and the stability of the political system. It appeared as though every sector was in a state of deterioration with the exception of Soledad, which was thriving.

Three weeks had passed when Raul returned to the hacienda to find his boss enjoying his afternoon nap. Upon awakening, he invited his trusted friend to join him for coffee in the den. It was outwardly apparent that Raul was a very troubled man. His mouth was tight, his face grim, his eyes glazed with a savage inner fire and his expression showed displeasure. "*Patron* (Boss), I have news for you. I ask that you sit while I make my report." Responding with a puzzled nod of accord, the *cacique* selected his favorite comfortable over-stuffed chair. Raul began by revealing, "My chief, I have the unpleasant duty to inform you that the information disclosed by Luis Rada is, indeed, correct. At this moment, there is an American trained union instigator in your bottling plant. He is attempting to rally the support of the workers to organize in order to provoke discontent. My chief, I see another Rio Negro in the making. It is my understanding that after the bottling plant, the procedure will move to another of your industries."

The *cacique* sat motionless, stunned, silenced with a dark angry expression. A muscle quivered in his jaw, his face still and serious. Eduardo responded, "A union organizer just doesn't walk in the front door and announce himself. There must be someone from within who is betraying us. Did you find any such person?"

Hesitating and with a look of discomfort crossing his face, Raul replied, "Yes, my boss, the betrayer is none other than your business manager, Armando Vilas. He has sold himself to the enemy. He has violated your confidence and trust. What is it you would like me to do?"

"Nothing for the moment. Allow me to digest what you have uncovered. I'm grateful for your loyalty and friendship." With that, Raul retired from the room while the *cacique* remained seated cogitating.

After several hours, he decided to go to his bedroom to lie down. As one might expect, he was not feeling his normal self after such mind-splintering news. While walking in the hallway to his bedroom, he collapsed. Mustering all of his strength, he called loudly for help. Responding to his cry, his domestic staff carried him to his room before Rosita arrived. She immediately ordered someone to return at once with the doctor who was quick to appear at the *cacique*'s bedside. After a thorough examination, the doctor diagnosed the ailment and administered medication. Glum faced, in private with Rosita, Raul and the valet, he pronounced that the patient had suffered his third cardiac arrest, which would require bed rest for an indefinite period. Rosita was visibly shaken; but it was Raul who was seen biting his lower lip in a display of anguish, perhaps because it was his revelation that brought on the attack. Confidentially, and behind closed doors, the physician informed Rosita that her husband was, indeed, in a most serious condition though not gravely ill. He insisted that the patient remain in bed for a protracted term.

Rosita reasoned that it would be wise to remain at *Casa* Rosita permanently. Once established at the hacienda, she was at her husband's bedside every day from early morning to late evening. Other business-related visitors and friends were admitted to see the *cacique* on an appointment only basis. Raul, who continued to feel culpable for his boss' illness, was permitted to visit for short periods each day. Father Agustin was on hand each morning at 10:00 A.M. and again at 7:00 P.M. to chat with his comrade and offer prayer for his rapid and complete recovery.

While there was little positive change in the *cacique*'s condition in the months that followed, there was, likewise, no significant improvement in Raul's suffering as related to his commiseration. He had privately conferred with both the doctor and the cleric exploring any action that might brighten the outlook of his respected employer who was enduring periods of depression. While he did not uncover a precise solution, it was during one of his many private conversations with his boss that a thought surfaced that could possibly be of benefit to his ailing friend. After a lengthy discussion with the parish priest, it was agreed that if the *cacique* could be influenced to order Maria and her family back to Soledad, the result might be therapeutically salutary. The priest agreed to delicately broach the subject of Maria's return.

Having chosen an appropriate time, Father Agustin initiated the discussion. It was, at times, quite emotional though not heated. The padre, having known his friend since he was a young college graduate, was most cautious to avoid any implication that the *cacique*'s concurrence would in any way imply weakness on the part of the monocrat. It was stressed that the return of his daughter would have a salubrious effect on his beloved, ailing Rosita.

The brain washing continued over a two-week

period when, with outward reluctance but delight within, the *cacique* consented to have the Garcia family—Maria, Nick and little Eduardo—return to Soledad. There were two conditions, however. The homecoming would take place on September 16, 1909, Maria's thirty-fifth birthday; and her return would be secret and a surprise for her mother.

In the meantime, Raul felt compelled to act in some constructive way to raise the spirits of the man he so admired. He would accomplish this in his own way.

One afternoon shortly thereafter, when the *cacique* had awakened from his daily nap, Raul appeared and requested permission to speak with his boss. As expected, permission was immediately granted. Once with the *cacique*, his words were brief and to the point. "My master, I hope you are feeling better. I wish to inform you that you shall never have to be concerned with the bottling plant instigator or Armando Vilas. They are both out of your life forever. I repeat, sir, forever." The *cacique* did not request an explanation to such a definitive statement. He merely thanked his good friend for his dedication and unremitting fidelity. Raul believed that those who had caused his patriarch's infirmity had been satisfactorily repaid.

With outward reluctance, the *cacique* dispatched a trusted courier on a twofold mission to the *Isla de Mujeres*. He was instructed to deliver a letter containing a note of appreciation and a sizeable amount of cash to Marta Moreno. In addition, he was to inform Maria and her family that they would be returning to Soledad on a pre-set date. The *cacique* then instructed Raul to have all in readiness for her homecoming. He took special precaution to insure that his beloved Rosita should have no knowledge of the forthcoming event.

Three weeks remained until her anticipated arrival, which would coincide with Mexico's Independence Day.

Inasmuch as the *cacique* would be unable to attend the normal festivities, his deputy city administrator would officiate in his stead. He was insistent that the celebration not be changed nor diminished in any way.

Meanwhile, with the aid of his loyal staff, he began accumulating gifts for the Garcias, particularly birthday gifts for Maria. Throughout the period of readying for her arrival, he directed those assisting while being extremely cautious not to display his emotional anxiety. Even while restricted to bed, he had his customary check-off list, which he would review with Raul. Throughout the house, with the exception of Rosita who was unaware of what was transpiring, inquietude reigned supreme.

As planned, the carriage carrying his daughter and her family arrived at *Casa* Rosita promptly at noon on September 16, 1909. Rosita, shocked though delighted, was the first to see, greet, embrace and kiss her "little girl." Tears flowed freely along with more hugs and kisses. Then she embraced her new son-in-law, after which she held and cuddled her grandson. This wonderful wife and mother, whose heart sang with delight, was enjoying a bottomless fountain of peace and happiness.

It was then on to the *cacique*'s bedroom. Maria rushed into her father's arms again hugging, kissing and crying with joy, exultant tears streaming down her cheeks. Her father, smothering a sob, could no longer restrain himself as he, too, embraced his daughter releasing tears of nostalgia. Next in line was his namesake, little eleven-year-old Eduardo, who was on the *cacique*'s bed being snuggled and kissed by his grandfather. Nick patiently stood by the door uncertain as to how he would be received. With a glance in Nick's direction and reaching toward him with an outstretched hand, Nick approached his father-in-law delivering a pope-like kiss on the *cacique*'s hand, after which they embraced.

The caressing, the clutching, the clinging and the

crying went on until all had regained their composure. Once calm had returned, the mountain of gifts was distributed to the three, including a small pony for the boy. Along with the ceaseless embracing, there were detailed explanations of all that had transpired in their lives during the thirteen years of separation. And so it went until the dinner hour when they departed the *cacique*'s bedroom, affording him an opportunity to rest. Finally, on this wonderful day in 1909, the entire Hernandez family was one and together for the first time.

After the family get-together, a routine was established specifically setting forth hours for visitation, dining and the special period set aside for prayer in the village chapel. For everyone, other than the master of the house, every unscheduled moment was dedicated to getting re-acquainted. All shared in the glorious moments of immense pleasure of just being together.

With family unit functioning in joyous harmony, the *cacique* lost little time in setting forth an organizational plan. Nick was appointed to an administrative position at the city hall. He was an intense worker who realized, at long last, that he and his father-in-law shared, to some degree, benevolence and tolerance for the working class. Maria and her mother were inseparable. Both of the young boy's idealistic parents were overjoyed to see their son romping and playing with the children of the workers in the village.

With each passing day, each grew closer to the other with the young boy serving as a bonding catalyst for all of the adults. Nick was proving to be an able administrator. He spent extended periods of time with his father-in-law who was never at a loss to offer words of wisdom.

"Always remember, my son, we are a mixture of Moctezuma and Cortés. We are the victims of a confused heritage; therefore, you must understand the inferior idiosyncrasies of your fellow Mexicans. When speaking with someone of higher authority and you wish to have your opinion prevail, refrain from a direct approach.

"Instead, make the person with whom you are conversing believe your point of view is of his creation. Simply say, 'Señor, you have just given me a great idea on how to resolve the situation.' He now feels inflated, and you will have accomplished what you intended to convey. As a subordinate race, our *machismo* must be inflated from time to time."

Through the ever-present rumor mill, the *cacique* learned that Nick, now in a responsible position in city government, had made an erroneous judgment decision. While his miscalculation was neither serious nor monetarily costly, it had left an imprint on Nick's self-assurance. It was even gossiped that he was suffering and in a depressed state. The *cacique*, disturbed when apprised of Nick's dilemma, decided that he would speak with the young man on a father to son basis. He called for Nick. After a few cordial words, the *cacique* explained that after the average person makes mistakes, all he learns from them is how to make excuses. He quickly reminded Nick that he was not average, but far superior.

It was his wish to instill confidence in the young man expressing his support by pronouncing, "You should be unafraid to attempt innovation and assume risk. In order for you to benefit from a mistake it is first necessary that you make one." Then holding Nick's hand and patting him on the shoulder, he concluded, "Nick, my son, the greatest mistake you can make in life is to continually fear that you will make one. Go out into this world and exercise your best judgment; for history has proven that in all great attempts, it's sometimes glorious to fail. Have no fear! You will not disappoint me. I am proud of you. You will be a great *cacique*!"

CHAPTER XXX

DON EDUARDO PASSES ON

Almost a year had passed and during those months, peace, contentment and happiness reigned in *Casa* Rosita. There were threatening movements in the *cacique*'s commercial empire, which was now under the watchful eye of Nick who, in addition, had assumed added responsibilities in the city administration. All was serene in Soledad.

Unfortunately, it was not so in the rest of the country. The administration of Porfirio Diaz had been indicted by Mexicans in all walks of life. In an attempt to soothe the inflamed nerves of the populace and hoping to avoid a revolution, the president shocked the country by issuing a declaration.

> "No matter what my friends and supporters say, I shall retire when my presidential term of office ends, and I shall not serve again. I shall be eighty years old then. I have waited patiently for the day when the people of the Mexican Republic would be prepared to choose and change their government at every election without danger of armed revolution and without injury to the national credit or interference with the national progress. I believe that day has come. I welcome an opposition party in the Mexican Republic."

Having made his pronouncement of retiring from public life, Diaz went into seclusion for one week. The approaching month of September would include his eightieth birthday as well as the one hundredth anniversary of the nation's Declaration of Independence. When he finally emerged from his self-imposed seclusion, it was apparent that he had spent the time detailing plans for both festive occasions.

He was, without dubiety, the continent's greatest egoistic individual, and he was not about to leave office without a never-to-be-forgotten bang. He directed that the entire month of September be dedicated to celebration and commemoration. On the first day of September, an enormous pillar topped by a figure of a gold-encrusted angel was dedicated on Mexico City's principal avenue, the Paseo de la Reforma. The impressive monument was a testimonial to Mexico's independence.

The president would spare no expense, for he invited distinguished guests from all parts of the world, all expenses paid, to participate in the month-long festivities. It was discretely conveyed to the visitors that the president expected everyone to attend every event. Being stricken with what was commonly termed "Moctezuma's revenge", tourist diarrhea, would be the only accepted excuse for absence.

The first major assemblage took place at the National University. Diaz was extremely proud of the fact that enrollment had multiplied during his years in office. He was particularly gratified that women, in great numbers, were attending the school, graduating and entering the professional work force. He boasted that the medical school graduated its first female doctor in 1888. He then went on to announce that there was continued impressive progress by women to the point that they were entering the fields of law, dentistry, pharmacy, education and journalism. As a result of the rapidly declining job market, unemployed male professionals had been among the president's harshest critics. It was believed by those present that this was Diaz's way of retaliation by his neglect to recognize their achievements and obliquely challenge their *machismo*.

There were theme balls of every description where imported food and wine flowed from evening to early the next day. The city was adorned in flags of all nations honoring the visitors while musicians strolled the streets to the enjoyment of all.

Wisely, the guests were confined to areas of the city where streets had been repaired, buildings scrubbed, and all beggars forcibly driven from view by the civil police and the *rurales*. Threatened demonstrations by students and unemployed professionals were prevented from transpiring.

The city was a metropolis of contrasts. While the privileged and attendees feasted on caviar and champagne, the forgotten masses were suffering from malnutrition and contaminated water. While the streets and buildings were spotless, the outlying districts were a congested mass of adobe huts, mud streets, accumulated garbage and rodents.

The opulence of Diaz's "September to remember" was, in the eyes of many, including the affluent, a portent that it was time for the president to go. He had served his purpose in elevating a suffering nation to one of world recognition. He had achieved, at least for the moment, economic prosperity along with law and order, without which there would be no flourishing tourist industry.

With his many positives, there were critical negatives. The solid foundation of his government was suspect with the fear of revolt and collapse. While there was enormous amassing of wealth by a few, he had not conveyed the promise for the rural masses who were in many ways even worse off under his autocratic rule than they were under the blundering governments that preceded him. Now with the economy declining, the jobless increasing in number, and the neglected impoverished, Mexico was a bomb waiting to explode. With the departure of Diaz, his absolute power and his *rurales*, the fuse had been ignited.

The *cacique*, completely cognizant of the existing state of deterioration, confided to his new-found son and the cleric declaring, "The president does not see what is transpiring. He is completely oblivious to the meaning of social reform. I see peace and prosperity as terribly fragile with our system in grave peril. I am alarmed and dread the thought that revolt is in the offing. Let us pray for the future." Father Agustin then led his friends in solemn prayer.

Even though he was bedridden, the *cacique* fully understood the gravity of the situation nationally, which, indubitably, was causing a regression in his physical condition. As a result, he suffered a number of minor heart attacks. It was readily evident to his family, the priest, the physician and Raul that there was a daily gradual weakening of their beloved *cacique*. They were all conscious of his deteriorating condition. After close examination, the doctor concluded that his patient's days on earth were numbered. He informed the priest who, in turn, could select the most prudent manner to advise the family.

After a day of soul searching, Father Agustin Diaz asked the family to assemble in the village chapel. Once together, he directed everyone to approach the statue of *San Eduardo el Martir* where he made known the opinion of the doctor. Grief stricken, they released their emotions, tightly embracing and counseling each other. The tears streamed down their faces. Once they regained their self-control, they joined the priest in an extended prayer service.

Eduardo could perceive his failing health just as he could distinguish the downheartedness of his loved ones. It was his wish to spend additional time with Rosita, Maria, his grandson and, particularly, Nick with whom he would detail the duties and responsibilities of a *cacique*. Discussion was directed, in great part, to the management of the family holdings. He stressed the fact that change had occurred since the tyrannical days of old and that social change must come about. He even questioned the system re-declaring that absolute or supreme rule was no longer acceptable for when an official, namely a dictator, had no opposition, the people have no choice.

He repeatedly asked that his young grandson be brought to his bed where he would nestle the boy to his side, occasionally kissing his forehead or hand. Word of his plight had reached the villagers who were indebted to the man who had given them a patron saint, a church and a respectable, relatively prosperous life. Each evening they would attend a prayer service at the church and then proceed to *Casa* Rosita to hold a candlelight vigil below the second floor window of their patriarch's bedroom. After all, he was their *cacique*, their benefactor, and they literally worshiped him.

For hours on end, Eduardo would lie and reminisce. He recalled his youth, his family, his successes, his failures his good fortune and misfortune. Regardless of where along the road of life he was in his reverie, he could never forget that as a young university graduate in Soledad, he received a letter from the president of Mexico that turned his life around. He wondered what his future would have been like had the letter not been sent. By dwelling on this incident so often, it had taken him prisoner.

With each day, he grew more fragile, losing consciousness for short periods of time. There was a family member at his bedside day and night. One evening, when his family and the priest were all assembled in his room, he raised himself on one elbow and with a magnetic smile and a satisfied light in his eyes whispered, "I have seen yesterday, I am content today and because of your love, I am not afraid of tomorrow." With that, the *cacique's* head fell to one side on his pillow as he left a world he had entered fifty-nine years earlier.

With their leader gone, it seemed as though a dead end of helplessness had engulfed the village, the hacienda and the city in an emotional period of mourning. Don Eduardo had been looked upon as the lord and master, not only in the community, but in the region as well. The villagers had placed him on a pedestal on a par with their patron saint.

Having been suddenly cast in the role of absolute ruler, Nick responded in a manner that would have made his predecessor proud. After meeting with the city's employees, he declared that there would be one month of mourning. He, personally, would direct all arrangements for the funeral, which would take place on the third day following Eduardo's passing—a funeral befitting a monarch.

It was ordered that all businesses would be closed for the three-day period prior to internment. The bells of all churches in the area would chime every half hour from sunrise to sunset until their leader was laid to rest.

Services on the day of burial commenced at noon at the village church of San José Marti. Eulogies would be delivered by Nick and Father Agustin Diaz. The mourners numbered in the thousands with only enough space for two hundred in the modest church. Loud speakers mounted on the exterior of the church would carry the speakers' words to the assembled throng. With good fortune, the day was ideal—cool, clear and cloud covered—which the masses believed was arranged for by their departed *cacique*.

From the outset, it was obvious this would be a most affectionate, heart-wrenching, solemn ritual. There was not a dry eye to be found.

The priest began the service with prayers, which were followed by the singing of hymns. Throughout the service, tears ran like rain down the faces of men and women alike. It was then time for the eulogies to begin. Nick took his place at the lectern, which was but a few feet from the villagers' patron saint. With tears filling his eyes, Nick delivered his tribute to his former adversary who had become an admired and respected friend. "Eduardo Hernandez Gonzalez was a man chosen by God to be our leader. While many apply, only a few are chosen. I could summarize his life by saying he was a great patriot, however, he is deserving of more than a few all-inclusive words to recall his magnitude.

"He believed that greatness was within one's power; and, therefore, he who would seek and accept a challenge, would achieve greatness. It was his opinion that most men possess more determination than they think they have. It was through his gift of determination that he was unafraid to act on his personal convictions. As a devout believer in God, he maintained that his acts were of his own certitude while the consequences of his actions belonged to the Almighty.

"He accepted the fact that the evil men do in their lives, lives on after them, while the good they have discharged is normally interred with their remains. He was not afraid of death for he knew that while a young man may die, an old man must die. He acknowledged that life was but a path that must be trod in order to pass to God. He further recognized that life was merely the commingling of time and eternity; and, if he were fortunate, he would envision eternity by looking through time.

> And so, Don Eduardo,
> While human hands have tried to save thee,
> Sighs and tears were all in vain.
> Happy angels came and bore thee
> From this weary world of pain.

> All is sad within our dwelling,
> Lonely are our hearts today,
> For the one we all loved so dearly,
> Like the dew on the mountain,
> Like the foam on the river,
> Like the bubbles on a fountain,
> Has forever passed away.

Having concluded his offering, Nick was replaced at the lectern by the beloved parish priest. After a short prayer, he commenced the eulogy, "I have lost a son whose name has been added to the honor roll of God. While gone in body, this community will never allow his name to die. The path to his grave will be traveled by the sandaled feet of those he befriended and who loved him dearly.

"Eduardo Hernandez Gonzalez made no claim to sainthood—perhaps he should have. He, like all mortal beings, was not perfect, for he asserted that men without faults are apt to be men without strength. Yes, not perfect but a good, caring and compassionate man who brought joy, well being and a renewed life to those in San José Martí.

"Nothing could be more distasteful to this honorable, modest soul while on earth and nothing more inappropriate to his memory, than fabricated embellishment. During his distinguished and illustrious life, he achieved success, fame and fortune. It was his postulate that the legacy a man left behind was simply a matter of dying at the right moment.

"Our *cacique* did not fear leaving us for his trip to heaven. And so, my dear brothers and sisters, I am certain that he would counsel that an excess of grief for the deceased is simply madness, for it is trauma for the living while the dead know it not. He would tell you that anything so necessary, so unavoidable as death, should not be looked upon as heinous to mankind for it is but a transition.

"You, my cherished son, Don Eduardo, have walked kindly throughout your life without knowing how long that life would last. While you have walked quickly, you have walked with love and compassion helping those along the way. Now, my son, you have found your way to heaven with God."

After a moving prayer for his departed friend, the cleric concluded the service.

The procession of mourners, led by a carriage carrying the deceased's body with pallbearers walking alongside, made its way to the burial site. Two parishioners carried the beautiful icon of *San Eduardo el Martir*. Eduardo would be interred on the grounds of Hacienda *San Eduardo* in the shade of a giant oak tree. Of his many holdings, he treasured his hacienda above and beyond all others for he had given birth to a community that would continue to live for time ever more.

With thousands in attendance, the deceased leader was laid to rest as his special man of God offered a brief, sensitive prayer.

Once interred, the family returned to *Casa* Rosita. The widow, pale and trembling, was overheard to say, "While I have lost my beloved Eduardo, I retain my most treasured gift—my fond memories of our life together. Something I shall always retain. Something that can never be taken from me. I shall never be alone." With no tears left to shed, the family consoled each other in a home of indescribable eeriness and emptiness.

While resolute direction in the household seemed lacking since the loss of its dominant leader, Nick, nevertheless, was making progress with dispatch. In addition to his hectic schedule since assuming the role of *cacique* with the sole responsibility as mayor of the city, he was, as well, administering the family's sixteen operating businesses. He enthusiastically forged ahead expeditiously.

It was only natural that at every turn, the intrusive shadow of Eduardo was present. The family, as best they could, was reorganizing their lives. In just three days, the court would remove and unlock Eduardo's safe deposit box from the bank vault for purposes of probate. All preparations were underway in the local courtroom for the examination of the depository's contents.

CHAPTER XXXI

PROBATE OF EDUARDO'S ESTATE

The day had arrived when the court would scrutinize the contents of the defunct's bank safe deposit box. Hours before the court opened its doors, hundreds of orderly prospective observers anxiously awaited entry hoping for one of the eighty available spectator seats. Promptly at 10:00 A.M., when the doors were opened, the more fortunate obtained seats while the overflow crowd was relegated to the standing room at the rear. The front row was reserved for family and close friends.

All departments of the government, including the court system, had been well indoctrinated in punctuality and a business-like manner in conducting their affairs. Consequently, at the prescribed hour of 10:15 A.M., the court clerk ordered all to rise for the judge, who, momentarily, would enter the courtroom.

The meticulous perusal of the box's contents would be performed by Judge Alonzo de Regil Mendez, a staunchly honorable man, whose firm belief was that as far as the law was concerned, moderation in the pursuit of the truth was unconscionable.

A normally smiling and cheerful man, the magistrate was different on this day. His countenance was taught with strain. The lines of concentration deepened along his brows and under his eyes while the tensing of his jaw portrayed his profound resolution.

After ordering the bailiff to fetch and open the box, the adjudicator initiated the process whereby he would remove each item in an orderly fashion. As per customary procedure, each testament, memorandum and missive would first be inspected by the judge and then read aloud. As expected, the bulk of the estate was bequeathed to Rosita. Not overlooked were Maria, Nick, little Eduardo, Raul and Father Agustin. After formally examining document after document, each having been read audibly and clearly to the courtroom, the judge noted an unusual looking envelope, semi-obscured in the rear of the box.

The envelope was face down, the flap of which bore a broken wax seal. Picking it up and scrutinizing it, he discovered the envelope to be of unusually fine parchment and timeworn. While the complete date of transmittal was obliterated, the year, 1873, was easily distinguishable.

With great care, the probate judge removed the letter and carefully read its contents after which there was a moment of hesitation. His hands trembled. There was perceptible tightening at the corners of his mouth. Within seconds, his features became grim. Apparently perplexed, the judge ordered a twenty-minute court recess whereupon he retired to his chambers.

Once seated in his high-back black leather chair, he meticulously read and digested the letter, word by word. Flustered, he shifted uneasily in his seat with face distorted by apprehension and nervous anxiety. With hands still trembling, he lit a cigarette, placing it on one side of his mouth, the smoke passing across his face.

He then proceeded to again punctiliously read the letter in the same manner as before. Once concluded, he sat silent, puffing on his cigarette. He leaned back in his huge chair gazing through the window. He observed a hustling, bustling, orderly Soledad that was prospering while virtually the rest of the nation was suffering from disorder and decline.

Thinking aloud he said, "What to do? Justice is peculiar, for it wears a different face for different people.

Everyone, even a judge, sees his own determination as just. I must do what I must do."

Stern faced and with a strained and haunting demeanor, he grasped the letter by the lower right hand corner with his right hand so that it stood upright. With great care, he very carefully ignited the upper left hand corner. As the flame devoured the letter, he scrutinized it from top to bottom for a last time.

National Palace, Mexico City
Office of the President of the Republic

August 29, 1873

Engineer Eduardo Hernandez Gonzalez
Hotel Emporio
Soledad, Chiapas

You were ordered to the town of Soledad commissioned with specific performance instructions. Inasmuch as you have failed to successfully carry out your mission, you are hereby discharged from further government service.

Sebastián Lerdo de Tejada, President

"The president does not see what is transpiring. He is completely oblivious to the meaning of social reform. I see peace and prosperity as terribly fragile with our system in grave peril. I am alarmed and dread the thought that revolt is in the offing. Let us pray for the future."

Eduardo Hernandez Gonzalez
October 5, 1910

Start of the Mexican Revolution
November 20, 1910

Notes

Notes

Notes

Notes

Notes

Notes